Dear Reader,

When I began to write historical romances,
I chose the Regency period for several reasons.
I had always enjoyed Georgette Heyer's novels—
still among the best—and had spent part of my
youth working at Newstead Abbey, the home of
Lord Byron, one of the Regency's most colorful
characters. It involved me in reading many of the
original letters and papers of a dynamic era in
English history.

Later on when I researched even further into the
period, I discovered that nothing I could invent
was more exciting—or outrageous—than what had
actually happened! What could be more natural,
then, than to write a Regency romance and send it
to Mills and Boon in England? It was accepted and
that started me on a new career.

Like Georgette Heyer I try to create fiction
out of and around fact for the enjoyment and
entertainment of myself and my readers. It is
often forgotten that the Regency men had equally
powerful wives, mothers and sisters—even if they
had no public role—so I make my heroines able
to match my heroes in their wit and courage.

Paula Marshall

Paula Marshall, married, with three children, has had a varied and interesting life. She began her career in a large library and ended it as a senior academic in charge of teaching history in a polytechnic. She has traveled widely, has been a swimming coach, embroiders, paints pictures and has appeared on quiz shows in Britain. She has always wanted to write, and likes her novels to be full of adventure and humor.

THE WOLFE'S MATE
PAULA MARSHALL

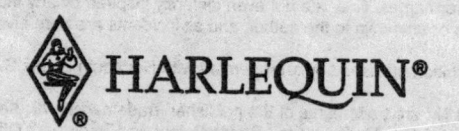

TORONTO • NEW YORK • LONDON
AMSTERDAM • PARIS • SYDNEY • HAMBURG
STOCKHOLM • ATHENS • TOKYO • MILAN • MADRID
PRAGUE • WARSAW • BUDAPEST • AUCKLAND

ISBN 0-373-51135-3

THE WOLFE'S MATE

Copyright © 1999 by Paula Marshall.

Visit us at www.eHarlequin.com

Printed in U.S.A.

Prologue

'Jilted!' screeched Mrs Mitchell, throwing herself carefully backwards into the nearest comfortable chair. 'That a child of mine should be left at the altar. Call him out, or horsewhip him, do, Mr Mitchell, it is all he deserves.'

'Difficult,' responded her husband drily, 'seeing that his letter informs us that he was setting sail for France last night!'

His restraint was all the more remarkable because, until an hour ago, he had been loudly congratulating himself on getting rid of his stepdaughter to a husband who was, all things considered, above her touch, he being a peer of the realm, and she a merchant's daughter and not very remarkable in the looks department.

His wife's only response was to drum her heels on the ground and announce that she was about to faint—which she did with as much panache as Mrs Siddons performing on stage. Her two young daughters by Mr Mitchell stood helplessly on each side of her, sobbing loudly. Mrs Mitchell's companion was wringing her hands, and exclaiming at intervals, 'Oh, the wretch, the wretch.'

The only calm person in the room was the jilted young

woman herself, nineteen-year-old Susanna Beverly, who coolly wrenched a feather from her mother's fan. She held it briefly in the fire and then placed it under Mrs Mitchell's nose to revive her.

Revive her it did. She started up, exclaiming loudly, 'Oh, Susanna, how can you be so unmoved when he has ruined you? The news will be all about town by tonight—it will be the sensation of the Season.'

'Really, Mother,' replied Susanna, who was clinging on to her self-possession for dear life, after just having been made the spectacle of the Season as well as its sensation, 'don't exaggerate. He hasn't seduced me, only left me at the altar.'

'Oh, Mr Mitchell,' shrieked her mother, sitting up at last, 'pray tell her that he might just as well have done so. Nobody, but nobody, will ever marry a jilted girl! Oh, whatever did you say to drive him away?'

She sank back into the chair again to be comforted by her companion, ignoring Susanna's quiet reply. 'Nothing, Mother, nothing. Perhaps that was what drove him away.' Only her iron will prevented her from behaving in the abandoned fashion of the rest of her family.

Her unnatural calm, however, annoyed her stepfather as well as her mother, however much it was enabling her not to shriek to the heavens at the insult which had been offered her. To arrive at the church, to wait for a bridegroom who had never turned up, and had sent a letter instead of himself—and what a letter!

'I have changed my mind and have no wish to be married, but have decided to set out for France this evening instead. Convey my respects to Susanna with the hope that she will soon find a more suitable bridegroom than Francis Sylvester.'

It had been handed to her by the best man who, to do him justice, had looked most unhappy while carrying out this quite untraditional role.

Susanna had read it, and then handed it to her stepfather who had been there to give her away. He had read it, then

flung it down with an oath, before shouting at the assembled
congregation, 'There will be no wedding. The bridegroom
has deloped and is no longer in the country!'

'Deloped!' Mrs Mitchell had shrieked. 'Whatever can you
mean, Mr Mitchell?'

'What I have just said,' he had roared. 'Lord Sylvester
has cried off. Failed to fire his pistol, or fired it in the air,
call it what you will. Come, Susanna and Mrs Mitchell, we
must return home before we become more of a laughing-
stock than we already are.'

Numbly Susanna had obeyed him. Noisily, Mrs Mitchell
had done the same, abusing her daughter whose fault she
claimed it to be.

Susanna scarcely heard her. Until an hour ago she had
been secure in the knowledge that a handsome young man
with a title and a moderate fortune, with whom she had just
enjoyed several happy summer months, was going to be her
husband. She had to confess that she did not love him
madly, but then, who did love their husbands madly—other
than the heroines of Minerva Press novels?

Nor did she think that he had loved her madly. Nevertheless, they had dealt well together, although their interests
differed greatly. Francis Sylvester's life had revolved around
Jackson's Boxing Salon and various racecourses in the day,
and the more swell of London's gaming hells, where he was
a moderate gambler, at night. Susanna's time, on the other
hand, was spent reading, playing the piano, and painting—
she was quite a considerable artist. These differences had
not troubled either of them for they were commonplace in
the marriages of the *ton*.

This being so, she could not imagine why he had behaved
in such a heartless fashion. He had had ample time to cry
off during the months of their betrothal when to have done
so would not have ruined her as completely as his leaving
her at the altar would do.

For Susanna knew full well that what her mother had said
was true: to be jilted in such a fashion meant social ruin.
Was it her looks? She knew that they were not remarkable—

other than her deep grey-blue eyes, that was, on which Francis had frequently complimented her. Her hair was an almost chestnut, her face an almost-perfect oval. Her nose and mouth, whilst not exactly distinguished, were not undistinguished, either.

Her height was neither short nor tall, but somewhere in between. Her carriage had often been called graceful. Susanna, however, knew full well that she was not a raving beauty in the fashionable style which her two half-sisters promised to be. Both of them were blonde, blue-eyed and slightly plump: 'my two cherubs,' her stepfather called them.

Nor was her fortune remarkable. Like herself, it might be described as comfortable, her father having died suddenly before he had been able to make it greater. Her stepfather, having daughters of his own to care for—and still hoping for a son—had not considered it his duty to enlarge it.

She straightened herself and held her head as high as she could. There was no use in repining. What was done, was done.

'I am going to my room,' she said. 'Send Mary to me, Mother. I wish to change out of these clothes. They have become hateful to me.'

Even as she spoke, she saw by the expressions on her mother's and stepfather's faces that she had become hateful to them: a symbol of their disappointment. Not only had they lost an aristocratic son-in-law, but they were saddled with a daughter who had become unmarriageable.

As her mother said mournfully as soon as she was out of the room, 'No one will marry her now, Mr Mitchell. Whatever is to become of her?'

He shrugged his shoulders. 'Do not distress yourself further, my dear. Leave everything to me. I shall make suitable arrangements for her. We cannot have Charlotte and Caroline's reputations muddied by her continued presence. I have great plans for them, as you know.'

His busy, cunning brain had been working out how to

deal with this *contretemps* ever since he had read Francis Sylvester's letter.

'Now follow Miss Beverly's example, my dear, and change out of your unsuitable bridal finery. Let us put this behind us. I shall speak to her in the morning.'

His tone was so firm that his wife immediately ceased her repining. Although he was usually indulgent towards her and all her three daughters, he invariably spoke to them as though they were recalcitrant clerks when he wished to make it plain that they must obey him immediately.

It was thus he addressed Susanna on the following morning when she arrived in his study in response to his request made over breakfast.

'It is necessary, Miss Beverly, that we discuss your unfortunate situation immediately. It brooks of no delay. I shall expect to see you in my room at eleven of the clock precisely.'

He had never called her Miss Beverly before. Indeed, in the past few months his manner to her had been particularly affectionate, but there was nothing left of that when he spoke to her then, or later on, when she arrived to find him seated at his desk writing furiously.

Nor did he stand up when she entered, nor cease to write, until he flung his pen down and said, 'This is a sad business, my dear. I was depending on this marriage to see you settled. I was prepared to find the money for your dowry, seeing that the match was such a splendid one, but, alas, now that your reputation has gone and you are unlikely to marry, such charity on my part is out of the question.'

Susanna listened to him in some bewilderment. She had always been under the impression that her father had left a large sum of money in a Trust for her which should have made it unnecessary for her stepfather to extend her any charity at all in the matter of a dowry.

And so she told him.

He smiled pityingly at her. 'Dear child, that was a kind fib I told you and your mother. Your father left little—he made many unfortunate investments before his untimely death. The Trust was consequently worthless. I was willing to keep you and even give you the dowry your father would have left you when I hoped that you would make a good marriage—as you so nearly did.

'But, alas, now that your reputation is blown—through no fault of yours, I freely allow—there is no point in me continuing this useful fiction. I have the unhappy task of informing you that, whilst I will assist you towards establishing yourself in a new life, I cannot afford to continue to provide you with either a large income or a dowry.'

Susanna was not to know that there was not a word of truth in what her stepfather was saying. It was he who had made the unfortunate investments, not her father. He had been stealing from the Trust to help to keep himself afloat ever since he had married Susanna's mother and he now saw a splendid opportunity to annex the whole of it to himself.

His wife would suspect nothing, for her way of life would continue unchanged: Susanna would be the only sufferer.

'I shall,' he continued, 'settle a small annual income on you, for I would not have my wife's daughter left in penury. Indeed, no. What I have also done is write a letter to an elderly friend of mine, a Miss Stanton, who lives in Yorkshire. She has asked me to find her a companion and I shall have no hesitation in recommending you to her. She will give you a comfortable home in exchange for a few, easily performed, duties. You may even be fortunate enough to meet someone who, not knowing of your sad history, will offer for you.'

He smiled at her, saying in the kindest voice he could assume, 'You see, my dear, I continue to have your best interests at heart.'

Susanna sat in stunned silence, her heart beating rapidly. 'I had no notion,' she began. 'Had I been aware of my true position, I would have thanked you before now—as it is...'

Samuel Mitchell raised a proprietorial—and hypocritical—finger. 'Think nothing of it, my dear. I was but doing

my duty. I shall send off the letter immediately, but have
no fear, I am sure that Miss Stanton will be only too happy
to employ you. Until then, continue to enjoy your position
in my home as one of my daughters.'

Susanna nodded her head numbly. She felt deprived of
the power of speech. The day before yesterday, she had been
the only child and heiress of a reasonably rich merchant of
good family. Yesterday, she had been about to become Lady
Sylvester. Today, she had been informed that she was a
poverty-stricken orphan who was to be sent away to be an
elderly lady's companion—with all that that entailed. Running errands, walking the pug: someone who was neither a
servant nor a gentlewoman, but something in-between.

Later, alone in her room, she began to question a little
what her stepfather had just told her. Was it really true that
her father had left her nothing? That the Trust had been
false, nothing but a lying fiction? That she had been living
for the past twelve years on her stepfather's charity? Surely
she and her mother would have been informed of that if
such had been the case.

She made up her mind to visit the family solicitors to
discover the truth. She would not tell Mr Mitchell of her
intentions, merely say that she needed to take the air in the
family carriage.

But her stepfather, knowing her strong and determined
character, so like her late father's, had foreseen that she
might wish to do such a thing, and was able to prevent it
by informing her mother that, until it was time for Susanna
to travel to Yorkshire, it would be unwise for her to go out
in public.

'The female mind is so delicate,' he said, 'that it might,
in such a situation as Susanna finds herself in, be inadvisable
for her to venture out of doors. A brief period at home,
before she makes the long journey to Yorkshire, will do her
a power of good.'

'If you say so,' her mother said falteringly.

'Oh, I do say so, Mrs Mitchell. After all, like you, I have her best interests at heart!'

It had been her mother who told Susanna of her stepfather's decision.

Susanna had stared at her, more sure than ever that something was wrong. She had been about to refuse to obey any such ban and even considered telling her mother of her suspicion that Mr Mitchell had been lying about the Trust and her father's not having left her anything.

Then she looked at her mother with newly opened eyes and knew that she would not believe that her husband was lying, would simply see Susanna as trouble-making and ungrateful towards a man who had graciously taken the place of her father ever since she had married Mr Mitchell.

Not only would Mr Mitchell make doubly sure that she was confined to the house, but she would make an enemy of them both, to no profit to herself. He would simply assert that the misery of being jilted had unhinged her mind—and she had no answer to that. She was helpless and knew it.

Susanna had taken her mother in her arms and kissed her childhood innocence goodbye. She would go to Yorkshire and try to make a new life there, far from the home which was no longer *her* home, and where she was not wanted.

Somehow, some day, God willing, she would try to repair the ruin which Francis Sylvester had made of her life...

Chapter One

⬥⬥⬥⬥

1819

It had been one of Lady Leominster's most successful balls, as she afterwards boasted to her lord the next morning, who merely grunted and continued to read the *Morning Post*. His wife's conversation was only wallpaper in the background of his busy life. It would never do to let her know how useful her balls and other entertainments were, she would only get above herself and, heaven knew, she was too much above herself as it was without his praise elevating her even further.

'And even the Wolf, the Nabob himself, came—after refusing everyone else's invitations, even Emily Exford's.'

M'lord grunted again. This time in appreciation. He had spent a happy half-hour with Benjamin Wolfe, discussing the current state of England, gaining advice on where he might profitably invest his money as the post-war depression roared on, showing no signs of breaking.

'Not a bad move, that,' he conceded grudgingly. 'The feller seems both knowledgeable and helpful. Invite him to our next dinner.'

'They say that he is looking for a wife.'

'Shouldn't have any difficulty finding one, my dear. With all that money.'

'True, m'lord, but his birth? What of that? Does anyone know of his family?'

'Well, I do, for one,' said Lord Leominster, smiling because for once he knew of a piece of gossip which his wife didn't. 'Same family as the General of that name. Poor gentry—went to India and made his pile there, or so he says. Besides, money sweetens everything. It's its own lineage, you know. Half the peerage goes back to nameless thrusters who received titles and consequence solely because of their newly gained riches—nothing wrong in that.'

Lord Leominster's distant ancestor had been a pirate with Francis Drake and was the founder of the family's wealth with loot wrested from Spanish treasure ships.

His wife shrugged and abandoned Ben Wolfe as a topic. 'They say that Darlington is about to offer for Amelia Western—that should be a meeting of money, and no mistake. He was paying her the most marked attention last night.'

She received no answer. Lord Leominster was not interested in idle gossip for its own sake. Ben Wolfe, now, was different. Such creatures had their uses.

Lady Leominster was almost right. The previous evening, George Wychwood, Viscount Darlington, had offered for Miss Amelia Western and been accepted. He had spoken to her father and received his blessing earlier in the day and had come to Leominster House solely to propose to her.

As usual, she had that dowdy goody of hers in tow. Well, she wouldn't be needing a duenna when she was his wife, as she surely would be soon, and the dowdy goody could be given her notice, move on either to be some old trot's companion or to shepherd some other innocent young woman and make sure that the wolves didn't get at her before the honest men did.

And speaking of wolves, wasn't that Ben Wolfe in earnest

conversation with their host? George Darlington frowned. He had mentioned Ben Wolfe's name to his father, the Earl of Babbacombe, earlier that day, and the Earl had made a wry face and said, 'You would do well to avoid him like the plague. His father was a wretch, and like father, like son, I always say—although there were rumours that he was not Charles Wolfe's son at all, just some by-blow brought in when Wolfe's own son died at birth. I thought that he had gone off to India—enlisted as a private in that skimble-skamble Company army. What can *he* be doing in decent society?'

Uninterested, George had shrugged. 'Made a fortune there, they say. Became a Nabob, no less. Been put up for White's and accepted.'

He had little time for his father's follies and foibles, having too many of his own to worry about.

'Money,' said his father disgustedly. 'Whitewashes everything.'

His tone was bitter. There were few to know that the Wychwood family was on its beam-ends and desperately needed the marriage which George was about to make. Lady Leominster had been wrong in her assumption that money was about to marry money.

Certainly George had no knowledge of how near his father was to drowning in the River Tick and, if he had, would have thought Ben Wolfe a useful man to ask for advice on matters financial, not someone to despise.

As it was, he passed him by and concentrated on looking for pretty Amelia, whom he found sitting in a corner, her companion by her side. He ignored the companion and asked Amelia to partner him in the next dance.

'After that,' he said, 'I have something particular to say to you, if Miss—' and he looked enquiringly at the companion '—will allow you to walk on the terrace with me—alone. It is most particular,' he added with a meaningful smile.

'Oh, Miss Beverly,' said Amelia, 'I'm sure that you will allow me to accompany George on the terrace alone if what he has to say to me is most particular. After all, we have known one another since childhood.'

Susanna, who had been Amelia Western's companion and somewhat youthful duenna since her previous employer, Miss Stanton, had suddenly died, knew perfectly well what it was that George Darlington wished to say to her charge. She also knew that, although she and George had met several times, and even conversed, he would not have known her had he met her in the street. He had twice been told her name, but it had made no impression on him.

She rose to answer him and, as it chanced, stood on George's left. He had Amelia on his right. At that very moment, Ben Wolfe, who was looking across the room at them, asked Lord Leominster, who had just been joined by his lady, 'Is that George Darlington over there?'

It was Lady Leominster who answered him eagerly, 'Oh, indeed.' She leaned forward confidentially, saying, 'He is speaking to Amelia Western, the great heiress. I am sure that he is about to propose to her tonight.'

'He is?' Ben looked at them again, and asked, apparently idly, 'I see that he has two young ladies with him. Which is the heiress?'

Never loath to pass on information, Lady Leominster answered, 'Oh, the young woman on his left.'

She was, of course, wrong—but then, she had never known her right from her left—but before Lord Leominster could open his mouth to correct her, she had seized Ben Wolfe's arm and exclaimed, 'Oh, do come and be introduced to Lady Camelford, she has two beautiful daughters, both unmarried, and both, I am assured, well endowed for marriage'—so the mistake went uncorrected.

She was never to know that her careless remark would profoundly alter the course of several lives.

Ben had no further opportunity to see George Darlington

or his future bride together, but later in the evening, as he was about to leave, Miss Western suddenly came out of one of the ballrooms. He was able to step back and inspect her briefly at close range.

She was modestly dressed, to be sure, but in quiet good taste in a dress of plain cream silk. She sported no other jewellery than a string of small pearls around her neck. She was no great beauty, either, but that was true of many heiresses, and he could only commend those who were responsible for her appearance in not succumbing to the desire to deck her about with the King's ransom which she undoubtedly owned.

Susanna, on her way back to the ballroom, was aware of his close scrutiny. She had seen him once or twice during the evening and his appearance had intrigued her. One of the other companions, to whom she had chatted while the musicians were playing and their charges were enjoying themselves in the dance, had told her who he was and that he was nicknamed the Wolf.

She thought that the name suited him. He was tall, with broad shoulders, a trim waist and narrow hips—in that, he was like many of the younger men present. But few had a face such as his. It was, she thought, a lived-in face, still tanned from the Indian sun, with a dominant jutting nose, a strong chin, a long firm mouth—and the coldest grey eyes which she had ever seen. His hair was jet-black, already slightly silvered although he was still in his early thirties.

Susanna had read that wolves bayed at the moon and that they were merciless with their prey. Well, the merciless bit fitted his face, so perhaps he bayed at the moon as well—although she couldn't imagine it.

Her mouth turned up at the corners as she thought this and the action transformed her own apparently undistinguished face, giving it both charm and character, which Ben Wolfe registered for a fleeting moment before she passed him.

So that was the young woman who was going to revive
Babbacombe's flagging fortunes. He had seen prettier, but
then, money gilded everything, even looks, as he knew only
too well. He laughed soundlessly to himself. Oh, but Amelia
Western's fortune was never going to gild Lord Babbacombe's empty coffers—as he would soon find out.

If Susanna could have read Ben Wolfe's most secret
thoughts she would have known exactly how accurate his
nickname was and how much he was truly to be feared. As
it was she returned to the ballroom feeling, not for the first
time, cheated of life: a duenna soon to reach her last prayers,
doomed to spinsterhood because of the callous behaviour of
a careless young man.

Francis Sylvester had never returned to England. He had
taken up residence in Naples and seemed set to stay there
for life.

Susanna shivered, but not with cold. She wanted to be a
child again, home in bed, all her life before her. After she
had been jilted, everyone had praised her coolness, the courage with which she had faced life, but once she had ceased
to be a nine days' wonder she had been forgotten. When
Miss Stanton died and she had returned to society as Amelia
Western's companion, there were few who remembered her.

She was perpetually doomed to sit at the back of the
room, unconsidered and overlooked. She had visited her old
home, but her mother and stepfather had made it plain that
they had no wish for her company, even though the scandal
surrounding her was long dead. There was no place for her
there, now.

'You're quiet tonight, Miss Beverly, are you feeling a
trifle overset?' asked one of her fellow companions kindly.

'Oh, no,' replied Susanna briskly. She had made a resolution long ago never to repine, always to put a brave face
on things. 'It's just that, sometimes, one does not feel in the
mood for idle chatter.'

'I know that feeling,' said her friend softly. 'You would

prefer a quiet room and a good book, no doubt, to being here.'

And someone kind and charming to dance with, thought Susanna rebelliously, not simply to sit mumchance and watch other young women dance with kind and charming young men.

But she said nothing, merely smiled and watched Ben Wolfe bearded again by Lady Leominster and handed over to Charlotte Cavender, one of the Season's crop of young beauties and young heiresses. For a big man who was rumoured to have few social graces he was a good dancer, remarkably light on his feet—as so many big men were, Susanna had already noticed.

She sometimes thought it a pity that her common sense, her understanding of the world and men and women, honed by her opportunities for ceaseless observation would never be put to good use.

Stop that! she told herself sternly, just at the moment that the patterns of the dance brought Ben Wolfe swinging past her. To her astonishment, he gave her a nod of the head and a small secret smile.

Now, whatever could that mean?

Probably nothing at all. He must have meant it for his partner, but she had gone by him before she had had time to receive it. Susanna watched him disappear into the crowd of dancers, and then she never saw him again.

It was a trick of the light, perhaps, or of her own brain which was demanding that someone acknowledge that she still lived other than as an appendage to Amelia, who, having been proposed to by young Darlington, would shortly not be needing her services any more.

Which would mean turning up at Miss Shanks's Employment Bureau off Oxford Street to discover whether she had any suitable posts as governess, companion or duenna for which she might apply.

The prospect did not appeal.

Now, if only she were a young man, similarly placed, there were a thousand things she could do. Ship herself off to India, perhaps, and make a fortune—like Ben Wolfe, for example.

Drat the man! Why was he haunting her? She had never looked at a man other than in loathing since Francis's betrayal and now she could not stop thinking about someone who, rumour said, was even more dubious than Francis.

And he wasn't even good-looking and she hadn't so much as spoken to him! She must be going mad with boredom—yes, that was it.

Fortunately, at this point, Amelia returned and said excitedly, 'Oh, Miss Beverly, I feel so happy now that George has finally proposed. It will mean that once I'm married I shall be my own mistress, do as I please, go where I wish, and not be everlastingly told how a young lady ought to behave.'

Susanna could not prevent herself from saying, 'You are not worried, then, that *George* might demand some say in where you go and what you do?'

'Oh, no.' Amelia was all charming eagerness. 'By no means. We have already agreed that we shall live our own lives—particularly after I have provided him with an heir. That is understood these days, is it not?'

And all this worldly wisdom between future husband and wife as to their married life had been agreed in less than an hour after the proposal!

'Of course,' said Amelia. 'It will mean that I shall not be needing a duenna after the wedding ceremony. But then, you knew that would be the case when you undertook the post. It's what duennas must expect, George says.'

Amelia's pretty face was all aglow at the prospect of the delights of being a married woman. She was a little surprised that Susanna wasn't sharing her pleasure.

'He's promised to drive me in the Park tomorrow and he's going to insist to Mama that I go without you now that it's understood that we are to marry. You can have the afternoon off to look for a post, George says. He's very considerate that way.'

Susanna could have thought of another word to describe him, but decided not to say it.

'If your mama agrees,' she said.

'Oh, of course she will,' exclaimed Amelia. 'Why ever not?'

And, of course, Mrs. Western did.

She also agreed with her daughter that Susanna should—as a great concession—take the afternoon off to visit Miss Shanks about another post. 'I would not like you to think us inconsiderate,' she finished.

She must have been talking to George Darlington was Susanna's sardonic inward comment. But, again, she said nothing, which was the common fate of duennas, she had discovered, when faced with the unacceptable and the impossibility of remarking on it.

Fortunately for both Amelia and Susanna the afternoon was a fine one. The sun was out, but it was not impossibly hot, and after Susanna had seen that Amelia was as spick and span as a young engaged girl ought to be, she dressed herself in her most dull and proper outfit in order to impress Miss Shanks with her severe suitability and set off for Oxford Street—on her own.

It never failed to amuse her that although Amelia, only a few years younger than herself, was never allowed to go out without someone accompanying her, it was always assumed that it was perfectly safe for Susanna to do so. Who, indeed, would wish to assault a plainish and badly dressed young woman who was visibly too old for a nighthouse and too poor to be kidnapped for her inheritance?

So it was that, enjoying the fine afternoon, the passing show and the freedom from needing to accommodate herself

to the whims of others, Susanna almost skipped along with
no thought as to her safety or otherwise.

Nor did she notice when she had reached Oxford Street
that she had been followed from Piccadilly by a closed carriage driven at a slow speed and with two burly men inside,
so that when she turned into the small side street and the
carriage and men followed her, she thought nothing of it
until one of the men, looking around him to see that no one
was about, acted violently and immediately.

He caught Susanna from behind, threw a blanket over her
head and, helped by his companion, bundled her into the
carriage, which drove off at twice its previous speed in the
direction of the Great North Road.

Chapter Two

Susanna started to scream—and then changed her mind. She only knew that she was inside a carriage and had been snatched off the street by two men. Best, perhaps, not to provoke them. She was about to try to remove the restraining blanket from her head when one of the men removed it for her.

She found herself inside a luxuriously appointed chaise whose window blinds were down so that she had no notion of where she was, or where she might be going. Facing her, on the opposite seat, were two large men, both well dressed, not at all like the kind of persons one might think went about kidnapping young women.

She said, trying not to let her voice betray her fear, 'Let me out, at once! At once, do you hear me! I cannot imagine why you should wish to kidnap me. There must be some mistake.'

The larger of the two men shook his head. 'No mistake, Miss Western. We had express orders to kidnap you and no one else. And there is no need to be frightened. No harm will come to you. I do assure you.'

Somehow the fact that he was well dressed and decently spoken made the whole business worse. And what did he mean by calling her Miss Western?

Her fright as well as her anger now plain in her voice Susanna exclaimed, 'You are quite mistaken. I am not Miss Western, so you may let me out at once. In any case, why should you wish to kidnap Miss Western?'

'Come, come, missy,' said the second man, whose speech was coarser and more familiar than that of the first, 'Don't waste your time trying to flummox us. Sit back and enjoy the ride. This 'ere carriage 'as the finest springs on the market.'

Susanna's voice soared. 'Enjoy the ride, indeed! I can't see a thing, and I have urgent business to attend to this afternoon. You have made a dreadful mistake, but if you let me go at once I shall not inform the Runners of what you have done, which I promise you I surely will once I am free again.'

Number One drawled, 'That's enough. You're a lively piece and no mistake, but we have a job to do and no tricks of yours will prevent us from doing it, so my advice to you is to behave yourself.'

'Indeed I won't!' Susanna leaned forward and began to tug at the window blind with one hand whilst trying to open the carriage door with the other. 'I have no intention of behaving myself,' she shouted at him as he caught her round the waist and pulled her back into her seat.

He laughed and said, rueful admiration written on his face, 'Oh, my employer is going to enjoy taming your spirit, I'm sure, but I haven't time to argue with you. I shall have to tie your hands if you continue to try to escape. Sit quiet and do as you're bid without any more nonsense, or I'll tie your ankles together and gag you as well. Even if I was ordered to handle you gently, you're leaving me no choice.'

He spoke quietly, even deferentially to her, but Susanna had no doubt that he would carry out his threats. She sank sullenly back into her seat and tried to put a brave face on things.

They thought that she was Amelia—if so, the reason why

they would want to kidnap her was plain. Amelia Western was a noted heiress and it would not be the first time that a man wanting money had carried off an heiress and married her. It was a risky business since the penalty for such an act was death or transportation if the parents or guardians of the girl pursued the matter. Some did not, preferring to accept the forced marriage, if the man were reasonably respectable, rather than have the girl's reputation destroyed.

Equally plainly they had mistaken her for Amelia—and how they had come to do so was a mystery. A further mystery was who could Amelia have possibly met in the recent past who was capable of carrying out such a criminal act? None of the men who had surrounded her since her entrance into society seemed likely candidates—or had Amelia been privately meeting an unknown lover and they had arranged this between them?

If so, why had she been snatched off the street? For, if Amelia had been conspiring with someone, it would have been simpler for her to have manufactured some excuse to meet him in secret to save him from risking exposure by kidnapping her in broad daylight.

Not that any of this speculation was of the slightest use when each yard the chaise travelled was carrying her further away from Oxford Street, Piccadilly and her temporary home there, and into the unknown.

And what in the world would be awaiting her at her journey's end?

She was not to know for some time. They changed horses at a posthouse on the edge of London where Number One put a hand over her mouth to prevent her from calling for help while Number Two made all the necessary arrangements at their stop—which included taking on board a hamper of food.

Number One unpacked the hamper and offered her a cooked chicken leg, which she refused indignantly.

'Don't like chicken, eh? How about this, then?' and he

held out a ham sandwich. She shook her head so he gifted Number Two with the chicken and the sandwich before rummaging around in the hamper and fishing out of it a roll filled with cold roast beef, saying, 'Beef, perhaps?'

She waved it away with as much hauteur as she could summon, announcing rebelliously, 'I don't want to eat. Under the circumstances it would choke me.'

'Suit yourself, my dear. No skin off my nose. More for us, eh, Tozzy? My employer will be most disappointed. He particularly wanted you to be properly fed on the way home.'

'How very gracious of him,' Susanna snapped back. 'Even more gracious of you if you turned the chaise round and took me back to Oxford Street.'

'Can't do that, I'm afraid,' said Number One indistinctly since his mouth was full of the beef sandwich which she had rejected. 'How about some pound cake? No?'

It might be childish of her, but Susanna found that the only way to demonstrate her displeasure at what was happening to her was to turn her back on him and sniff loudly, like the cook in the Westerns' kitchen when something had happened to cause her aggravation—an event which occurred at least five times a day.

Eating over, silence fell.

Susanna resumed a more normal position, folded her arms, leaned back against the cushions and closed her eyes. She felt as exhausted as though she were a child again and had been running and jumping all afternoon with her cousin William—and whatever had happened to him? He had disappeared from her life when her mother had married again. And what a time to think of him!

The lack of light and the swaying of the chaise lulled her so that she was on the verge of dozing.

Number Two said softly to Number One, 'She's a good plucked 'un and no mistake. She'll be a match for 'im, that's for sure.'

'Oh, I doubt that very much,' yawned Number One. 'Never met anyone who was a match for him in all the years I've been with him. Pass a bottle of wine over, Tozzy, kidnapping's thirsty work.'

Even through her half-sleep Susanna heard what he said and was fired with indignation. Just let this journey be over so that she could tell their employer—whoever he might be—exactly what she thought of him for arranging a kidnapping at all, let alone one in which the wrong woman had been carried off!

Ben Wolfe was looking out of the window in the library of his great house in Buckinghamshire which had been known as The Den ever since six generations of Wolfes had lived there. Before that it had simply been called the Hall. It had been left derelict when his father had died and he had gone to India, but since his return he had spared no expense in returning it to its former glory.

He looked at his fob watch. If everything had gone as he had ordered—and he assumed that it had since Jess Fitzroy had never botched a job for him yet—it should not be long before the chaise turned into the sweep before the front of the house. He could then begin to take his revenge for the wrongs which had destroyed not only his family's wealth, but had driven his father into an early grave.

It was a pity that the girl was not particularly beautiful, but then, one could not have everything. He smiled as he thought of Babbacombe's anger when the splendid match for his son fell through and he was left penniless, ruin staring him in the face. He was absolutely sure that, even though he had carried their daughter off in order to marry her, the Westerns would find him an even more suitable husband for her than Darlington—once they had discovered the astonishing extent of his wealth and the Wychwood family's lack of it, that was, for he would take good care to let them know of it.

Even acquiring an Earl's title would not make up for that lack. Especially since someone as rich as Ben was—and with an old name into the bargain—would almost certainly be a candidate for a title of his own before very long.

Not that Ben cared about titles and all that flimflam, but the Westerns did.

He had just reached this point in his musings when the chaise turned into the sweep. As he had hoped, Jess had successfully carried out yet another task for him—and would be suitably rewarded. He had given orders for Miss Western, soon to be Mrs Ben Wolfe, to be taken initially to her suite of rooms on the first floor so that she might refresh herself after the journey.

After that she would be conducted to the Turkish drawing room—a salon designed and furnished by a seventeenth-century Wolfe who had been an Ambassador to that country—where the teaboard would be ready and where he would at last introduce himself to her.

As was his usual habit, he had planned everything carefully to the last detail so that nothing would go wrong and all would go right. Even the clothes he was wearing had been chosen with great care to give off the right aura of effortless self-command and good taste. They were neither careless nor were they dandified, but somewhere in between. His boots, whilst black and shiny, bore no gold tassels. His clothes had been cut for him by a tailor whose taste was impeccable—there were to be no wasp-waisted jackets or garish waistcoats for Mr Ben Wolfe.

He sat himself down to wait for Jess to report to him, after which he would visit the drawing room where Miss Western would be waiting for him.

Susanna stared numbly at the beautiful façade of The Den when a footman opened the chaise door and Number One helped her out. When she had first been kidnapped she had supposed that she might be taken off to some low nighthouse either in the Haymarket or London's East End. When, instead, they had obviously been driving into the country, she could form no idea of what her ultimate destination might be like.

Such splendour as Susanna saw all about her in the house and gardens awed her, and for the life of her she could not imagine why it had been necessary to carry Amelia off and bring her here. Surely the owner of such magnificence would be able to court Amelia in proper form, with no need to treat her so cavalierly? And surely, also, the owner of it would be shocked to learn that he had merely acquired a plain and poverty-stricken duenna and not the wealthy heiress she had been guarding for the past half-year.

When she walked up the steps to the double doors held open by splendidly liveried footmen she found herself shuddering slightly, not from cold or fright, but for some reason which passed her understanding. It was as though, once she walked through them, she knew that, somehow, she would find herself in a totally new world, where nothing that had happened to her in the past mattered, only what would happen in the future.

And then this sensation disappeared as though it had never been and she was plain-spoken, downright, sane and sensible Miss Susanna Beverly again, who never suffered from whim-whams or premonitions and was about to give a piece of her mind to the fool or knave who had caused her to be kidnapped.

But not yet. She had to endure a fluttering little maid and a pleasant middle-aged woman who led her upstairs to a suite of rooms so beautiful and grand that she was overset all over again. Indeed, the splendours she saw all about her temporarily silenced her so that she did not complain of her mistreatment to the women even when they called her Miss Western and tried to persuade her to change into the beautiful garments laid out on the bed.

She shook her head in refusal dazedly, but she did use

the other facilities offered her—to put it delicately—and finally washed herself and allowed her hair to be ordered a
little by the maid.

Then she was taken downstairs by the motherly body into
a drawing room which was even grander than the upstairs
rooms, where she was offered a seat and tea, which she also
refused. When the motherly body, shaking her head a little
at her silence, retreated, she sat down at last—to stare at a
wall full of beautiful paintings and prints of a foreign civili-
sation such as she had never seen before.

Outside the sun was shining. In the distance a fountain
was playing. Standing in the window through which she was
looking was a new pianoforte. Objects of great beauty and
vertu surrounded her. It would almost be like living in a
rare and well-arranged museum to take up residence here,
she thought in confusion.

And then the double doors were thrown open, and a man
walked in.

A man who was her captor—and he was, of all people,
Mr Ben Wolfe looking his most wolfish.

Mr Ben Wolfe, who had nodded and smiled at her at Lady
Leominster's ball.

This must, Susanna decided, be a nightmare. She would
shortly wake up to find herself safely back in bed in the
Westerns' Piccadilly home. Except that everything about her
seemed as sharp and well defined as objects are in real life,
not at all cloudy and shifting like those in a dream. Only
Mr Ben Wolfe's presence partook of the dream.

And if he were truly here, in this disturbing and unreal
present, then she would give him as short shrift as she was
capable of offering in her unfortunate position. She could
form no notion at all of why he had had her kidnapped or
why he was bowing and smiling at her in a manner he
doubtless considered ingratiating.

Well, she would not be ingratiated, not she! He could go
straight to the devil and ingratiate himself with him if he

could. She would demand to be sent straight back home, at once, on the instant...

Except, except...it was already late afternoon. There was no way in which she could be returned before nightfall and offer any reasonable explanation of where she had been and what she had been doing. Indeed, by now, her absence would already have been discovered.

If anything, this dreadful thought inflamed her the further. So she said nothing, merely stared at Mr Ben Wolfe, who was bowing low to her. That over, he motioned her to a seat before a low table on which a teaboard was set out, saying, 'Pray be seated, Miss Western. You are doubtless wondering why you are here. May I say that I intend you no harm. Quite the contrary.'

It was the first time she had heard him speak. He had a deep gravel voice, eminently suited to his harsh features. Susanna's first impulse was to inform him immediately that he was much mistaken: she was not Miss Western, his hired villains having carried off the wrong woman.

She wondered briefly why Amelia was the right woman. For what purpose would *she* have been brought here? She made an instant and daring decision: she would not tell him straight away that she was not Amelia, and then only after she had discovered what his wicked game was. It would be a pleasure to wrongfoot him.

Aloud she said, 'No, I will not be seated. And I do so hope, Mr Ben Wolfe—you are Mr Ben Wolfe, are you not?—that you have a satisfactory explanation for my forced presence here.'

He smiled at her, displaying strong white teeth—all the better to eat you with, my dear, being Susanna's inward response to *that* for was he not behaving exactly like the wolf whose name he bore in the fairy tale *Red Riding Hood*?

Mr Ben Wolfe, on the other hand, evidently thought that he was the good fairy in *Cinderella*, murmuring in a kind voice, 'Do not be frightened. Miss Western. My intentions

towards you are strictly honourable, I do assure you. As for
my reasons for bringing you here thus abruptly, you will
forgive me if I leave any necessary explanation for them
until later.'

'No, indeed, I do not forgive you at all. I don't believe
in your so-called honourable intentions; I have no notion of
whether you intend to wed me or bed me. Or neither. I do
so hope it's neither. I should like very much to return home
untouched—and as soon as possible.'

His smile this time was rueful. 'No, I'm afraid I can't
allow that, Miss Western. You see, I wish to marry you, to
make you the wife of one of the richest men in England
instead of one of the poorest. I'm sure, on mature and ra-
tional consideration, you—and your family—would prefer
that.'

Susanna stared at all six foot one of masculine bravura,
superbly turned out from the top of his glossy black head
to the tips of his glossy black boots.

'Then, in the name of wonder, Mr Benjamin Wolfe, why
did you not approach my parents in proper form and make
an honourable offer in an honourable fashion instead of having me carried off, hugger-mugger, like a parcel from the
post office?'

She was beginning to enjoy herself, hugging gleefully to
her bosom the knowledge that he was not talking to his
proposed forced bride at all but to her unconsidered and
poverty-stricken governess. He evidently believed her to be
Amelia and had no suspicion that he was mistaken. The
longer she continued to deceive him, the more her pleasure
grew.

On the other hand, by the looks of him he had a fine and
wilful temper, which offered her the problem of how he
would react when she finally enlightened him as to her true
identity. But that could wait. Susanna had endured her disas-
trous fall into penury by living only for the moment and

ignoring the future. What will come, would come, being her motto.

Mr Ben Wolfe bowed to her again. 'My dear girl, I have already informed you that I have my reasons and will reveal them to you on a suitable occasion. That occasion is not now. Now is the time for us to come to know one another better. To that end, pray pour us some tea before it grows cold. We shall both feel better for it.'

'There are only two things wrong with your last remark, Mr Ben Wolfe,' returned Susanna, all sweetness and light. 'The first is that I have no wish to know you any better—quite the contrary. The second is that I have no wish either to pour you tea, or drink it myself—*I* should certainly not feel any better for it. A fast post-chaise and an immediate return to London are the only requests I have to make of you.'

They were standing at some distance apart, for Mr Ben Wolfe had entered with no immediate desire to frighten his captive. On the other hand, he had expected to meet a young girl whom he could easily control by the gentlest of means. Instead, he was confronted with a talkative, self-possessed creature, older than her eighteen years in her command of language, who was evidently going to take a deal of coaxing before she agreed to become Mrs. Ben Wolfe without making overmuch fuss.

He decided to continue being agreeable and charming, praying that his patience would not run out. 'I regret,' he told her, bowing, 'that is one of the few requests which you might make of me which I must refuse. My plans for you involve you remaining here for the time being. Later, perhaps.'

'Later will not do at all!' said Susanna, who wished most heartily that he would stop bowing at her. Most unsuitable when all he did was contradict her. 'I have my reputation to consider.'

Mr Ben Wolfe suddenly overwhelmed her with what she

could only consider was the most inappropriate gallantry, all things considered. 'No need to trouble yourself about that. I shall take the greatest care of you.'

'Indeed? I am pleased to hear it—but I am a little at a loss to grasp the finer details of that statement. I ask you again do you intend to wed me—or to bed me?'

This unbecoming frankness from a single female of gentle nurture almost overset Ben Wolfe. Nothing had prepared him for it. Might it not, he momentarily considered, have been more useful for him to have been equally as frank with her from the beginning of this interview?

No matter. He smiled, and if the smile was a trifle strained, which it was, then damn him, thought Susanna uncharitably, it is all he deserves.

'Oh, my intentions are quite honourable. I mean to marry you and to that end I have already procured a special licence from the Archbishop of Canterbury himself.'

Marriage! He proposed to marry her—or rather Amelia. In the cat-and-mouse game she was playing with him Susanna had almost forgotten that she was not the target of Mr Ben Wolfe's plans. For a moment she considered enlightening him immediately, but he deserved to live in his fool's paradise a little longer, for was there not an interesting reply which she could make to his last confident declaration?

'You do surprise me, sir. First of all, you seem to forget that you have not yet asked me whether I wish to marry you and, all things considered, I'm sure that I don't; secondly, aren't you forgetting that I am already betrothed to George Darlington?'

'No, indeed—for that is precisely why you are here.'

His eyes gleamed as he came out with this, and the look he gave her was so predatory that Susanna shuddered. She was playing with a tiger. A tiger who had intended to kidnap an innocent young girl and force her to marry him in order, apparently, to prevent her from marrying George, Viscount Darlington.

Now Susanna did not like George Darlington and, by the look on his face when he had uttered his name, neither, for some reason, did Ben Wolfe, but she didn't think that he deserved to be treated quite so scurvily as to lose his proposed bride, and when she had finally confessed who she truly was she would so inform her captor.

If he was prepared to let her get a word in edgeways, that was—for she was beginning to understand that Mr Ben Wolfe in a thwarted rage might be a very formidable creature, indeed.

Unconsciously they had moved closer and closer together so that, when Susanna echoed him again by murmuring 'By saying "Precisely why you are here", you mean—I take it—that you have kidnapped me in order to thwart George Darlington by depriving him of his bride—and her money,' he bent down to take her hand, saying,

'Yes—and you are a clever child to have worked that out so quickly. I think that I may be gaining a real prize in marrying you, Miss Western.'

Susanna smiled up into his inclined face. 'Oh, I think not, Mr Ben Wolfe. All of this would be very fine if I *were* Amelia Western but, seeing that I am not, you have given yourself a great deal of trouble for exactly nothing.

'Your hirelings have only succeeded in kidnapping not Miss Western, but her poverty-stricken nothing of a governess, Susanna Beverly, who possesses no fortune and no reputation, either. By carrying me off by mistake you have destroyed the last remnants of *that* for good—and gained only frustration for yourself.'

His response to this bold and truthful declaration was to smile down at her and say gently, 'Well tried, my dear. You surely don't expect me to believe that Banbury tale!'

Really! He was being as impossibly stupid as his two hired bravos—which was not his reputation at all.

'Of course I do—for that is the truth. I told those two
bruisers of yours that they had snatched the wrong woman—
but would they listen to me? Oh, no, not they!—and now
you are as bad as they were.'

His face proclaimed his disbelief. She had carried being
Amelia off so well that she risked being stuck with her false
identity, if not for life, for the time being at least. So much
for his immediately exploding into anger when she made
her belated revelation!

Instead it was she who stamped her foot. 'Of course I'm
not Amelia. Do I look like a simple-minded eighteen-year-
old? Do I speak like one? Come to your senses, sir, if you
have any, which I beg leave to doubt on the evidence of
what I have seen of you so far. It is time that you recognised
that you have organised the kidnapping of the wrong woman
and are now unlikely to carry off the right one, for once I
am free again I shall proclaim your villainy to the world.
The punishment for kidnapping an heiress is either death or
transportation. I have no notion what the penalty is for a
mistaken kidnapping, but it ought to be pretty severe, don't
you think? Unless, of course, you could manage to get it
lessened on the grounds of your insanity.'

Susanna's transformation from a reasonably spoken
young woman of good birth into a flaming virago was a
complete one—inspired by the fear that, will she, nil she,
having been kidnapped by mistake she was going to find
herself married by mistake as well!

Ben Wolfe's face changed, became thunderous. He controlled himself with difficulty, and murmured through his
teeth, 'Tell me, madam, were you playing with me then—
or now? Was Amelia Western the pretence, or Susanna Beverly? Answer me.'

'I have already answered you. I am Susanna Beverly and
therefore nothing to your purpose at all.'

The look he gave her would have stopped the late Em-
peror of France in his tracks it was so inimical, so truly

wolf-like as he barked out, 'And how do I know that that *is* the truth? I assure you that you look and sound like no duenna I have ever had the misfortune to encounter. You are far too young to begin with. No, I fear that this is but a clever ploy to persuade me to let you go.'

'Well, I assure you that I don't find *you* clever at all. Quite the contrary,' exclaimed Susanna, exasperation plain in her voice. 'Call in that big man of yours and he will inform you that from the moment he threw me into your carriage I never stopped trying to tell him that he had carried off the wrong woman.'

Ben Wolfe knew at once that, whoever she was, there was no intimidating her—short of silencing her by throttling her—and he was not quite ready to do that, although heaven knew, if she taunted him much more, he might lose his self-control and have at her.

Choosing his words carefully, he said, 'Let us sit down, enjoy a cup of tea and talk this matter over quietly and rationally.'

Biting each word out as coldly as she could, Susanna said, 'If you offer me a cup of tea again, Mr Ben Wolfe, I shall scream!'

His answer was, oddly enough, to throw his head back and laugh. 'Well, I don't fancy tea, either. Would a glass of Madeira tempt you at all?'

'It might tempt me, but I shan't fall. A wise friend of mine once said that an offer of a glass of Madeira from a gentleman when you were alone with him was the first step on the road to ruin, so thank you, no.'

'Very prudent of you, I'm sure. Although, if you are Miss Western, you may be certain that I shall not attempt to ruin you. As I said earlier, my intentions towards you—or her—are strictly honourable. I intend to marry you—or her.'

'But since I am Miss Beverly, what will be your intentions towards *me*? Seeing that, by your reckless act, I shall have been irrevocably ruined?'

Before he could answer, Susanna added quickly, 'What I am at a loss to understand, Mr Wolfe, is how you came to mistake me for her. We are not at all alike. How did you discover who I was—or rather, who you thought I was?'

'Oh, that is not difficult to explain,' he returned, although for the first time an element of doubt had crept into his voice. 'At my express wish you were pointed out to me by Lady Leominster herself on the occasion of her grand ball the other evening. You were standing next to George Darlington at the time.'

'Was I, indeed? On the other side of the room? With another woman on his other hand?'

'Does that matter? But, yes—or so I seem to remember.'

Susanna began to laugh. 'Oh, it matters very much. One thing I know of Lady Leominster, but not many do, is that she cannot distinguish between her right or her left. Be certain, Mr Wolfe, that you have indeed carried off the duenna and not her charge. You should have asked to be introduced to Miss Western—but you had no wish to do that, did you? It would have saved you a deal of trouble and no mistake.'

Ben Wolfe, his mind whirling, tried to remember the exact circumstances in which he had seen the supposed Miss Western. Yes, it had been as she said. George Darlington had been standing between two women, and Lady Leominster had pointed out the wrong one—if the woman before him was telling the truth.

He smothered an oath. Her proud defiance was beginning to work on him—and had she not earlier told him to ask his 'big man' whom she had claimed to be when they had first captured her?

'For heaven's sake, woman,' he exclaimed, being coarse and abrupt with her for the first time now that it began to appear that she really might be only the duenna of his intended prey, 'sit down, do, don't stand there like Nemesis in person, and I'll send for Jess Fitzroy and question him. But that doesn't mean that I accept your changed story.'

'Pray do,' replied Susanna, whose legs were beginning to fail her and who badly needed the relief and comfort of one of the room's many comfortable chairs, 'and I will do as you ask. As a great concession, I might even drink some of the tea which you keep offering me.'

'Oh, damn the tea,' half-snarled Ben Wolfe before going to the door, summoning a footman and bidding him to bring Fitzroy and Tozzy to him at the double.

'By the way, before the footman leaves,' carolled Susanna, who was beginning to enjoy herself in a manic kind of way, very like someone embracing ruin because it was inevitable rather than trying to repel it, 'tell him to bring the reticule which flew from my hand on to the floor after I was dragged into the chaise. There is something in it which might help you to make up your mind about me.'

'Oh, I've already done that,' ground out Ben Wolfe through gritted teeth as he handed her a cup of tea. 'A more noisy and talkative shrew it has seldom been my misfortune to meet.'

'Twice,' riposted Susanna, drinking tea with an air, 'you've already said that twice now—you earlier announced that you had a similar misfortune with duennas. When I was a little girl, my tutor told me to avoid such repetition in speech or writing. It is the mark of a careless mind he said.'

She drank a little more tea before assuring the smouldering man before her, 'Not surprising, though, seeing that your careless mind has secured you the wrong young woman. You would do well to be a little more careful in future.'

This was teasing the wolf whom Ben so greatly resembled with a vengeance but, seeing that she had so little to lose, Susanna thought that she might as well enjoy herself before the heavens fell in.

Afterwards! Well, afterwards was afterwards—and to the devil with it.

Ben Wolfe, leaning against the wall as though he needed its support, looked as though he were ready to send her to the devil on the instant. He did not deign to answer her because he was beginning to believe that she wasn't Amelia Western, and that, for once, he had made an unholy botch of things.

No, not for once—for the very first time. He had always prided himself on his ability to plan matters so meticulously that events always went exactly as he had intended them to and he had built a massive fortune for himself on that very basis.

The glare he gave Miss Who-ever-she-was was baleful in the extreme, but appeared to worry her not one whit. There was a plate of macaroons on the teaboard and Susanna began to devour them with a will. She hadn't eaten since breakfast and all this untoward excitement was making her hungry.

It was thus Ben Wolfe who greeted the arrival of his henchman with relief. Tozzy, the junior of the two, was carrying a woman's reticule, a grin on his stupid face. Fitzroy, more acute, knew at once that his employer was in one of his rare, but legendary, tempers and assumed the most serious expression he could.

'Is that your reticule?' demanded Ben of Susanna, who was busy pouring herself another cup of tea. 'I thought that you didn't care for tea,' he added accusingly, mindful of her former refusals.

'Oh, it wasn't the tea I didn't care for,' Susanna told him smugly, 'it was the company and the occasion on which I was drinking it which incurred my dislike. I'm much happier now,' she added untruthfully, 'and, yes, that is my reticule.'

'Then hand it to her, man,' roared Ben who, being gentleman enough, just, not to shout at Susanna, shouted at Tozzy instead.

Tozzy, having handed the reticule back to Susanna, opened his mouth to speak, but was forestalled by the beleaguered Ben saying to Fitzroy, 'Look here, Jess, Miss

Who-ever-she-is says that when you picked her up in Oxford Street—'

'Kidnapped me,' corrected Susanna, who was now inspecting the contents of her little bag and smiling at them as she did so.

'You picked her up in Oxford Street,' repeated Ben through his excellent teeth, 'and she told you that she was not Miss Western. Is that true?'

Jess looked away from his employer before saying, 'Yes. I called her Miss Western and she immediately informed me that she was not.'

'And who did she say that she was?'

'She claimed to be Miss Western's duenna, Miss Beverly. But you had pointed her out to me as Miss Western yesterday in Hyde Park so I knew that she was only saying that in order to try to make me let her go. So I took no notice of her.'

'You took no notice of her,' said Ben, who found that he had recently acquired the distressing habit of repeating not only what he had said, but everything said to him. 'Didn't it occur to you to tell me that she had made such a claim?'

'Not exactly, no. You've never, to my knowledge, ever made such a mistake before—indeed, I can't remember you ever making a mistake of any kind in any enterprise we've been engaged on, it's not your way, not your way at all...'

'Jess!' said Ben awefully. 'Shut up, will you? Just tell me this. Which do you think she is? She has, in the last half-hour, claimed to be both Miss Western and Miss Beverly.'

Jess was too fascinated to be tactful. 'Both? How could she do that?'

'Easily,' said Ben. 'Damme, man. Answer the question.'

Jess looked Susanna up and down as though she were a prize horse. 'Well,' he said doubtfully, 'she's only supposed to be eighteen. I'd put her as a little older than that. On the other hand, she claimed to be a duenna and, in my experience, duennas are usually middle-aged; she certainly doesn't resemble or behave like any duenna I've ever met and—'

'Jess! Stop it. You're blithering. I know what duennas look like. Give me a straight answer.'

'Wouldn't it be simpler if you listened to me?' Susanna was all helpfulness. 'Perhaps you could explain why, if I'm Miss Western, heiress, I should be kidnapped outside an office for the placement of young gentlewomen needing employment, i.e. Miss Shanks's Employment Bureau, and carry its card in my reticule. Look,' and she handed it to Ben Wolfe who stared at it as though it were a grenade about to go off at any moment.

'She has a point,' observed Jess gloomily.

'Does that mean, yes, she's Miss Western or, no, she's Miss Beverly?' snapped Ben, tossing Jess the card.

'No, she's Miss Beverly.'

'God help me, I think so, too. You picked up the wrong woman.'

'Kidnapped her, on your orders, which he faithfully carried out,' interrupted Susanna, her mouth full of the last macaroon. 'You really can't pretend that you're not the one responsible for me being here.'

Master and man stared at one another.

'Apart from gagging her to stop her everlasting nagging, what the hell do we do now?' asked Mr Ben Wolfe of Mr Jess Fitzroy, who slowly shook his head.

Chapter Three

'Missing?' said Mrs Western to Amelia's maid, who had been sent to remind Miss Beverly that she should have been in attendance on Amelia at six of the clock precisely to see that she was turned out *à point* in order to attend the little supper party which the Earl, George's father, was giving for them at Babbacombe House that evening.

'She's not in her room, madam, and the housekeeper says that she went out early this afternoon, saying that it would not be long before she returned. She has not been seen since.'

'You visited her room, I collect. Was there any sign that she had intended to be away for some time?'

The maid shook her head. 'Not at all, madam. The ensemble which she proposed to wear this evening was laid out on her bed, together with her slippers, evening reticule and fan.'

Mrs Western heaved a great sigh. 'How provoking of her! You are sure that she is not in the house—hiding in the library, perhaps? She spends a great deal of time there which would be better spent with Miss Western.'

'I enquired of the librarian, madam, but she has not visited it today.'

'I should never have hired her—although, until now, she

has carried out her duties well enough—but tigers do not
change their spots…or do I mean leopards? What are you
smiling at, Amelia?'

'It's leopards, mama, I'm sure—or so Miss Beverly always says. But it's no great thing that she's missing. I am
to marry soon and shall not be needing a duenna—and in
any case, young women about to be married are always
allowed greater freedom than those who are not. We could
let her go immediately. I, for one, shall not miss her.'

'Not until you're married,' moaned Mrs Western. 'We
must be seen to do the right thing.'

She snapped her fingers at the maid. 'Keep a watch out
for Miss Beverly and tell her to report to me the moment
she returns—she cannot be long now, surely. Her absence
is most inconvenient.'

The maid bobbed a curtsy and said, 'Yes, madam.' Later,
after the maid had spoken to the housekeeper, they agreed
with Mrs Western that the duenna would shortly turn up.
But no, time wore on—the Westerns left for Babbacombe
House and still the duenna had not reappeared.

'Run off with someone, no doubt,' offered Mr Western
when they reached home again and she was still missing.
'If she's not back by morning, we'll inform the Runners of
her absence—just in case something odd might have occurred.'

'Never mind that, Mr Western—whatever the circumstances, you will agree with me that she's to be turned away
without a reference.'

'Indeed, my dear. Amelia is right. She no longer needs a
duenna for these last few weeks before she marries.'

Susanna was not to know—although she had already
guessed—the manner in which her disappearance was
treated by the Western family and the way in which it would
complete the ruin which Francis Sylvester had begun.

While Mrs Western and Amelia were discussing her fate

so callously, she was sitting alone before the now-empty teaboard, Ben Wolfe and his chief henchman having retreated to Ben's study in order to discuss how to extricate themselves from the quagmire into which they had fallen as a result of kidnapping the wrong woman.

Not, Susanna concluded, wondering whether to ring the bell and ask for something more to eat, that there was such a thing as the right woman where kidnapping was concerned! And why was Mr Wolfe so bent on depriving George Darlington of his bride? There was a fine puzzle for her to solve.

The secret little smile she gave when she thought of what the two men might be planning in order to repair their present unhappy situation was quite a naughty one.

I really should not be amused, she told herself severely, for I can think of no happy way out of this brouhaha for myself. On the other hand... She paused, and thought carefully for some minutes. On the other hand, I must admit that Ben Wolfe seems to be a man of great resourcefulness, but he will need all of that to disentangle himself from the spider's web which he has created.

She was not far wrong about Ben. Once out of the sound of Susanna's mocking voice, constantly reminding him of what a cake he had made of himself, he had recovered the cold-blooded and cold-hearted equanimity which had taken him from poverty to immense riches.

'Don't say anything, Jess,' he had commanded, his right hand raised, when they reached his study, a comfortable room that was all oak, leather and bookshelves. 'I freely acknowledge my error. I am entirely to blame, and conceit has been my undoing. You carried out my orders to the letter and the only thing I can fault you for is not reporting to me the lady's reaction when you kidnapped her. What I have to do now is save the situation from becoming even worse than it already is.

'I cannot allow this innocent young woman to suffer as a consequence of my folly, but how to rescue her poses a number of difficulties. If you have any suggestions to offer, pray make them now.'

He flung himself into a high-backed chair which stood before a large oak desk on which pens, papers, sand, sealing wax, rulers and a large ledger were carefully arranged. As elsewhere in the house the room was meticulously ordered, a monument to the care with which Ben Wolfe normally arranged his life and that of those around him.

Jess looked down at him, a rueful smile on his face. 'If I had a magic sentence which, once uttered, put all to rights again, then I would offer it to you,' he said. 'But for the life of me I cannot think what would mend matters—or, indeed, if they could be mended. The young woman is here, will be missed by her employers and will have no tale to offer them which would not end in ruining us all—including her.'

'Job,' said Ben bitterly. 'I might have known that you would be Job's comforter. One thing, she cannot stay here long, in a house of men, with no duenna for herself, so that must be the first remedy—but how?'

He leaned forward, his elbows on the desk, his eyes closed. Jess had seen him do this many times before when he was concentrating, so he remained as still and silent as he could.

Ben began by reproaching himself for his carelessness. The young woman, Susanna, had the right of it. But enough of that. He needed a duenna for the duenna. But who? And how? How much time passed as he cleared his mind of thought and waited for inspiration to strike he never knew.

He lifted his head, looked at Jess, and said, 'I have it. Celeste. I wonder that I did not think of her before.'

'Celeste?' asked Jess, puzzled.

'Yes. Celeste. Madame la Comtesse de Saulx who is living not two miles away and whose reputation is beyond reproach.'

'You mean the Frenchwoman who has rented the Hall outside Lavendon. She is the epitome of all that is proper,' returned Jess. 'I had no notion that you knew her.'

'I know her, and she is not French—although she sounds as though she is.'

'And you think that she would agree to help us?'

Ben smiled. He had never looked so wolfish. 'Oh, I think she might be persuaded.'

He did not say, I know that she will and for reasons which I cannot discuss with you—or anyone else. All that remained was for him to ride over to her home, Primrose Hall, and ask her to help him—and immediately.

Jess watched him as he rose, saying, 'Ask Nicholson to have my curricle and my best pair of chestnuts ready as soon as possible. I'll drive over immediately. It's only a short run and she can come back with me straight away. Tell the housekeeper to prepare another suite of rooms for her and for her maid—and possibly an attendant if she wishes to stay overnight. I doubt that she will, but one never knows.

'In her hands, Miss Beverly's reputation should be quite safe.'

He bounded out of the room, all his usual violent energy restored.

Jess called after him, 'And I am to tell Miss Beverly of what you are planning?'

'You are to tell Miss Beverly nothing of that. Tell Mrs Ashton to attend on her and suggest that she goes to her room, change into the clothing provided for her, and be ready to eat an early supper with you, myself, and at least one other guest. That is all.'

Jess watched him go. Now, how in the world had he come to know Madame de Saulx? And know her well enough to demand such a favour of her? She was too old, surely, to be, or have been, his mistress; in any case, she was widely known for her virtue as well as her strong sense of propriety.

He shook his head. He had known and worked for Ben Wolfe for many years—but he still had no real notion of the true man he was, or of the many secret affairs which his employer chose to keep to himself.

Ben himself, cursing his folly, made short work of his visit to Madame de Saulx. He drove at a pace which, although it could not exactly be described as *ventre à terre*, was near to it. He knew that *Madame* would receive him immediately, not keep him waiting, at whatever hour he chose to arrive.

He was shown into a drawing room which already bore the marks of *Madame*'s impeccable taste, and it was not long before she appeared. She was in her middle fifties, was tall beyond the common height of women, and bore the remains of a great beauty. She was dressed modestly, although her turnout had that air of *je ne sais quoi* which most Frenchwomen of noble birth possessed.

Her shrewdness was demonstrated immediately when, after Ben had performed the common courtesies which a gentleman owed to the lady whom he was visiting, she said gently, 'Pray, sit down. I know by your face that you must have come on some matter of great moment, but we can still discuss it in comfort. I have no mind to have you pacing my drawing room like a caged tiger!'

Ben gave a short laugh and did as he was bid. 'How well you know me! I have come, as you have doubtless guessed, to ask a great favour of you.'

'You may ask as many favours of me as you please, great or small. Nothing I can do for you could equal the one great favour you did for me.'

'You exaggerate, but let me come to the meat of my problem as soon as may be,' and he immediately began to tell her the sad tale of how he had, by chance, come to kidnap the wrong woman, and how urgently he needed her assistance to save three reputations.

'*Bien sûr,*' she said, her voice and manner grave, 'that I shall certainly not ask you why you chose to do such a thing—but I can guess. What do you propose that will mend matters?'

'That you will come immediately to The Den to be introduced to Miss Susanna Beverly as a French noblewoman of impeccable birth, who is ready to assist her in every way after hearing of the sad mischance which I have so carelessly brought about. I have concocted an explanation which I believe will do the trick of allowing her to retain her reputation and which will also disassociate her completely from any connection with me—that is, if you agree to it.

'It goes as follows. You were being driven along Oxford Street when you saw this young gentlewoman overcome by faintness. Of your infinite compassion you stopped, assisted her into your chaise and took care of her. She did not recover for some time and, when she did, she was temporarily afflicted with a distressing loss of memory. Again, of your compassion, you drove her to your *pied à terre* in Stanhope Street near Regent's Park, where you cared for her until her memory returned. After which you immediately arranged to restore her to the family by whom she is at present employed.'

Madame clapped her hands together gently.

'Excellent. You should be writing plays for Drury Lane! I shall, of course, need to drive the young woman secretly back to London and make it known that I had recently arrived there in order to take part in the Season. I shall be happy to oblige you, seeing that I need to visit the capital in order to renew my wardrobe and visit a few old friends.'

'Excellent,' echoed Ben, looking happy for the first time for several hours. 'All that remains is for you to meet Miss Beverly as soon as possible. She seems a most respectable young woman, except that she said something rather odd to me, to the effect that, if it were known that she had apparently run off with me, it would finally destroy her reputation which was damaged already. Have you heard of any scandal relating to a young woman of that name? If you have, I think that you ought to tell me. It would be as well to know exactly where we stand.'

'Very true,' nodded *Madame* gravely. 'You and I, of all people, know the necessity of guarding our backs. The name is a little familiar—but I will try to gain her confidence this evening; if anything important crops up, I shall not hesitate to inform you.'

She smiled and said after a fashion as cool as his, 'By the by, I must congratulate you on your choice of words to describe the criminal act which you have just committed! To describe an innocent young lady's forcible kidnapping as "a sad mischance" is a feat worthy of the late Dr Johnson himself!'

Ben's grin was somewhat shamefaced. 'You never spare me, *Madame*,' he told her.

'Indeed not. There ought to be someone in the world who is capable of compelling you to face the truth about yourself occasionally, *mon cher*.'

And so it was arranged. On the one hand, in London, Susanna's future was being busily destroyed whilst, in the country, a practised pair of conspirators were equally busily trying to rebuild it!

Chapter Four

Whilst Ben was occupying himself at Lavendon by covering up his blunder, Susanna, at the urgings of Mr Jess Fitzroy, allowed the housekeeper, Mrs Ashton, and the little maid to accompany her upstairs, bathe her, and dress her in the modish clothing which lay on the bed in her suite of rooms.

It was many years since she had worn anything so fine, so expensive and yet so ladylike. Looking in the long mirror, she saw herself transformed. Mrs Ashton who had been a lady's maid herself long ago, not only dressed her hair for her, but also applied a *soupçon* of rouge with a fine hare's-foot brush, despite Susanna exclaiming that she never used it.

'You are a little wan, my dear. The tiniest application of colour to your cheeks will soon remedy that. There—' and she swung Susanna towards the mirror again so that she could see for herself that the ravages of the afternoon had been repaired.

'Now, you must go downstairs,' said her new guardian. 'I understand that it will not be long before the Master returns and, shortly after that, dinner will be served. It will be at an odd hour, to be sure, but then, Mr Wolfe has his own ways of going on—as you have doubtless discovered.'

Oh, yes, Miss Susanna Beverly had already discovered
that! She arrived in the drawing room to find Mr Jess Fitzroy
there, dressed in a superfine blue jacket, cream pantaloons
and the most elegant evening slippers—to say nothing of an
artistically tied cravat and suitably dishevelled hair in the
latest fashion.

He bowed to her gracefully. 'Allow me to congratulate
you on your appearance, Miss Beverly. Most fitting.'

'Fitting for what, Mr Fitzroy—to be kidnapped again?
And maltreated into the bargain?'

He bowed again. 'I pray you, forgive me for that—but
do admit…my unfortunate behaviour to you was based on
a complete misunderstanding.'

'And am I to infer from that, that all would have been
well if you had carried off Miss Western and not myself?
If so, I wonder at your morality, sir, as well as your common
sense.'

By Jove, Ben had been right. The woman had a tongue
like a viper and did not hesitate to use it!

Nevertheless, Jess Fitzroy had the grace to look a trifle
ashamed of himself before he muttered, 'Why, as to that,
Miss Beverly, there are reasons—'

He got no further before Susanna exclaimed, 'Pray do not
enlarge on them, sir, for I am sure that I should neither
approve of them nor like them!'

Jess was saved from having to reply by the arrival of Ben
Wolfe, with Celeste, Comtesse de Saulx, on his arm. Both
of them were dressed in the latest stare of fashion appro-
priate to their sex and to their different ages.

Ben, indeed, had for once allowed his valet to do his best
for him—why, he did not know. It was not that he wished
to attract Miss Susanna Beverly in any way, far from it,
simply that he wished to reassure both the Comtesse and
her as to his claims to respectability.

The Comtesse had not only acceded to his demand that
she return to The Den with him immediately, but she had

also had herself dressed for dinner with exemplary speed after her arrival there. Ben's valet had passed on to him the welcome news that Miss Beverly had joined Mr Fitzroy in the Turkish drawing room where they were awaiting his arrival.

At least the argumentative virago had had the grace to give way over something. Ben had not relished the thought of another slanging match occasioned by his unwanted guest refusing to oblige him by dining with him. Not only that, when he walked in, he saw immediately that she had also obliged him by assuming the clothes which she had earlier refused.

But that was not all that he saw—or experienced—either when she rose to greet him, or when he took her hand to kiss its back after the continental fashion of which he knew Madame la Comtesse would approve. For, seeing Susanna for the first time as a woman, and neither as an object destined to bring about his long-awaited revenge on the Wychwoods, nor as the wretched nuisance who had been carried off as the result of his own folly, had the oddest effect on him.

That indomitable spirit, which had allowed Susanna to overcome the series of disasters which had afflicted her since her father's death, shone through the envelope of flesh which clothed it, and, in doing so, touched Ben Wolfe's own proud and unyielding soul.

There was nothing of the flesh about this experience for either of them. It affected Ben the more strongly and immediately precisely because it was so different from anything he had ever known before. It was not Susanna's fine eyes, or her tender mouth, nor her carefully arranged and lustrous hair, or even the delicate figure revealed by the arts of a Parisian dressmaker, attractive though these were, which were having such a strong effect on him.

No, it was something more, something which passed his understanding and which made him see Susanna in a totally new light. And when he took her small hand in his to kiss the back of it, a shudder passed through both of them.

Susanna's eyes widened and she withdrew her hand as though it had been stung. Nevertheless, so instantaneous was their reaction that even the keen-eyed Comtesse did not notice that Ben Wolfe and the pretty young woman whom he was now presenting to her were sharing something which neither of them could explain.

Why meeting Ben Wolfe again after a short absence should affect her so differently and so profoundly from her first sight of him, Susanna did not know. Perhaps, she told herself, it was my anger at being so vilely mistreated on his orders which made my first reaction to him one of acute distaste. That, and the harsh manner in which we both attacked one another.

But I must not trust him until he has proved that he is worthy to be trusted—he and this *grande dame* who has sprung from nowhere and whose reputation for virtue is such that the whole world knows of it.

As though he had just read her mind, Ben said, 'Madame de Saulx has kindly consented to join with me in arranging that you shall suffer nothing from the mischance which has befallen you today. We shall speak of it later at our leisure, after we have enjoyed the excellent meal which the butler tells me the chef has prepared for us.'

Thus, she had no alternative but to fall in with his wishes when Madame de Saulx said approvingly in her prettily accented English, 'What a splendid notion, *cher* Ben. I hope Miss Beverly will understand that all her troubles are now over, and that she has nothing more to fear.'

'Other than that when I *do* return to the Westerns, whatever explanation we may offer them, they will almost certainly terminate my employment,' Susanna could not prevent herself from saying.

'Oh, as to that, my dear young lady,' *Madame* reassured her, 'you need have no fear. One way or another you will be taken care of. It is the very least that Mr Wolfe can do for you after causing you so much mental and physical agony as a consequence of his foolishness. Is not that so, *cher* Ben?'

Susanna was pleased to see that, for once, '*cher* Ben' looked a trifle discomfited by this rebuke. Jess Fitzroy even smiled a little at it, only to earn from *Madame* a rebuke of his own. 'And you need not smirk so condescendingly at your employer, Mr Fitzroy, for your own part in this unhappy business is not without its share of blame.'

Bravo, *Madame*, was Susanna's inward comment, even as the butler entered to inform them that dinner was served, and Mr Fitzroy proceeded to offer her his arm so that they might properly follow Madame la Comtesse and Mr Wolfe into the dining room where she might forget for a time her unfortunate predicament.

'Allow me, Miss Beverly,' said Ben, 'to inform you at length of the measures which I have taken to explain your strange disappearance from London earlier today.'

They were all back in the Turkish drawing room again; the inevitable teaboard before them. They had just enjoyed the excellent meal which Ben had promised them. During it they had spoken only of the lightest matters, such as the health of the present monarch; the latest scandal about that old and faded figure, the Prince Regent; of his equally faded and scandalous wife, Princess Caroline of Wales; the recent birth of the Princess Victoria and even, at *Madame*'s instigation, of the change in women's dress brought about by the slight lowering of the waistline.

'So there you have it, Miss Beverly,' said Ben, after he had finished outlining his plans for Susanna's immediate future. '*Madame* has agreed to be our saviour and we can but hope that you will approve of the arrangements which we have made to bring about such a happy outcome.'

'I am struck dumb by your ingenuity,' returned Susanna,

'and can only hope that it will impress the Westerns sufficiently to save me. Were anyone with a reputation less than that of *Madame*'s to sponsor me, I believe that the task might be difficult, nay, impossible, but, as it is—' she shrugged her shoulders '—I can only thank her for her kindness and condescension in offering to assist me at such short notice.'

Madame's glance for her was an approving one. 'Properly and graciously spoken,' she said, 'as I am sure Mr Wolfe will acknowledge.'

Ben put down a china teacup which was so small that his big hand dwarfed it. 'With one small rider,' he added. 'Much, I fear, depends on the fact that Miss Beverly's own reputation is a spotless one. I was a little perturbed by a statement which she made to me earlier this afternoon to the effect that she possessed neither fortune nor reputation, and that by carrying her off I had destroyed the last remnants of the latter. I wonder if you would care to enlarge on that, Miss Beverly, so that we might all know where we stand?'

The white smile which he offered Susanna as he asked his question had her mentally echoing Red Riding Hood again: Oh, Grandma, what big teeth you have! It was plain that little said or done escaped him, and although she had no wish to tell Ben Wolfe of all people her sad story, let alone two other strangers on whose charity she now depended, tell it she must.

What was it that her father had said to her when she was a child? 'Speak the truth and shame the devil, my dear.' Well, she would do exactly that.

Aloud, after a little hesitation, she said, 'The explanation for my remark is a simple one. I believe that what happened to me should cause no one to think any the worse of me, but the world chooses to believe quite otherwise. Four years ago I was jilted by Lord Sylvester. He was cruel enough to leave me waiting for him at the altar where I received, not my bridegroom, but a letter informing me that he no longer wished to marry me.

'You must all be aware of what such an action does to the reputation of a woman, however innocent she might be, and I was truly innocent—but I was ruined, none the less. No man wishes to marry a woman who has been jilted.'

Madame said thoughtfully. 'So, you are *that* Miss Beverly, the late William Beverly's only child and heiress. I did wonder if you might be, but I thought it would be considered tactless to question you on the matter if you proved not to be her.'

Ben Wolfe, however, leaned forward in his chair, intent it seemed, on quizzing her further.

'You say that you are employed by the Westerns as a duenna. I was out of England at the time and consequently knew nothing of the scandal which followed. But if you *are* the India merchant William Beverly's heiress, how is it that you have descended into becoming a duenna, a paid servant? He was as rich as Croesus, to my certain knowledge.'

However painful it might be to tell them more of her sad situation, Susanna had no alternative but to do so.

'And so I thought when he died, some twelve years before I was to have married Lord Sylvester. My mother married again, one Samuel Mitchell, soon after my father's death, but after I was jilted my stepfather informed me that, contrary to public—and my—belief, my father had died a ruined man, and he had been keeping me since my mother's marriage.

'It was, he said, he who was providing my ample dowry in the hope that I would make a good marriage. Now that my chance of making any sort of marriage had gone, he was no longer prepared either to keep me or to be responsible for my dowry. Consequently it was necessary for me to find employment.'

No one spoke for a moment. *Madame* said gently, '*En effet*, he turned you out?'

'I suppose you might say so.'

'Oh, I do say so.' It was not *Madame* who answered her, but Ben Wolfe, and the look he gave her was quite different from any he had offered her before. There was pity in it for the first time.

Damn his pity! She didn't want it, or anything else from him—especially the odd sensations which she was feeling every time she looked at him.

'You were not to know,' she told him.

'No, but nor should I have treated you so harshly this afternoon—but, in fairness to myself you did, at first, lead me to think that you were Amelia Western, which made it difficult for me to believe that you were telling the truth when you finally claimed to be Susanna Beverly. My apology to you for carrying you off, and then vilifying you, may be late but, believe me, it is sincere.'

They might as well have been alone in the room, so intent was each on the other. His grey eyes were no longer cold, his harsh features had softened into a smile. Susanna found it difficult to offer him one back. What she did do was acknowledge to him her own complicity in creating the situation which had set them so distressfully at odds.

'I should not have claimed to be Miss Western,' she admitted, 'but your cavalier attitude towards me—and indirectly towards her—angered me beyond reason. I am still at a loss as to why you should plan to do anything so wicked as carry off a young girl in order to make her your forced wife.'

As she said this, Susanna registered that Madame la Comtesse de Saulx was nodding her elegant head in agreement.

'That is neither here, nor there,' riposted Ben loftily.

Rightly or wrongly, Susanna could not leave it at that. 'And do you still intend to kidnap poor Amelia? If so, then regardless of anything which is done to assist me, I must inform the Westerns—'

Ben said, his tone regretful, 'Alas, no, that plan has been

thwarted forever by the mistake which I made in identifying the wrong woman. Miss Western has nothing further to fear from me. More than that I cannot promise.'

So he was still considering further action of a lawless kind and, judging by what he had said in their first furious interview, it must concern the Wychwoods. But this was no business of hers. She owed them nothing. Her one concern was that young and innocent—even if silly and selfish—Amelia Western should be protected from the predator named Ben Wolfe.

Something of her emotions showed on her face, or Ben Wolfe was mind reading, for he said gravely, 'What are you thinking of, Miss Beverly, that causes your smooth young brow to furrow and your eyes to harden as they examine me in my own drawing room?'

'That you are a ruthless man, Mr Wolfe, and that I should not like you for an enemy—and that once you have set out to perform some action, whether lawful or lawless you are not easily deterred from carrying it through.'

'Bravo, Miss Beverly!' exclaimed Madame de Saulx, 'our friend Ben Wolfe is often in need of hearing some plain speaking and in this case you are the right person to supply it!'

Susanna's eyes glowed with honest indignation. 'He is not my friend, *Madame*, and it was an ill day when he mistook me for another woman. I shall accept his help in restoring myself, unstained, to society again, for he owes me that favour, but afterwards I shall thank him, bid him goodbye and try to forget that I ever met him.'

This brave and spirited declaration was admired by all three of her hearers, including Ben Wolfe. *Madame* clapped her hands together, and Jess could not restrain himself from saying, 'Well spoken, Miss Beverly, but may I be excepted from the interdict which you have proclaimed against Mr Wolfe since I should so wish to meet you again under happier circumstances?'

He avoided looking at Ben as he came out with this small act of defiance. His reward for it came when Susanna, regarding him thoughtfully, said, 'So soon as I am settled in life again, Mr Fitzroy, you may call upon me. More than that I cannot say. I must remember that you were merely carrying out your employer's orders, and only those like myself who are in a similar subordinate position can sympathise with the necessity to do so in order to earn one's bread.'

'Earn one's bread!' exclaimed Ben sourly, glaring at Jess's peacock-like splendour. 'I pay him much more than that, I think, if he can turn himself out like a Bond Street dandy, ready to make eyes at any pretty woman.'

Jealous! thought *Madame*, he's jealous because Miss Beverly spoke kindly to his aide, but not to him. Whoever would have guessed it? Now, what does that tell me? She examined Ben with knowing eyes. That's the first time in our long acquaintance that I have ever known him display such an emotion or care two pins about what any woman thought of him—or any man, either. Always excepting myself, that is.

Goodness, does that mean that he thinks of me as pretty? was Susanna's response. And could he possibly have been hurt because I spoke kindly to Mr Fitzroy and not to him?

Ben, indeed, scarcely knew what to think of himself. He waved a hand at Jess who opened his mouth to answer him. 'No,' he said, 'forgive me. I have made enough mistakes, as well as one unwanted enemy today, without my being graceless to my most faithful friend—for that, Miss Beverly,' he added, turning to her, 'is how I think of Jess.'

Jess, surprised by this unwonted declaration mumbled, 'You do me too much honour, Ben,' while Susanna murmured,

'So you can be kind, Mr Wolfe, and, after a fashion, you have reprimanded me, for the Lord tells us to forgive our enemies, and now that you are not even my enemy I should have answered you more kindly.'

'And that,' announced *Madame* firmly, 'is enough of that. Heartsearching is a thankless occupation if overdone. Do you sing or play, Miss Beverly? Ben has a fine Broadwood piano and I have a mind either to play it, or to hear you play.'

'I can play a little, but I am a better singer,' answered Susanna.

'Good,' said *Madame*, 'then we shall entertain the company. Are you acquainted with Mr Tom Moore's songs?'

'Certainly. My favourite is "The Last Rose of Summer."'

'How fortunate, for it is also one of mine! And, that being so, let us perform it first of all. Shakespeare has said that music hath charms to soothe the savage breast. Let it soothe ours and we shall all sleep the more easily.'

Was it a coincidence that *Madame* was gazing at Ben Wolfe when she came out with this? Ben thought not. As he listened to Susanna's pure young soprano soar effortlessly towards the painted ceiling, the power of the music lulled his restless mind and his busy plotting brain into temporary tranquillity, as well as increasing his unwilling admiration for his unwanted guest.

What had he done to his calmly controlled existence by dragging Miss Susanna Beverly into it? For the first time in his life he found himself considering a woman as something more than someone there to entertain him briefly and then be forgotten.

Chapter Five

'Has no one any notion where the wretched woman was going?'

Mr Western, on the urgings of his wife, was interviewing the servants two days after Miss Beverly's disappearance. Any hope that she might suddenly return was fading, and since an examination of her room had shown that she had taken nothing with her except the clothes in which she had left the house, it was beginning to appear extremely likely that some misfortune had befallen her.

The butler answered for his staff. 'None at all, sir. As you know, we had little to do with Miss Beverly, nor she with us. She exchanged no confidences with anybody—indeed, until she failed to return, no one was quite sure why she had left the house.'

'Then we must inform the authorities of her disappearance,' said Mr Western gloomily. 'She is, after all, of good family, and we must not appear to be negligent or careless concerning her safety.'

'Oh, we must be seen to be doing the proper thing,' said his wife contemptuously. 'For my part, I still think that she has run off with someone. Such creatures are more trouble than they are worth.'

'I'm sure I don't want her back,' offered Amelia.

'I shall start matters in train this afternoon,' said Mr Western. 'But first tell Cook to provide us with some nuncheon. Such matters are best discussed on a full stomach.'

'Or not at all,' commented his wife acidly.

They were about to enjoy the nuncheon when the butler entered, a strange expression on his face.

'Madame la Comtesse de Saulx has arrived, sir, and has asked to see you at once. She says that the matter is most urgent.'

'Madame de Saulx!' exclaimed Mrs Western, throwing down her napkin. 'What can she want with us?'

'She might have come at a more convenient time,' moaned Mr Western. 'Have you any notion,' he demanded of the butler, 'what this most urgent matter might be?'

'Only that she has Miss Beverly with her.'

'What?' exclaimed Mr Western, throwing his napkin down, too, and leaping to his feet. 'Have you admitted them?'

'Indeed, they are in the drawing room.' The butler smirked. 'One does not turn away such as *Madame*.'

'True, true,' said Mr Western. 'Come, my dear. As the young woman was our daughter's duenna, you must accompany me.'

'May I come too?' asked Amelia. 'I'm sure that I wish to know what Miss Beverly can be doing with the Comtesse de Saulx.'

Both her parents said together, 'No, it would not be proper.'

Mrs Western added, 'I promise to tell you all that transpires, my dear.'

'Not the same as being there,' grumbled Amelia, subsiding into her chair and picking up a buttered roll.

'Be sure not to overeat, my love,' ordered her mother. 'You are already a trifle too plump to be fashionable.'

Amelia made a face behind her mother's back as the door

closed on it. It was bad enough that the duenna had bullied her about her eating habits, but it would be the outside of enough if her mother started singing the same tune!

Mrs Western was not singing any tune when she walked into the drawing room on her husband's arm to find there, as the butler had promised, not only the Comtesse, but also their duenna, dressed *à point*, although looking a trifle pale.

Susanna had been amused when, earlier that day, *Madame* had entered her bedroom in Stanhope Street carrying a bowl full of a fine white powder, a pot of oil and a large powder puff on the end of a stick.

'You look altogether too healthy, my love,' she proclaimed, 'for a young woman suffering from an unexplained fainting fit in Oxford Street. Permit me to remedy the matter.'

With that she sat Susanna down and tied a shawl around her shoulders before smearing oil gently on her face. Next she swirled the puff in the white powder before applying it to Susanna's too-rosy cheeks. She then produced a smaller puff with which she removed the surplus powder, leaving Susanna with an interesting pallor suitable for a convalescent from a sudden attack of some unknown, but mercifully brief, illness.

'Much better,' pronounced *Madame*, removing the shawl. 'Try not to rub it off and your late employer will have no suspicion of the truth.'

'My late employer,' echoed Susanna, a trifle bemused. 'She has not yet dismissed me—although she doubtless will.'

'I assure you that she will not have the opportunity to do so, for Mr Wolfe and I are adamant that you shall not return to the Westerns. The reason, of course, being that you need to recuperate and, after that, you will become my companion—saving me the trouble of going to Miss Shanks's excellent bureau to find one.'

The mention of Mr Wolfe had Susanna up in arms immediately. 'Since when did he gain the right to decide my future?' she exclaimed, her eyes shooting fire.

Madame regarded her with approval. 'I admire your spirit, my dear, but he gained that right when he did you such a great wrong. To make up for that he has decided, with my help, to safeguard your future. Do I understand that you do not wish to become my companion?'

There was nothing Susanna would like better. From what she had seen of *Madame* and of her home, her own life would be infinitely more pleasant in *Madame*'s establishment than in any other in which she had ever worked. It was only Mr Wolfe's meddling hand that she resented.

'Of course,' she admitted. 'You are being most generous, and I must sound thankless, but—' She stopped, not sure how to continue.

'But you dislike the notion that Mr Wolfe had a hand in things. Believe me, he has a hand in more things than you can possibly imagine. Forgive him—particularly since to my certain knowledge it is rare for him to condescend to repair his mistakes—not that he makes many.'

Well, it would have to do and, sitting in the Westerns' drawing room, Mrs Western's baleful eyes on her, she was grateful to both him and *Madame* as *Madame* poured treacle over them, admitted to being Miss Beverly's good Samaritan and detailed the brief loss of memory which had resulted in her delay in returning Miss Beverly to them.

'Not that that return will be permanent, I hope,' she ended, bathing her hearers in smiling condescension. 'My physician has urged rest and recuperation for Miss Beverly before she returns to any duties she may have to perform. I understand that your daughter is soon to marry and that consequently you will have little further need of Miss Beverly's services. I suggest that it would be to the benefit of us all if you were to allow Miss Beverly to resign from your employment immediately so that she can become my companion as soon as her recovered health permits. I fear that at the moment she is still feeling weak.'

This last sentence was a signal for Susanna to lean back in her chair, hang her head while sighing gently before fetching one of *Madame*'s fine lace kerchiefs from her reticule in order to hold it before her eyes as though overcome.

This artistic manoeuvre was the result of some careful coaching by *Madame* before they left Stanhope Street for Piccadilly.

'I really do feel the most awful fraud,' Susanna had said whilst being instructed, 'and I am also fearful that I shall give myself away by laughing at the wrong moment.'

'Nonsense, child,' said *Madame* briskly. 'Only imagine that you are contemplating the death of your pet dog or bird—if you ever had one—and even tears will not be beyond you. Do you think that you *could* manage tears?' she added hopefully.

'I'd rather not,' said Susanna, wondering how *Madame* had gained such a reputation for virtue when she was the mistress of so many artful tricks. Nevertheless, in the Westerns' drawing room, she achieved the appearance of one suffering a major attack of the vapours by remembering her poor pug who had expired twelve years ago and whom she had forgotten until this moment.

Only *Madame*, thrusting a bottle of smelling salts under her nose and saying, 'There, there, dear child, we shall soon be home again where you may rest. We can collect your belongings on another day if you do not feel equal to the task today,' prevented her from succumbing to a severe attack of the giggles, something from which she had not suffered since she was thirteen.

Both Mr and Mrs Western were grateful to *Madame* for disposing of the duenna so easily and leaving them with nothing to reproach themselves had they turned her out with nowhere to go.

They parted with mutual expressions of admiration as

though all four of them had been oldest and dearest friends
for years—and Susanna was free once again.

Not before, however, Mrs Western, quite overcome by
the graciousness of a grand personage whom she had never
expected to find in her home, begged to be allowed to present Amelia to *Madame* while arrangements were being
made to collect Susanna's few possessions and stow them
in the boot of *Madame's* chaise.

'By all means, nothing would please me more,' trilled
Madame untruthfully. 'And I am sure that Miss Beverly
would wish to make her adieux to her late charge.'

Susanna was not sure that she would but, since polite
deceit appeared to be the order of the day, she smiled her
assent. She was not quite capable, she decided, of uttering
an outright lie.

Her late charge, though, was delighted to be admitted to
the great lady's presence and to discover that she was to
lose her duenna immediately. Nothing would satisfy her but
that *Madame* should recite all over again the saga of Susanna's misadventure and rescue.

'How convenient,' she exclaimed, 'for her to be able to
turn a sad accident into something so fortunate in its consequences for us all! You are aware, I suppose, that I am
about to marry Viscount Darlington, Lord Babbacombe's
heir, in the near future.'

This was an arrogant statement, not a question, and *Madame's* reply, had anyone cared to examine it, possessed
more than a touch of ambiguity.

'Oh, then,' she murmured, 'you will truly be needing all
the good wishes which I can offer you, my dear.'

'You are too gracious, Madame la Comtesse,' Amelia
simpered back at her, oblivious of any double meaning—as
were her parents.

Only Susanna understood that one was there for anyone
who was acute enough to hear it. She wondered briefly why
Madame should choose to exercise her wit on the Westerns,

but decided that it was merely her idea of amusement. She was beginning to understand why she and Ben Wolfe were such great friends.

Thinking of him made her wonder what he was doing and where he was—and at the same time reproach herself for thinking about him at all.

Back in London again Ben Wolfe was reproaching himself for his inability to forget Miss Susanna Beverly. There were few idle moments in his busy days, but when they came along he found himself remembering her and the way in which she had sparked at him, had refused to bend before his will and had gallantly held her own in every one of their verbal encounters.

He had met prettier women—beautiful ones, even—but none of them had lingered in his memory as she had done. Standing before his desk in the house he owned off Piccadilly, he remembered the morning on which she and *Madame* had left The Den.

From the window of his study he had watched their chaise and the following heavy coach containing *Madame*'s most important servants and their luggage travel along the drive towards the main gates of The Den in order to make for the London Road.

He had let the heavy curtain fall as the carriages disappeared and turned to Jess Fitzroy, saying, 'And that's the end of that. Now I shall have to make new plans to deal with Babbacombe and his cub.'

Jess said, his voice as unemotional as he could make it, 'Do you think that's wise? Was yesterday's débâcle meant to be a warning to you from the gods? And is your interest in Miss Beverly truly at an end?'

'I don't pay you to quiz me,' returned Ben, seating himself at his desk, 'but for once I shall allow it—only don't let it become a habit.'

'Most gracious,' smiled Jess. 'But it would be wrong of

me not to point out that the pitcher which too often to the well—you don't need me to finish that old saying, but you have gone to a great many wells lately.'

'Which, translated into plain English, means that you are advising me to abandon my vendetta against the Wych-woods because you fear that my luck may be running out. Am I right?'

'That's about the sum of it,' replied Jess carelessly.

'I can't do that, Jess,' he said. 'I've waited long years for this, made myself a fortune to accomplish it. You have no idea what this means to me.'

'No,' agreed Jess. 'I don't want to know your reasons—unless you tell me them, nor will I refuse to carry out your orders. But a man must speak his mind occasionally.'

'Very true. And to your last question about Miss Beverly I will reply with another. Did you mean what you said when you asked if you might call on her?'

'Indeed. There is something about her which—'

'You needn't elaborate,' Ben growled. 'I accept that she might have certain attractions—for those who like noisy, self-assertive women, that is. So you want an argumentative wife?'

'Oh, matters haven't gone as far as that yet,' said Jess, grinning. 'But I would be pleased to meet her in happier circumstances.'

'Well, you are very likely to, for I need to return to London tomorrow, now that this business has fallen through. Be ready to leave before noon.'

'So noted,' returned Jess. 'Do you think,' he added provocatively, 'that there is anything significant in the fact that you refused to answer my question about her?'

The look Ben gave him was as fierce as his surname—which was unfair, he knew, for he could not have asked for a better lieutenant: a poor, but clever, gentleman who was willing to work for his living and whose loyalty was un-questioned.

So he said, a trifle less curtly, but still severe, 'Now that is a question which I shall not dignify with an answer!'

In reply, Jess threw his hands into the air, exclaiming, 'Pax, I shall say no more—and carry out your orders to the letter!'

'See to it that you do. When we return to London I need to visit the Rothschilds, and you will immediately begin—most discreetly—to investigate the financial affairs of Bertram Wychwood, Third Earl of Babbacombe. I have lost one lever I intended to use against him and must now contrive to find another.'

He had said no more. Jess, who had hoped that he might learn the reason for the implacable hate Ben felt for the Earl, had shrugged his shoulders and left to prepare to return to the capital.

Ben was recalled to the present by the butler informing him that the chaise was waiting to take him on his delayed visit to Nathan Rothschild. He had called on him earlier before the attempted kidnapping of Amelia Western, only to find that he was away on business in the country but would return shortly when he would be informed of Mr Benjamin Wolfe's visit.

Shortly might mean now, and his business was urgent. Which meant that Ben was relieved to find Mr Nathan back at his desk and willing to receive him immediately.

The two men, young as the financial world counted youth, bowed and surveyed one another warily.

'I assume,' said Mr Nathan, 'that you have come to do business here, which does not surprise me, knowing of your operations in India. You are to be congratulated in achieving so much in so short a time.'

Ben was not to be patronised. He smiled, showing his teeth. 'Oh, I had the excellent example of you and your family to urge me on,' he returned airily. 'I have not come for a loan, but to discuss the extension of my operations to the Port of London and to gain your co-operation—for a consideration, of course.'

'Of course,' said Mr Nathan smoothly. 'But something tells me that that is not the only reason for your presence here.'

'Ah,' returned Ben, showing his teeth again. 'You are determined to live up to your family's reputation for shrewdness, I see. No, I have a favour, perhaps two favours, to ask of you. If you are prepared to assist me, then I have further business to throw your way—if you care to accept it, that is.'

This polite form of blackmail secretly amused Mr Nathan, who was rapidly becoming aware that Mr Wolfe was as formidable as his reputation and his name.

'I will help you,' he said, 'if it is in my power to do so.'

'Excellent. I see that doing business with you, sir, will be a pleasure. My first request is this: do you have any knowledge of the affairs of the late Mr William Beverly who, I understand, was a merchant of some wealth who died about ten years ago? Most particularly as to the extent of his wealth at his death.''

'Beverly?' replied Mr Nathan reflectively. 'The name is familiar, but as to the details of him, no. But take heart— my chief clerk, Willis, is a mine of such information. One moment.'

He rang a small bell on his desk. The door opened and an elderly man, a quill pen behind his ear, entered.

'Willis,' said Mr Nathan without preamble, 'this is Mr Wolfe who wishes to know if we have any knowledge of the affairs of the late merchant, Mr William Beverly.'

'Mr William Beverly, sir? Oh, a very warm gentleman was Mr Beverly. Made a fortune in the late wars whilst others were losing theirs. Came from poor gentry stock as I recall. Had one daughter, an heiress—oh, very warm she was, too. I have not heard what became of her. Married well,

I'll be bound. Brought her here once when she was a little one, Mr Beverly did.'

He beamed at both men. 'Is there anything more you wish to know, sir?'

Mr Nathan said proudly, 'Willis has the most remarkable memory—you may question him at your will.'

Ben said slowly, 'Then it would not be true to say that he died a poor man and that his widow and his daughter needed financial assistance.'

'Indeed, not. A very Banbury tale that, I do assure you. Very warm, Mr William Beverly.'

'Interesting,' murmured Ben, after listening to a tale very different from the one Susanna had told him. 'One further question, Mr Willis, of your goodness. Do you know aught of Mr Samuel Mitchell, whom I believe the Widow Beverly later married?'

'Oh, Mr Samuel Mitchell, a very sad story that. He lost where Mr Beverly gained. Lately, his career has been different, very different. He has recouped his losses, one supposes, since he, too, is a very warm man these days. Will that be all, sir?'

Ben nodded. 'I think so. May I compliment you on your knowledge. I will not demean you by asking whether you are sure of your facts: that Mr Beverly died rich, and that Mr Samuel Mitchell, who was poor, has recently become rich. On second thoughts, perhaps you could tell me of the source of his new-found wealth.'

'There, sir, I must confess that I am nonplussed. A small mystery attaches to it.'

This guarded answer amused Ben. He smiled, and said smoothly. 'Your discretion is as remarkable as your knowledge. My thanks to you, sir.'

He bowed and, gratified, Mr Willis bowed back. He then looked at Mr Nathan for instruction, who nodded his head to indicate that he might return to his desk.

Mr Nathan said when the door closed behind Willis, 'You are thinking along the same lines as I am, Mr Wolfe?'

'Oh, I am sure of it, sir.' Ben's voice was grim. He said nothing further on the matter, although he was already turning over in his mind how he could use, on Miss Susanna Beverly's behalf, the disturbing information offered him by Mr Willis. Instead, he entered into business discussions with Mr Nathan over his own affairs at the Port of London.

He would have relished asking the knowledgeable Mr Willis about the financial affairs of the Earl of Babbacombe, except that the fewer people who knew of his interest in the Earl, the better.

What he did not admit to himself was that one of the benefits of the interview with Mr Willis was that it gave him an excuse to see Miss Susanna Beverly again—and soon.

Chapter Six

'I think,' said Jesse Fitzroy to Ben some days later, 'that you will be pleased to learn what I have discovered, both about Lord Babbacombe and the ineffable Mr Mitchell.'

After learning of Samuel Mitchell's sudden acquisition of wealth shortly after the death of Susanna's father and his marriage to Mrs Beverly, Ben had given orders to Jess to find out as much as possible about Mitchell and his firm.

'Do you want me to drop further enquiries about Lord Babbacombe, then?'

'Not at all. Carry on with them side by side—but give priority to Mitchell's business if there is any conflict of time. The other can wait a little. After all, it's waited for the last twenty-odd years.'

'Which do you want me to report on first?' asked Jess.

'Mitchell first,' replied Ben. 'That has more urgency and is probably more easily remedied—if matters are as I think they are.'

Jess pulled a piece of paper from his pocket and began to read from it. 'Before he married Mrs Beverly, Samuel Mitchell was almost in Queer Street, only just staving off bankruptcy.' Echoing Mr Willis, he went on to elaborate, 'After that he became very warm indeed. He paid off his debts and launched several new enterprises but, some years later, shortly before he arranged his stepdaughter's marriage to Lord Sylvester, he started to fail again.'

He paused. Ben said impatiently, 'Spit it out, man—or is that all?'

'By no means. I contacted a friend of mine who has a connection with Mitchell's solicitors and another at Coutts where Mitchell and William Beverly banked. I also contacted the late Mr William Beverly's solicitors. I had to pay out good money to discover details from these and other contacts who prefer to be nameless. It appears that shortly after his marriage Mitchell paid into Coutts a large sum of money. He did the same at the time of Miss Beverly's proposed marriage. The sums were of an equal size, and added together they tally exactly with the sum of money left in trust to his daughter by Mr William Beverly. Mr Mitchell, who had been a friend and associate of Mr Beverly, was the chief trustee of Susanna Beverly's fortune.

'Further enquiries revealed that Mr Mitchell had, indeed, twice stolen from the trust, emptying it at the second time, after which he told Miss Beverly that she was penniless—without, of course, informing her that it was he who had made her so. My informant added that it is sadly true that money left in trust to young women heiresses is frequently stolen by the very trustees who are supposed to protect them.'

'As I thought.' Ben smiled wolfishly, adding, 'I won't ask how you penetrated Coutts's supposedly sacred records, I'd rather not know. What you can do for me now is set up a meeting with Samuel Mitchell—pretending that I am interested in doing business with him. On second thoughts, you won't be pretending, I shall be doing business with him—but not of a nature he will relish. I don't like swindlers who leave young women helpless and unprotected.'

'And Lord Babbacombe? You wish to hear of him?'

'Very much so.'

'Few details, I am afraid. He is virtually penniless, as you suspected. His son is to marry Miss Western in an effort to recoup the family fortunes—both of which facts you already know. What you may not be aware of is that he has mortgaged the family home and all his estates and that his lawyers have not informed the Westerns of that fact when drawing up the marriage settlements since that interesting piece of news has been kept from them by m'lord and his advisers. Were the Westerns to know, the marriage would, of course, fall through. Wealthy though Miss Western might be, her fortune would scarcely cover Babbacombe's losses.'

'Excellent, Jess,' said Ben, rising from his chair as he spoke. 'Remind me to give you a bonus for good work well done. Now, set about the Mitchell business at once. I would like to see Miss Beverly comfortable again as soon as possible.'

Unaware of the interest which Ben Wolfe was taking in her affairs, Susanna was finding life with *Madame* very different from life either in her stepfather's home or in the Westerns. She was being treated neither as somewhat of a cuckoo in the nest nor as a servant to be used and exploited.

Madame's paid companion she might be, but *Madame* treated her as a friend and as an equal. She insisted on buying Susanna an entirely new wardrobe, 'For,' she said, 'I cannot be accompanied by a young lady dressed like the under-housekeeper. Pray do not take that as a criticism of yourself, my dear. I know perfectly well the manner in which poor young duennas and companions are treated by their more thoughtless employers—and, from what I saw of the Westerns they were among the more careless it has been my misfortune to meet.'

She must have been talking to Ben Wolfe to come out with that piece of English slang, thought Susanna a trifle irreverently, or she is not quite so purely French as she claims to be. She was shrewd enough to notice that *Madame* occasionally forgot that she was a Frenchwoman and spoke perfect English without her pretty accent—although never in company, only when she was alone with Susanna.

As a consequence of *Madame*'s kindness, Susanna, when attending Lady Exford's ball for the French Ambassador a week or so after Ben's visit to Nathan Rothschild, was splendour itself. She was dressed in a deep rose silk turnout come fresh from Paris, beautifully cut and sporting the new lower waist and V-shaped neck. Its delicate colour flattered her dark hair and grey-blue eyes and gave a rosy flush to her creamy skin.

Although *Madame* had offered to lend her some jewels to go with it, Susanna had refused them, wearing only her small pearl necklace with its matching drop earrings and bracelet. Her fan, another present from *Madame*, was of a creamy parchment decorated with delicately painted rose-buds.

Thus attired, she came, early on in the evening, face to face with Amelia Western, who was on George Darlington's arm.

'Good gracious, what a surprise to find you here, Miss Beverly! I had rather thought that such an occasion would be beyond you,' was Amelia's graceless comment.

'But not beyond Madame la Comtesse de Saulx, I think,' retorted Susanna sweetly.

George Darlington, who had been staring at Susanna as though he had never really seen her before—but liked what he now saw—said gently to Amelia, 'Come, my dear. I am sure that—Miss Beverly, is it not?—will accept your congratulations on her good fortune in securing such a kind mistress. *Madame*'s reputation is a peerless one.'

Susanna was not sure that she cared for the look in George's eye. He had always previously passed by the somewhat dowdy and wan young person in a duenna's cap whom she had so recently been, and she was not sure that she wished him to notice her.

On the other hand, he was beginning to teach Amelia the

good manners in which her parents were so singularly lacking, so he must be congratulated for that if for nothing else.

Amelia muttered something which could be construed as following her betrothed's advice. Her betrothed smiled fondly at her, saying to Susanna, 'We hope to see you, and *Madame*, later again this evening, but I have a duty to attend on my father as soon as possible to report to him on an errand which he asked me to perform this morning.'

His bow was low, but his eye was insolent and the look he gave Susanna was a meaningful one which she chose to ignore. She was helped in this by the arrival of someone whom she had not expected to see: Mr Wolfe.

Ben was turned out *à point* and was more overwhelming than ever with his combination of size and sartorial splendour, above which his harsh face seemed even stronger in a roomful of soft and over-civilised men.

He bowed most graciously to the three of them, finally turning to George, who was staring at his formidable presence, and saying, 'Forgive me for introducing myself, Lord Darlington. My name is Ben Wolfe. We have not been presented to one another, but you were pointed out to me by no less than our host, Lord Exford. I understand that you and your father have certain business interests in India—although we shall not talk of such affairs before the ladies.

'And, speaking of ladies, I hope that you will forgive me for ignoring the usual conventions by coming up to you as I did, and will consent to honour me by introducing me to your fair companions.'

He bowed again, straightening up to hear a trifle bemused George saying, 'Oh, as to the conventions, if Lord Exford is your sponsor here, then we may forget them. Allow me to present to you the lady on my arm: Miss Amelia Western, to whom I have the good fortune to be affianced. On her right is Miss Beverly, late Miss Western's duenna and now, I understand, the companion of Madame la Comtesse de Saulx.'

Ben bowed to each woman in turn, muttering, 'Charmed, madam.' To Susanna he said, lying in his teeth, 'I am acquainted with Madame de Saulx, but I have not yet had the honour of meeting her companion. I must compliment you, Miss Beverly, on becoming part of *Madame*'s household. She is a most gracious lady, as I am sure you have already discovered.'

Amelia, who did not look at all honoured by having to meet Ben Wolfe, pulled mannerlessly at George's arm, annoyed that it was Susanna who was engaging Ben's interest.

'Oh, do come along, George,' she said with a pout. 'We have wasted enough time here and your father will be expecting us. I am sure that Mr Wolfe will be only too happy to entertain Miss Beverly—if she needs entertaining, that is.'

George said, 'Yes, my dear, Mr Wolfe will forgive us for leaving him after such a short time together, but we—that is, my father and I—may hope to meet him for a longer discussion.'

He bowed again to both Ben and Susanna before leading Amelia away. Ben watched them disappear through the double doors at the far end of the room, a wry smile on his face.

'Good God,' he exclaimed once they were out of earshot, 'is that little shrew the woman I was trying to kidnap? Thank the Lord I had you made off with instead! I should have strangled her within ten minutes of meeting her. I could not help overhearing the manner in which she spoke to you before I announced myself. It quite bore out what Madame de Saulx told me of her lack of manners.

'As for her fiancé, I disliked exceedingly the way he looked at you. His reputation is bad—I advise you to avoid him.'

This last came out in Ben's most imperious manner.

Susanna began to laugh. 'A fine case of the pot calling the kettle black, if I may say so, Mr Wolfe. Whatever Lord

Darlington's reputation may be, I have not yet heard that it includes kidnapping young women.'

'Oh, pray do not hold that against me. After meeting Miss Western, I shall certainly never try to kidnap a woman again unless I have it on good authority that she is the most docile creature whom a man might want for a wife.'

There was no doubt that his eyes were mocking and challenging her as he said this. He was trying to provoke her, no doubt of that, either. Well, she would not oblige him, not she!

Susanna cast her eyes down and said, 'I shall remember that, Mr Wolfe, so it will not surprise you that I have no intention of becoming docile lest you try to kidnap me again. Once was quite enough. On top of that, you have involved me in telling a farrago of lies when I publicly pretended that we had never met one another before tonight. Even to save my reputation I find that a trifle above my touch.'

Ben leaned forward and said softly so that none might hear, 'Oh, no, it's not above your touch. You played your part to the manner born, my dear. And enjoyed yourself while you did. Now, let us find *Madame* and tell her that we have just met for the first time in Lord Exford's ballroom and that your reputation is therefore safe and sound.'

What could Susanna say to that? She opened her mouth to offer him a swift retort, but before she could she caught his wicked eye upon her. Consequently all that she could do was splutter, 'Oh, you are impossible, quite impossible!'

And all he said in answer was, 'So I am often told. Now let us find *Madame*.'

There was no putting him down. On the other hand, Susanna flattered herself that he was not able to put her down either.

'Shall we cry quits,' she murmured to him, 'the past quite forgotten and start again, as though we truly had met for the first time when George Darlington presented me to you?'

Ben said nothing for a moment before looking down at her from his great height. 'There is only one problem with that. I do not wish to forget the spirited young miss who sparked at me from the moment we first met. I think that I prefer her to tonight's proper young lady who only says what she ought.'

'Really, Mr Wolfe? Really? In that case am I to understand that you are giving me leave to be as impertinent to you *as* I please—*whenever* I please?'

'I would prefer that to being in the company of a bread-and-butter Miss Prim, so I suppose the answer is, yes, I am.'

This was becoming dangerous, was it not? Was Mr Wolfe descending from kidnapping her to engaging in a lesser, but more subtle, form of seduction? Did he find the newly polished Miss Beverly attractive? Or had George Darlington's obvious interest in her made him jealous?

'Dear, dear,' Susanna said, almost ruefully. 'I seem to have uttered a challenge to you which I had not intended. You were meant to say, "Oh, no, my dear Miss Beverly, you misunderstood me quite," or some such nonsense, not fling the ball of conversation back at me quite so strongly.'

It was his head Ben flung back as he laughed aloud. Other heads turned to look at him in surprise. 'Ah, Miss Beverly, have you not yet discovered that I never do what is expected of me? No, no, that is not my way. And may I add that you possess the same talent—or, if you prefer, the same fault. It all depends upon one's point of view, does it not?'

To have discovered in a man whom she ought to despise someone who said aloud what she sometimes thought secretly overset Susanna a little. To hold him off, she decided to be impersonal, to put the conversation on a higher plane—if she could.'

'Ah, then you agree with Prince Hamlet: "There is nothing either good or bad but thinking makes it so."'

'Prince Hamlet—who the devil's he?' asked Ben. 'Oh, I do beg your pardon, Miss Beverly. I should have said,

"Pray, who is Prince Hamlet? And of what country is he a Prince?"''

Susanna could not tell whether he was joking or not, so she answered him in true Miss Prim fashion. 'Shakespeare's Prince Hamlet in the play of that name. I should not advise you to imitate him. He ended the play as a corpse on the stage—a noble corpse, but dead as a doornail all the same.'

'Oh, I do so agree with you. I have a rooted objection to ending up as a corpse—either on a stage or anywhere else— before my time, that is. I know little of Shakespeare, but I gather that a large number of the characters in his plays do come to an unfortunate end. By the by—you never told me of Hamlet's nationality.'

'He was a Dane, Mr Wolfe, and I do believe that you have been bamming me.'

'Not at all. A Dane, eh? I have never done business with a Dane. If one arrives in my counting house, I shall be sure to consult you as an expert on them. As it is, we have almost reached *Madame* and I must pay her my respects and relinquish you to the company of others. One thing before we part. Do you think that you could possibly refer to me as Ben in future?'

Susanna laughed up at him, unaware of how enchanting she looked and of how Mr Wolfe's heart twisted in his breast at the very sight of her as she teased him.

'What is it they say in the House of Commons? I demand notice of that question. And do we have a future—other than in chance meetings at balls and other public functions? For the moment I think that you must remain Mr Wolfe.'

'Oh, yes,' he said softly, 'we do have a future, you may be sure of that. It is that future of which I wish to speak to *Madame*. Oh, I almost forgot, Mr Fitzroy has had the impudence to ask me to pass on his respects to you—by which he showed his lack of respect for me. I hereby do so, and ask you to respect me by not respecting him.'

What impudence! 'You may be sure that I shall respect

whomsoever I please, Mr Wolfe, and if I choose to respect Mr Fitzroy, so be it.'

'Oh, bravo,' he replied, and gave her one of his deep bows. 'We must cross swords again soon.'

'Whenever you please.'

Thus they parted, Ben to speak to *Madame*, who had been watching them approach, a curious smile on her face, and Susanna to carry out the errand *Madame* had asked her to perform earlier and which meeting George and Amelia had interrupted.

'Whenever you have a moment, child,' she had said, 'you might find the library for me and discover whether the Exfords possess a copy of *Les Maximes du M. le duc de la Rochefoucauld*. If so, I would wish to ask Lord Exford's permission to borrow it.'

The library was in a room at the end of a corridor just off the Grand Salon. Not surprisingly Susanna found herself alone in it. Books lined every wall and window ledge. A map table stood in the centre. Standing by it was a small man clad in the dark clothes of a scholar or a clerk. He looked up as Susanna entered and bowed in her direction.

'Ah,' he said, 'a refugee from the ball. How may I help you? If help you need.'

He was so quaint and old-fashioned that Susanna smiled. 'My name is Miss Beverly. I am here at the request of my friend and mistress, Madame la Comtesse de Saulx. She wishes to know whether the library contains a copy of M. de la Rochefoucauld's *Maximes*.'

He smiled at her. 'Indeed it does.'

'And would Lord Exford be prepared to lend it to her?'

'If Madame la Comtesse made such a request of him in proper form, I have little doubt but that he would agree to it.'

Susanna thanked him prettily, and looked wistfully around the room. She would have liked to explore the bookshelves filled with such treasures, but she had a duty to return.

On the other hand, she felt that there was one question which she could ask. 'I wonder if, before I leave, you would show me M. de la Rochefoucauld's treatise?'

'By all means,' he said. 'I will bring it to the map table for you. You must not soil your dress by carrying it. Pray take a seat.'

Susanna did as she was bid and presently the librarian, whose name, he told her, was Dr Strong, placed before her two elegant volumes bound in splendid red leather decorated in gold leaf, with the coat of arms of the Exfords on the front.

He opened the first volume for her, saying, 'I hope that you are a strong-minded young lady, Miss Beverly. The Duke was a very sardonic gentleman and his Maximes are cynical in the extreme.'

Susanna said gaily, 'You need have no fear, Dr Strong. Time and chance have shown me that the world is not a bed of roses.'

The books had been published in France and the type, though elegant and beautiful was a trifle difficult to read. And Dr Strong was right, Susanna soon found. *M. le duc* was indeed cynical. She laughed out loud at one gem. 'We all have strength enough to endure the troubles of others.'

Regretfully Susanna closed the book. She would read it when *Madame* borrowed it. Before she did so, however, she turned to the title page—to discover there an inscription in a woman's elegant handwriting.

'To Eleanor Exford on her marriage, from her true friends, Charles and Margaret Wolfe.' Beneath it a date had been written: 14th July, 1780. The book had been given to the present Lord Exford's late mother and father.

She stared at it. Were they in any way related to Ben Wolfe? And was it a coincidence that Madame de Saulx, who was Ben Wolfe's friend, should wish to borrow a book which had been the gift of persons called Wolfe?

Susanna shook her head. She was probably seeing mysteries where none existed. After thanking Dr Strong prettily, she made her way back to the Grand Salon and was about to enter it when she was stopped by a gentleman coming from the opposite direction. It was George Darlington, without Amelia hanging on his arm. It was not long since she had seen him, but now his face was flushed as though with drink.

Susanna knew that at such occasions there was often a small private room to which bored gentlemen retired to drink away from women and ceremony. She would have liked to avoid him but, on seeing her, he held out his arm, saying, his voice slightly slurred, 'Well met, Miss Beverly. Allow me to escort you back to the Salon. Or would you prefer that we delayed our return a little?'

'By no means, Lord Darlington. I have been performing an errand for Madame la Comtesse and I am already somewhat late returning…'

'Oh, come, *Madame* is not an ogre. She could spare you a few moments more. There is an anteroom not far away where we could enjoy ourselves a little. Neither of us would be missed, I am sure.'

He had taken a firm hold of her hand without her even willing it. Susanna tried to withdraw it, but in vain. He began walking her briskly towards the little anteroom which he had mentioned.

'Please release me,' said Susanna, trying to deter him by sounding as matter-of-fact as possible. 'I have no wish to accompany you anywhere, least of all to a small private room where we shall be alone. Pray remember that you are betrothed—and to the young lady who was recently my charge.'

'That has nothing to do with this,' said George. 'I had no notion that you were such a brisk little piece. Why should we not enjoy ourselves? Others do,' and he grasped her hand more firmly than ever.

This is ridiculous, thought Susanna, trying not to panic. First Ben Wolfe kidnaps me, thinking that I am Miss Amelia Western, and now Amelia's betrothed is trying to seduce me while Amelia is otherwise engaged in the Grand Salon!

Her adventures, or rather her misadventures, were rapidly becoming the subject of farce—except that George's intentions were not really farce at all. She couldn't scream for help—to do so would create a scandal which she would not survive, though George might.

Nevertheless she said, 'If you will not be a gentleman, sir, and release me, I shall be compelled to call for help.'

'Scream away,' said George unkindly, 'and complete the ruin which your being jilted started on its way.'

No doubt Amelia had informed him of that, which was why he was being so bold with her. They had reached the door to the anteroom and George began to drag her through it. The drink might have destroyed his common sense, but it seemed to have had little effect on his strength.

Afterwards Susanna wondered whether M. de la Rochefoucauld would have found a clever little phrase to describe or illuminate what happened next so far as its unexpectedness was concerned.

She had just begun to kick George's shins, hard, exclaiming, 'I really shall scream if you don't desist on the instant,' when a voice behind them said, 'What the devil's going on here?'

It was Mr Ben Wolfe. Before he had finished speaking, he seized George by his cravat and began methodically to strangle him. George, gasping for breath and slowly turning blue, was compelled to release Susanna in order to try to dislodge Ben's hands by pulling them away with both of his own.

George was not a small man, but he was no match for Ben. Susanna, released, staggered backwards. Ben said to her, over his shoulder, 'Leave us, Miss Beverly. I wish to teach Lord Darlington a lesson, but not in your presence.'

Feebly, as she afterwards thought, Susanna said, 'You won't kill him, will you? Think of the scandal.'

'What and hang for him?' said Ben through his teeth. 'Credit me with some common sense, Miss Beverly, and display your own by returning to *Madame*, and saying nothing to anyone of this.'

So they were conspirators yet again in a plot to save her good name. And common sense said that she obey him. Her last sight of George was as he sank to his knees when Ben loosened his murderous grip on his neck.

He didn't stay there long. Ben pulled him to his feet, thrust his face into George's and said in a voice which would have cut steel, 'Listen to me, Darlington, as you value your life. You are not to approach Miss Beverly again, neither are you to allow that wretched shrew whom you are doomed to marry to bait her in public or in private. Fail to oblige me in this and I will find an excuse to call you out and dispose of you for good.

'Now, give me your word and I will let you go, unscathed. Were we other than at a public function in Lord Exford's home I would have given you the thrashing you deserve, but I have no intention of providing society with a scandal to titter about.'

'Yes,' croaked George, fingering his abused throat. Ben had been careful not to mark him in any way.

'Yes, what?' exclaimed Ben, grabbing him by the cravat again. 'Say it clearly and plainly, if you please. I, George, Viscount Darlington, promise not to approach Miss Beverly again and I will also prevent Miss Amelia Western from abusing her. I also apologise for any unhappiness or distress I may have caused her.'

'Damme,' moaned George. 'You hardly leave a fellow a voice to say all that,' but he said it all the same.

'Good,' said Ben. 'Now, get out of my sight before I'm tempted to give a fellow what he deserves.'

George staggered away, to turn at the door and say, 'You'll pay for this, Ben Wolfe, see if you don't.'

'Oh, please,' returned Ben, 'pray try to make me pay as soon as possible. I shall enjoy giving you a second lesson in manners much more than the first.'

His victim could think of no clever answer to that but to give his tormentor his back and leave.

Susanna had made her way back to *Madame*, who was seated with a small crowd around her. *Madame* signalled to her to sit beside her before enquiring whether her errand had been a successful one.

'Very,' replied Susanna. 'The librarian, Dr Strong, will ask Lord Exford whether you may borrow M. de la Roche-foucauld's *Maximes*. He supposes that m'lord will give his consent.' She said nothing of the inscription which had intrigued her.

'Excellent,' said *Madame*. 'Mr Wolfe grew a trifle perturbed when you were so late in returning. He thought that you might have met with some mischance, so I suggested that he look for you in the library although I scarcely thought that you were in any danger there. He must have missed you on the way back.'

Susanna did not correct her. Secretly she was shocked at how greatly her ability to deceive had grown since she had met Ben Wolfe. His many naughtinesses must be catching, she decided.

Madame showed no sign that she thought that Susanna might not be telling the absolute truth. Indeed, when Ben returned she said brightly, 'You see, sir, your agitation over Miss Beverly's late return was unwarranted. Here she is, quite unruffled.'

Ben raised his thick eyebrows. 'Agitated? I was scarcely that. In any case, I never reached the library. I met an old friend and we had a most fruitful discussion. At least, I found it so. We were so long that I decided to return immediately, thinking that Miss Beverly might well be with you again by now. I see that I was right.'

Well, manhandling George was one way of having a fruitful discussion—on Mr Wolfe's terms! Susanna supposed. She wondered what having an unfruitful one with him might entail! George left dead on the floor, perhaps.

Aloud she said, 'Your care for me is exemplary, Mr Wolfe. I thank you for it.'

By the twitch of his lips Susanna knew that he had taken her double meaning.

'Not at all, Miss Beverly. I am always happy to be of service. I am not a dancing man, but I would be honoured to take the floor with you this evening—if you would so oblige me.'

His bow as he said this was a deep one. Susanna found herself trembling as he straightened up and she met his magnetic gaze. She had read of Dr Mesmer and his experiments, that it was possible to bend someone to your will by the power of that will. She could well believe that Ben Wolfe possessed that power.

It was the only explanation which she could find for the extraordinary effect which he had on her. Her mouth opened slightly, she licked her lips and swayed forward. She had a hard task preventing herself from stammering like a green girl at her first ball.

At the back of her mind was the memory of the summary manner in which he had treated that cur, George Darlington. Far from being horrified at his disposal of George, she had felt excited. Knights of old protected their ladies, she knew, but she was scarcely Ben Wolfe's lady. All the same it was comforting that someone cared enough about her to punish anyone who was mistreating her.

On the other hand, even as Ben led her on to the floor, she was remembering the harsh way in which he had spoken of Lord Babbacombe's family when he had been under the impression that she was Amelia—as well as his summary kidnapping of her. Perhaps there was more to his treatment of George than met the eye.

For a big man who claimed that he did not care for dancing, he danced surprisingly well, being very light on his feet as she had already noticed at the Leominster's ball. What disconcerted Susanna—and although she did not know it, Ben also—was that, as they touched, something like Dr Mesmer's famed electric response in frogs ran through them. That it was to do with Ben alone was made apparent by the fact that no other man's touch had ever brought about the same response.

But I am not a frog, Susanna thought wildly, so what can it mean? She tried not to catch Ben's eye as they moved through the stately parading of the dance, because if she did, that, too, possessed the power to excite her. And when they met, face to face, she had the oddest and most dreadful impression that all her clothes had fallen off. And if that was not bad enough, she found herself wondering what Ben Wolfe might look like with *his* clothes gone.

Of all improper thoughts for a respectable young lady to have! She would not have found any consolation in knowing that the totally unrespectable Mr Wolfe was having similar ones about her.

Unknowingly, her eyes dilated and shone. Her mouth opened itself slightly and the tip of a small pink tongue peeped out—a sight which drove Ben Wolfe mad. Like Susanna, he asked what was happening to him. Not because he was inexperienced in the ways of sex, but because, although he had always been kind to the women he was involved with, he had never felt anything for them such as he was beginning to feel for Susanna.

Mixed with an intense desire to have her in his arms or in his bed, was an equally intense desire to protect her. She had been right to see murder in his eye when he had attacked George. It had taken him all his willpower not to beat the wretch senseless for daring to distress her. He had no idea how to respond to such strange and new emotions. Particularly when they were so contrary.

Neither Ben nor Susanna had ever found dancing so exciting before. It certainly added spice to an otherwise rather formalised ritual. Susanna had heard that no less a person than Lord Byron had founded waltzing immoral. What *was* surprising was that she felt immoral performing the quadrille—his lordship had never gone so far as to suggest that!

As if that was not enough, further spice was added to an already interesting evening immediately after the dance was over. Ben had scarcely had time to escort Susanna back to her place beside *Madame* when he was accosted by a large middle-aged gentleman wearing a star on his breast.

'Lord Babbacombe,' whispered *Madame* to Susanna. 'Lord Darlington's father. Whatever can he want with Mr Wolfe?'

To pick a quarrel with him, apparently, for he said in a high, angry voice. 'A word with you, Wolfe, I will not call you sir. I wonder that Lord Exford has invited you to pollute his home. He cannot know of your dubious reputation or he would not allow you to cross his threshold. I understand that you have had the impudence to make yourself obnoxious to my son. Let me inform you that, if I have my way, every decent house in London will be closed to you.'

By the time that he had finished speaking he was scarlet in the face. The object of his anger remained impassive. Ben's face had never before looked quite so carved out of granite.

'I am here, as you are, I suppose, as a friend of Lord Exford, and I must inform you that, if your son conducts himself in good society as though his true home is a nighthouse in the Seven Dials rather than a gentleman's mansion, I shall be as obnoxious to him as I please whenever I find him misbehaving. Although I have to say that his deplorable conduct does not surprise me for I have always found ''like father, like son'' to be a useful maxim in the conduct of life—and of business.'

Lord Babbacombe was now, to Susanna's fascination, turning purple. 'Oh, business,' he snarled. 'Hardly the stuff of conversation in the company of gentlemen. Well, never say that I did not warn you what your fate might be. And, speaking of fathers and sons, your own father's conduct would scarcely bare inspection.'

Ben's expression fascinated Susanna. It never altered. He was as calm as Lord Babbacombe was noisy, and his calm did not desert him now.

'I trust that you have finished,' he said politely, 'since I came here to enjoy myself, not to listen to sermons from stupid old gentlemen. And as to business, I can understand your distaste for it, since you have been so unsuccessful in the practice of it. I bid you good evening, m'lord, in the hope that another day may find you in a better temper and your son likewise.'

He bowed and turned back to *Madame* and Susanna. Lord Babbacombe, now gobbling like a turkey, had no alternative but to accept the insults put upon him, or challenge Ben to a duel. As he had neither the mind nor the courage to do the latter he was left in a quandary.

What he would have liked to do was to order his footman to give Ben a beating, and throw him out of Exford House, but that being impossible, he turned on his heel and left, silently promising himself to take all the steps necessary to drive Ben Wolfe out of society.

Madame said gently, 'Was that wise Mr Wolfe? Lord Babbacombe is a power in London society.'

'So much the worse for London society, then,' returned Ben, his face implacable. 'My only regret is that you and Miss Beverly—to say nothing of several spectators—were compelled to listen to such an ill-tempered to-do. I hope,

Miss Beverly, that my plain speaking will not result in you refusing to stand up with me in the next dance.'

'Oh, I am well acquainted with your plain speaking, Mr Wolfe, and I am in the best position to know that your remarks concerning Lord Darlington were no worse than he deserved.' She felt, rather than saw, that *Madame* was intrigued by her forthright defence of Ben, but had decided that, for once, she might indulge in a little plain speaking of her own.

'And I shall certainly agree to stand up with you in the next dance,' she added.

Susanna surprised even herself by her behaviour. On the face of it she should have been shocked but, after his failed kidnapping of her, the rest of Ben Wolfe's conduct seemed to her to be small beer at the very least.

Which was a piece of internal vulgarity she had better keep to herself!

'I wonder that you dare commit yourself to such a bad hat as I am, Miss Beverly,' said Ben with a wry smile, 'knowing, as you do, the very worst of what I am capable of performing. Who knows what might happen next?'

'Surely, sir, the evening can hold no more shocks for me, either verbal or otherwise,' she riposted.

But she was wrong. Ben had taken her hand and they stood side by side waiting for an opposite couple to appear so that the dance might begin. A tall gentleman with one of Lord Exford's sisters on his arm arrived to take his place. He was so busy talking to her that he did not turn to face Ben and Susanna until the very moment that the music began and it was too late for Susanna to react to his sudden appearance.

Ben Wolfe felt her tremble, but did not know that what had disturbed Susanna was the arrival of the latecomer.

He was Francis Sylvester, whom she had last seen the night before he had left her at the altar.

Chapter Seven

'Susanna,' said Francis agitatedly as he passed her in the dance, 'can it possibly be you?'

As he ought to have known she could not answer him immediately for the dance had rapidly returned her to Ben's side. Nor, when they were next face to face again, hands held high, did he allow her to speak, bursting out instead with, 'I had heard that you had left your parents' house and were no longer in society.'

She barely had time to retort, 'Then you were wrongly informed,' before she was back with Ben, who hissed at her,

'Who the devil is that fellow who is pestering you each time you pass him?'

Fortunately the dance took her away from him, too. And who gave him leave to question her so summarily? Or Francis, either, for that matter. Both men had glared at her as though she had offended them. She decided to speak to neither of them, treading through the patterns of the dance in silence.

So when Francis asked her as they crossed again, 'Whose party are you with, Susanna, to whom I may pay my respects when the dance is over?' she said nothing, turning her head away from him before rejoining Ben—who demanded of her exasperatedly,

'Is that fellow still troubling you?'

She didn't answer him either—which was all that they both deserved, seeing that Francis had jilted her, and Ben had kidnapped her, neither of which acts could possibly be described as gentlemanly. Her temper wasn't helped by her noticing that both men were now scowling blackly at one another whenever they crossed.

'What in the world are you doing with *him?*' Francis snorted at her. 'Don't you know how dubious his reputation is?'

Susanna could not prevent herself from riposting, 'No more than mine was and is, Francis, after you had finished with me.'

That should have finished *him* but, judging by his wounded expression, hadn't, for when he next twirled her around he came out with, 'I never intended that, you know.'

'Then what did you intend?' she shot back at him before moving on to Ben, who muttered at her,

'Is he *still* importuning you? Do you want me to deal with him also, when the dance is over?'

Susanna nearly came out with, 'Heaven forfend', murmuring instead, 'Best not, he's Lord Sylvester.'

This made matters worse, for Ben immediately hissed at her, 'The swine who jilted you, eh? I will deal with him as he deserves.'

'Oh, not that,' she said. 'What little good reputation we still possess would be quite destroyed, and having escaped hanging for George, you would swing for Francis instead. Neither of them are worth it and I should have to retire to a nunnery to escape public obloquy.'

Fortunately Ben's sense of humour revived itself when he saw that she was smiling as she spoke. 'True,' he said, his lips twitching again and his harsh face lightening a little. 'I admit that I am being somewhat extreme, but he's exactly the kind of soft fool I most dislike.'

Susanna refrained from pointing out to him that most of

the men in the room were soft fools if you compared them with Mr Ben Wolfe, but that didn't justify him threatening them all with violent death as a consequence. She also reflected that, until she had met him, her life had been conducted after a fashion which could only be described as dull and boring, whereas now even attending a ball at Exford House had become almost dangerously exciting!

There was no time for further talk with him, or with Francis either, who next had the impudence to ask, 'Are you married, Susanna? I trust that that great oaf, Ben Wolfe, is not your husband if you are.'

'No business of yours if he is,' she told him briskly, over her shoulder, as she left him for the last time.

The dance over, Ben seized her arm proprietorially and virtually dragged her over to where *Madame* was sitting, but he didn't succeed in throwing Francis off the scent. He doggedly followed them, bowing to *Madame* and ostentatiously avoiding any eye contact with Ben who had been compelled to release Susanna once she was under *Madame*'s wing again.

Francis bowed to them all. He was, Susanna noticed, as superbly turned out as he had been when he had been her supposedly faithful suitor. Yet Ben was right: his face was soft, something which she had not noticed when she had been a green girl. His public manners, however, were still superb.

'We met in Paris, I believe, Madame la Comtesse,' he said, 'at a reception given by M. de Talleyrand. I am happy to renew your acquaintance, and would wish to renew that of Miss Beverly—if she is still Miss Beverly, that is.'

Madame's manners were, as always, impeccable. 'Lord Sylvester,' she acknowledged. 'Yes, I remember the occasion. And Miss Beverly is not married, but I am not sure whether she will wish to renew her acquaintance with you. She must speak for herself.'

'Then I must beg of her that she will allow me to speak

privately to her—for a few moments only,' he said hastily, 'for I have to inform her of something meant for her ears alone.'

Susanna looked away from him. 'This comes a trifle late, m'lord, if it is an explanation of your behaviour of four years ago.' Or an apology, she was going to add, but he did not allow her to finish, saying,

'I know that I did you a great wrong, but I wish to remedy that. I ask you to allow me to speak to you in memory of what we once were to one another.'

She could almost feel Ben Wolfe's hard eyes on her, willing her to refuse him, but that very fact compelled her to accede to Francis Sylvester's wishes. To neither of them would she give the right to determine her conduct. She would speak to Francis of her free will, and that same free will would determine the nature of her reply to him. Her decisions would be her own.

'Very well, Lord Sylvester,' she said, rising. 'I will allow you to address me privately, but for a few moments only, and on the understanding that you will make no attempt to detain, or control me, physically.'

'He'd better not,' growled Ben under his breath, earning himself a sharp tap of her fan from *Madame* who was watching with interest the play of emotion on his usually impassive face.

Lord Sylvester held out his hand. Susanna shook her head as she joined him, and, not touching, they walked out of the Grand Salon and into the self-same anteroom into which George had earlier dragged her.

He turned to face her, indicating that he wished her to sit while he spoke to her. Susanna shook her head again. 'I would prefer to remain standing,' she said, as coolly as she could.

Francis inclined his handsome blond head. His looks were the exact opposite of those of Ben Wolfe—but they had lost the power to attract Susanna.

'Very well,' he said, his voice melancholy. 'I wish to tell you how sorry I am that I behaved to you as I did four years ago. But I had no alternative. I was heavily in debt, but the moneylenders, knowing of our marriage, were holding off. And then, two days before the wedding your guardian, Mr Samuel Mitchell, came to me and told me that, contrary to public belief, you were not an heiress. That he had discovered that your father had left you nothing, and that consequently I was right up the River Tick again. That the moneylenders had word of this and there was a writ out against me, consigning me to the Marshalsea since I would now be unable to pay my debts.

'Consequently, to escape imprisonment I would have to fly the country at once. He said that he would help me on condition that I said nothing of this, for he would put matters right with you and ensure that you did not suffer as a consequence of your marriage failing. He told me what to say in my letter to you, and I set sail for the Continent on the following day. You may judge of my surprise when I heard not long ago that you had left your home soon after we should have married.'

Susanna, shocked by this surprising news, stared blankly at him. Could Francis possibly be speaking the truth? Had her stepfather been playing a double game with her? And if so, why? She remembered that, immediately after Francis Sylvester's rejection of her Samuel Mitchell had informed her that he had known since her father's death that he had died penniless and had deliberately kept the truth from her until Francis's dereliction had made that impossible.

Could she trust no one? Was everyone lying to her? Samuel Mitchell, Ben Wolfe and now Francis Sylvester. The room swung about her. She put out a hand to grasp the back of an armchair in order to steady herself.

'Am I to believe a word that you are saying?' was all she could manage.

Francis, shocked by her pallor, said, 'I swear to you, by

all I hold holy, that I am telling you the truth. I loved you then, and I love you now. I fled because I could not condemn you to a marriage with a man who would shortly enter a debtors' prison, or to a narrow life in Calais never to revisit your home again. Forgive me for deceiving you so vilely four years ago, but, seeing how much I loved you, I thought that it was for the best.'

He might, perhaps, be telling her the truth, but Susanna dared not trust him. Her common sense, which rarely deserted her, had her asking him, 'If that is so, why are you able to return now?'

'Because an old aunt, whom I scarcely knew, died, leaving everything to me. Enough to pay my debts and enable me to live a decent life again in England. I have forsworn gambling and the wild life which went with it. I am a reformed character, and I wish to make a new start—with you, if you will accept me.'

He made a move to take her hand, but she pushed him away. She could not bear to be touched by him.

'Accept you!' she exclaimed bitterly. 'You do not know what you are asking, nor what my life has been since you left me at the altar. As for forgiveness, you may have that, but only because I must not forget the Christian faith by which I live and which bids us to forgive sinners. But marry you! Never, not if you were the last man in the world.'

To her horror, for horror it was, he went down on his knees before her, half-moaning, 'You cannot mean that.' This time he clutched at her hands and would not let them go. Susanna sought to release herself, but he was obdurate. He was not yet trying to force her as George had done, but she feared that he might.

'Listen to me—' he began.

Attempting to pull away, she exclaimed, 'No, I will not…'

At which point the door opened and it was Ben Wolfe again who strode in saying, 'For a short talk, you said, and you promised not to detain her, but, damme, I find you at it after all.'

His expression was so ugly that Susanna, freeing herself from a startled Francis Sylvester, caught him by the arm, exclaiming, 'No, Mr Wolfe, do not attack him, I was only trying to prevent him from proposing to me and from holding my hand while he was about it.'

'What! And give himself the pleasure of jilting you twice, I suppose,' was all the answer she got, but he made no further attempt to assault Francis, simply adding, 'If you dislike his advances, then I offer you my arm to escort you out of his unwanted presence.'

Francis, his face white now, said angrily, 'I was merely trying to make Miss Beverly an honourable proposal. Can you claim to wish to do as much?'

'Certainly,' almost shouted Ben, coming out with something which he had never thought to hear himself say. 'Miss Beverly, if you will only consent to marry me, I shall apply for a special licence tomorrow.'

The look which he threw Francis was a triumphant one.

But he did not triumph with Susanna.

She jumped back from the pair of them, exclaiming, 'Oh, you are impossible, both of you—and for quite different reasons. You are only alike in wishing to make my life miserable, and I certainly don't want to marry either of you.'

Which, she later dismally acknowledged, was not a true statement at all so far as one of them was concerned, but she wasn't going to allow anyone—even someone she was beginning to love—to bully her into doing anything.

And as the two men turned to her, both speaking at once, she said as coldly as she could, 'As you claim to be gentlemen, pray allow me to depart without troubling me further.'

Her head high, she walked past them to the door, pacing slowly along the corridor, delaying her return to the Grand Salon, for after what she had just passed through she did not know whether to laugh or to cry.

After that, the evening resumed the normal course of such evenings. Francis Sylvester disappeared, not to reappear again. Susanna could only imagine what Ben had said to him before he returned to talk to her and *Madame* as though nothing untoward had occurred. She could not help wondering of what he was thinking—and all the time she spoke and laughed and danced without an apparent care in the world, although not again with Ben, who stood silent behind *Madame*'s chair.

Was he regretting his rash proposal—or her rejection of it? At the end of the evening when *Madame* rose to take her leave, Ben bent over Susanna's hand in farewell, murmuring in a voice doubtless meant to be reassuring, 'I do not think that that fellow will trouble you again, Miss Beverly. If he does, pray inform me immediately.'

Miss Beverly! So they had returned to their previous relationship with one another as though his proposal of marriage had never been made. In theory, this should have pleased Susanna but, in practice, made her feel cold and desolate.

He had only proposed to her in order to annoy Francis and to put him off—and he had succeeded. It was simply one more of Mr Wolfe's many deceits performed to allow him to remain in control of his life—and the lives of others.

She took this sad and lonely thought to bed with her.

As for Ben Wolfe, his night was spent in wondering at himself. In the name of all that was holy, how had he come to propose marriage to Miss Susanna Beverly when he had always told himself that—other than for revenge on the Babbacombe—he would never marry? In retrospect, his rashness appalled him. She might have accepted him on the spot, then where would he have been?

Properly caught—but she had not accepted him. Instead of being pleased, he was feeling glum—which was ridiculous, for he had had no real desire to marry her, had he?

He had merely been putting down that ass Francis Sylvester, hadn't he?

So why was it that he couldn't sleep, and was behaving like a moonstruck boy whose love had turned him down flat? Yes, he must be moonstruck, fit for Bedlam: hard Ben Wolfe, who was slowly being overcome by a pair of fine eyes and a brave spirit such as he had never met in a woman before.

And, when sleep came at last, his dreams were filled with visions of Susanna.

'A letter for you, my dear,' said *Madame*, passing it across the breakfast table to her several days later when the Exfords' ball and its many incidents was becoming a memory.

'For me?' Susanna looked up in surprise. She could not remember when she had last received a letter. The invitations to the many social events which she was attending were made to *Madame*: and she had lost all her friends from her old life after Francis had jilted her.

The letter looked official. It was addressed to her in a clerk's copperplate script and it invited her to attend the offices of Messrs Herriott and Bracewell as soon as possible, where she might learn something to her advantage. She passed it over to *Madame*, saying, 'Whatever can it mean? Do you know anything of this?'

Madame shook her head. 'No, my dear. I am as surprised as you are. Do you know of the firm?'

'Only that it was Papa's. I never had dealings with them after he died. Everything was done by Mr Mitchell even before he married Mama.'

'Indeed,' remarked *Madame* drily, thinking of a conversation which she had had with Ben Wolfe. 'I think that you ought to visit them as soon as possible. You may take the carriage this afternoon.'

'But you were going to the Park…'

'Oh, that can wait,' said *Madame* airily. 'This is more important.'

It was a somewhat puzzled Susanna who was shown into Mr Herriott's office later that day. He rose to meet her, offering her a chair and a glass of Madeira in that order.

'Thank you, no,' she said to the Madeira. She saw that Mr Herriott had another portly middle-aged gentleman with him and assumed that it was his partner, Mr Bracewell. Stranger and stranger, she thought, surely my business cannot be so important that it needs the two senior partners to conduct it.

'First of all,' began Mr Herriott, whose face looked as though he had drunk more than his share of Madeira in his time, 'we are here to offer you an apology for what is a dereliction of duty on our part. It has recently come to our notice that you have been under the misapprehension that your father left you a pauper. That the money set out in his will was non-existent and had been lost by him before he died.

'Regrettably we were unaware of this but, once it was brought to our notice that your stepfather, Mr Samuel Mitchell, had misappropriated a sum upwards of one hundred thousand pounds, it was our duty to remedy the matter, in so far as we could.'

Susanna was not so innocent that she did not grasp that Mr Herriott was using grand language to obscure his own share of guilt in the matter. It had been his duty to protect her interests—something which he had singularly failed to do.

'Immediately we became aware of the true situation, we set matters in train. Mr Mitchell has been compelled to make over to you the balance of your fortune left after his depredations had reduced it. You will immediately receive the sum of some sixty thousand pounds—or, rather, the yearly interest of that sum. As for Mr Mitchell, he will escape conviction and transportation only because he has co-operated with us in restoring your fortune to you, and because we believe that you would not wish your mother and your half-sisters to be left in penury and without a husband and a father. He has sufficient capital left to enable them to live in modest comfort.

'If, of course, you felt that this punishment was not enough, then we would inform the proper authorities, but we believed that you would not wish your mother to be punished as well.'

Susanna hardly knew what to say. Mr Herriott rose and poured her a glass of water. 'Drink this, Miss Beverly, I am sure that this news has come as a great shock to you.'

She drank the water greedily down before saying, 'So, when my stepfather virtually turned me out of the house in order to earn my own living, he was actually using my money to improve his own circumstances?'

'Yes. It appeared that, shortly before he married your mother, he had lost a great deal of money in speculation and he used part of your inheritance to overcome that. Later, after your marriage with Lord Sylvester was arranged, he had another run of bad luck, he said, and embezzled most of the rest of it to make up his losses.'

Susanna thought of what Francis had told her at the Exfords' ball—and knew that he had been speaking the truth.

Her distress was patent. Not so much because of the loss of the money itself, but because of the hard life she had led until Ben Wolfe had had her kidnapped. The only good thing in the whole vile business was that it had prevented her from marrying Francis Sylvester.

'Does my mother know?' she asked at last.

'I fear so.'

'I ought to help them…' she began.

'Indeed not,' said Mr Herriott vigorously. 'He has caused you a great deal of misery and I understand that neither he nor your mother ever offered you any help during your last

few difficult years. They are not in penury and must learn
to live on what is theirs and not on what was stolen from
you.'

'But surely my mother had no notion of Mr Mitchell's
wickedness?'

'Possibly not.'

Susanna stared at the breakfront bookcase opposite to her,
filled with law books.

'How did you come to know of this?'

'Oh, only recently—and our sources must remain secret.
Legal etiquette, you understand.'

Susanna didn't; it all seemed most odd to her. Since Madeira had not served its purpose in preparing her for such
good news, Mr Bracewell joined in the discussion by ring-
ing for tea instead and offering Miss Beverly both congratulations and condolences.

'I understand that you are comfortably placed at the moment,' he said kindly.

'Yes, I am the companion of a very gracious French noblewoman, Madame la Comtesse de Saulx.'

'So we understand. You realise that the house in which
Mr and Mrs Mitchell have been living is yours, part of the
estate which your father left you. They quitted it today.'

So Mr Mitchell had turned her out of her own home.

'Time's whirligig,' she said aloud.

'I beg your pardon?' said Mr Bracewell gently.

'Shakespeare,' answered Susanna numbly. '"Thus the
whirligig of time brings in his revenges."'

'Ah, yes,' he answered her, smiling. 'The ancients' Wheel
of Fortune. First we are down and then we are up.'

'Or the reverse in Mr Mitchell's case,' put in Mr Herriott,
who appeared to be enjoying the Mitchells' downfall.

'May I assure you, Miss Beverly,' he continued, 'that the
interest on your fortune will be paid to you quarterly, and
that you may return to your home as soon as it is convenient
to you. You may call on us for any assistance you may

require when you take up your new life. Before you leave, I must ask you to sign some necessary documents to enable us to do so.'

What a difference a fortune makes to the manner in which you are treated, thought Susanna sardonically. Yesterday I was an unconsidered nobody, grateful for *Madame*'s kindness, and today, all is changed. The world is bowing and scraping to me and my lightest wish is law.

This was not the sort of comment she cared to make to the Messrs Herriott and Bracewell, however.

She drank her tea and signed the necessary documents, both gentlemen assuring her of their good wishes and their desire to help her at all times. Mr Herriott, as the senior partner, escorted her to her carriage, returning to his office to find that Mr Bracewell had been joined by a third party, Mr Ben Wolfe, who had slipped in from another room.

'Your partner assures me,' he said to Mr Herriott, 'that all went swimmingly this afternoon, and that Miss Beverly is now in command of her fortune again.'

'Indeed,' said Mr Herriott, bowing slightly. 'I wish that you had allowed Mr Samuel Mitchell to be prosecuted for his misdeeds—even if you did compel him to make restitution. It is a bad principle, I fear, to allow the wicked to go unpunished.'

'Not exactly unpunished,' drawled Ben comfortably, drinking the Madeira which Susanna had refused, 'seeing that he was compelled to disgorge himself of virtually everything he possessed. Furthermore, I wished, as I am sure you do, to spare Miss Beverly as much public pain as possible, as well as ensuring that she remains unaware that it was I who uncovered Mr Mitchell's wrong doing. I have no wish to profit from that.'

'Very noble of you,' returned Mr Herriott insincerely, for he thought that Mr Ben Wolfe was as devious a schemer as he had ever encountered. 'It does you nothing but credit, sir.'

'It does, doesn't it,' agreed Mr Wolfe amiably, 'which was probably why I did it, don't you think?' He threw his head back and laughed. 'But of course, you do. Who knows how it may yet profit me? At the moment, though, I must thank you both for your co-operation in this matter, especially insofar as it relates to keeping my intervention a secret.'

He refrained from pointing out that, despite their dereliction of duty in allowing Mr Mitchell to deceive them, he was allowing them to take the credit for unmasking him.

Allies were always useful, especially in the game he was about to play—and now he had two powerful ones.

Chapter Eight

Susanna was seated in *Madame*'s small drawing room, trying to come to terms with the sudden recovery of her fortune, when the butler announced that Mrs Mitchell had arrived and wished to speak to Miss Beverly.

She put her canvaswork down and composed herself. Ever since she had told *Madame* of her good news she had felt that she was living in a dream. *Madame* had begged her to remain with her as a friend, rather than as a companion, 'Although,' she had added, 'I shall quite understand if you wish to return to your old home immediately.'

'I don't know what I wish,' Susanna had told her. 'If I am honest, I would like to accept your kind invitation, if only because it will give me time to consider my future arrangements.'

She was not sure that she wanted to return to her old home: it held too many unhappy memories—and she certainly didn't want to live there on her own. She was contemplating a number of possibilities when her mother was announced.

Mrs Mitchell scarcely waited for the butler to depart before she rounded on Susanna—*Madame* had already tactfully left the room so that mother and daughter might be alone together.

'Was it you who ruined poor Mr Mitchell and banished us to a back street in Islington? Someone must have told a pack of lies to condemn us to poverty so that you might live in splendour. We were given an hour to leave our own home and were not allowed to take anything with us except the clothes we stood up in. Your poor sisters were even compelled to leave their little treasures behind. Such unkindness! I would never have thought a daughter of mine would treat me so cruelly.'

She paused to draw breath before continuing her tirade, looking around the room and exclaiming, 'You seem to be comfortable enough here without needing to vent your spite on us in order to make yourself more comfortable still.'

After hurling this dart at Susanna, Mrs Mitchell threw herself on to the nearest sofa and began to howl into one of the cushions on it in the most abandoned fashion, before throwing it on one side and preparing to reproach her daughter again.

Susanna, her face white, had retreated a couple of paces backwards, fearful that her mother might attack her physically. She said, as gently as she could, before Mrs Mitchell could speak again, 'I had no knowledge of Mr Mitchell's theft of my inheritance until three days ago, nor was I aware that you had already had to leave your home. But aren't you forgetting something, Mother?'

'Forgetting! I!' screamed her mother. 'No, I am forgetting nothing. Oh, the humiliation! The pain!'

'You are forgetting,' said Susanna steadily, 'that your husband, Mr Samuel Mitchell, not only stole my inheritance, he also made sure that my marriage with Francis Sylvester would fail, and after that he turned me out of my home—not yours or his—to earn my own living. My father left you a fortune of your own which passed to Mr Mitchell when you married him, but, not content with that, he made sure that he enjoyed mine. I lost everything—my inheritance, my good name, and my home—through his machinations. It is you who should apologise to me for the wrongs I have suffered, not me apologise to you.'

'Oh, "How sharper than a serpent's tooth it is / To have a thankless child,"' intoned her mother, quoting from Shakespeare and rolling her eyes towards heaven. 'Your father had no business leaving so much to you. Mr Mitchell has five of us to keep and there is only one of you.'

'Well, Mr Mitchell made sure that I remained only one when he wrecked my marriage, so you had better reproach him. No, Mother—' as her mother raised her arms to heaven like an Old Testament prophet, ready to rain fire and brimstone on her '—I am sorry that Mr Mitchell has brought this disaster on you. It was none of my doing, and I agreed with my lawyers that he should not be arrested for his misdeeds. Had I insisted, he would have either been hanged or transported, for those are the punishments for embezzlement. Be thankful that you still have him, and pray that he uses his talents for business more honestly in the future.'

'No,' said her mother, pushing her open hands at Susanna as though she was about to attack her, 'no, I will not listen to you. I am sure that my poor husband is innocent and that the truth will come out one day. Until then I have no wish to see you again.'

'Well, you have lived without seeing me for the last four years, so a longer parting will make little odds.'

She stopped, and then tried to take one of her mother's hands, 'Oh, Mother, remember that I am your child as well, and try to understand how I must have felt when I learned the dreadful truth. And how I feel now when you disown me so cruelly although I have done you no wrong—and have even saved your husband from the implacable hands of the law despite all that he has done to me.'

Her mother pushed her away. 'That is enough. I won't hear any more. Stay with your fancy Frenchwoman—oh, how it hurts me to think that she may be enjoying herself in my home while I suffer the privations of poverty.'

Ignoring Susanna's pleading face, she walked to the door. 'You need not have me shown out. I want no favours from you or anyone who lives with you. I know that you disliked Mr Mitchell, but I never thought that you would have gone so far as to ruin him—and us.'

She went. Susanna sank on to the sofa which her mother had briefly inhabited and found that, broken though she was, she could not cry. Or rather, she thought grimly, I will not.

Madame came in a few moments later, took one look at her and rang for the teaboard.

'Dear child,' she said kindly, 'I will not ask you what passed. Knowing the world as I do, I assume that your mother was far from kind to you. No, do not answer me. There is nothing which either of us can say at present other than to admit that life is often too difficult for us to bear. The only comfort which I can offer you is one that I have found to be true—"This, too, will pass," which is cold comfort enough, I admit. Now, drink your tea.'

Susanna reflected sadly that these days everyone seemed determined to make her drink some liquid or other. Mr Wolfe had begun this apparent ritual and everyone else she had encountered had followed his example. Nevertheless she did as she was bid, wondering what else the afternoon had in store for her.

She was not in the least surprised when Mr Wolfe was announced—he seemed to haunt her these days. Even her refusal of his proposal—of which she had not informed *Madame*—did not seem to have deterred him.

In *Madame*'s little drawing room he seemed larger than ever. He refused the tea which *Madame* offered him, saying, 'Another time, perhaps. It is a fine day, I have a new carriage outside and four splendid horses and am determined that, if you have no other engagement, you will allow me to drive you both to Hyde Park to enjoy the sun.'

He could have said nothing more calculated to allow Susanna to recover herself. Before her mother's unhappy visit she would have thought that her reaction to it would have been to wish to hide herself away. Instead, she was possessed with a fierce determination to show the world that she would not be put down. Which was stupid, she thought wryly, because no one but her mother and herself were aware of what had so recently passed between them.

Knowing Ben Wolfe as well as she did, she also knew that his new carriage would be as splendid as his horses and that it would be a privilege to sit behind them. Nevertheless, having agreed almost immediately, she was a little perturbed to hear *Madame* say that she was suffering from a light megrim and would prefer not to sit in the hot sun—if Mr Wolfe would be so good as to allow her to make her excuses.

'In that case,' began Susanna, a trifle unhappily, 'perhaps I—'

For once *Madame*'s perfect manners deserted her. She cut Susanna off in mid-sentence, announcing briskly, 'Do not allow my malaise to prevent you from enjoying a well-earned excursion, my dear. Without yet being past your last prayers, you are mature enough to sit beside Mr Wolfe in a public place such as Hyde Park without causing scandal.'

'Or perhaps because I have already caused so much,' Susanna riposted lightly, 'one more *bêtise* will not count against me!'

'Nonsense,' said *Madame* and Ben together.

'Your presence in *Madame*'s home,' said the latter, 'will suffice to stifle any scandal. And you need a run in the Park. You are a trifle pale this afternoon—too much staying indoors, I presume.'

Madame again answered for her. 'You mistake, Mr Wolfe. Miss Beverly has recently received two pieces of news, one good and the other much less so. The first is that she has received notice that her fortune, which her lawyers had allowed her to be cheated of by her stepfather, has been restored to her, so she is no longer dependent on cold charity. The second is that her mother has visited her and has been most unkind to her because of the change in her own circumstances. Not that she has told me so directly—it is what I have gathered from her manner.'

'Is this true, Miss Beverly?' asked Ben, his face grim. He had, at *Madame*'s urgings, taken a seat, and he leaned forward from it to add, 'Most unwarranted, if so, seeing that by all accounts her husband stole your inheritance from you.'

'Both statements are true,' she told him, 'but I confess to feeling a trifle unhappy that my good luck is at the expense of my mother and half-sisters' bad luck.'

'Do not reproach yourself,' he said earnestly. 'You have had a great wrong done to you, and your mother and sisters have been living a comfortable life while you have been struggling. You were turned out of your home, were you not?'

Susanna nodded a brief agreement.

'Well, then!' said Ben sturdily. 'Your sentiments do your soft heart credit, but I advise you to forget the unhappy past, accept my invitation and tell me what you think of my carriage and four.'

'But I am not really dressed to go to the Park,' objected Susanna.

'Nonsense, you look as you always do whatever you wear, quite *à point*. You simply need to equip yourself with a parasol to arm yourself against the sun and a light shawl to protect your arms.'

Madame nodded agreement and sent her away to dress herself as Ben had advised. Once Susanna was out of the room, *Madame* rose and walked to the mantelpiece to rearrange some objects of *vertu* there.

'Do I detect your fine Italian hand in this sudden access of wealth which Miss Beverly is enjoying?'

'Now, why in the world should you think that?'

'You forget how well I know you, *cher ami*! What I don't understand is why you don't simply propose to her and have done with it.'

Ben said in his most winning voice, 'Oh, but I have, and…' He paused tantalisingly.

Madame turned to face him. 'You really are provoking,' and her voice had quite lost its pretty French accent and was disturbingly downright in the English fashion. 'I am growing too old to be teased.'

'Never—you are timeless, as you well know,' he said. 'But, all the same, I will oblige you and finish my sentence. She refused me. Perhaps because neither the manner of it, nor the occasion on which it was made, could be described as either tactful or auspicious.'

'You are, as usual, being remarkably cold-blooded about the whole business,' said *Madame* sternly, 'but that is your way. Are you cold-blooded about her? Do you feel anything for her?'

'You are not to ask me that. I can only tell you that I would not hurt her for the world. She has been hurt enough.'

'Only that? Is that all you feel for her?'

'Better that than loud protestations of undying love which mean nothing.'

If *Madame* thought that he was not quite telling her the truth, she did not say so. In any case, the arrival of Susanna, looking enchanting in cool pale blue and cream, with kid shoes, bonnet and parasol to match, brought an end to their conversation.

'Charming,' said Ben, bending over to kiss her hand. 'Quite charming. I shall be the envy of Hyde Park.'

He was not far wrong. On his own he would have created gossip, because all the world was excitedly chattering about the mysterious nabob, and the new *on dit* running around the *ton* suggested that he was not a member of the Wolfe family at all, but merely an adventurer who had assumed the name and had subsequently misappropriated what was left of the Wolfe estates.

Escorting Susanna, however, who had remained anonymous for the four years since her jilting when she had made such a scandalous, if fleeting, impression on the London scene, he was the subject of even more gossip and interest. Pieces of excited conversation flew around the Park such as:

'Who is he with?'

'Oh, is that the young woman whom Sylvester jilted? What a beauty she is now. Where has she been?'

'Madame la Comtesse de Saulx is sponsoring her, you say? Then what is she doing with *him*? *Madame* is respectability itself.'

'Had her fortune restored to her, I understand. Is that why Wolfe is with her?'

'And *Madame* is sponsoring Wolfe, as well, is she? Odd, that! Best go over and pay our respects. Wouldn't want to be backward in coming forward if he is the coming man, which they say he is.'

And so on...

Susanna was sublimely unaware of the excitement which she was creating. She only knew that she was happy. Ben had driven the carriage into the shade of some trees and his two grooms were holding the horses steady. She and Ben became the subject of a little court. Men and women on foot, either because they had walked to the Park or had left their horse or carriage for the moment, made their way to them out of sheer curiosity if nothing else.

'I had no notion that you were so popular, Mr Wolfe,' said Susanna, intrigued by all this excitement.

'I am a novelty,' he whispered to her. 'In a few months I shall become a commonplace and a new sensation will be found to exclaim over. And you are a novelty as well, a beautiful woman whom, I dare say, few know. And remember, the story of your lost-and-found inheritance is probably

an *on dit* already. Prepare to be boarded by ambitious and
fortune-hunting suitors.'

'I hadn't thought of that,' Susanna admitted artlessly. She
had been so busy worrying about all the other implications
of her new-found wealth that she had forgotten that one.

'Best to remember it.' Ben's voice was now sober, its
usually wryly jesting overtones absent for once.

'Yes, I suppose so.' She sighed. 'Ah, well, I suppose
every silver lining has its cloud.'

Before he could answer her, a mature beauty on the arm
of a large man in the uniform of a Hussar approached them
and began to gush at Ben as though he were alone.

'So happy to see you. You remember me from India, I
trust. Charlotte Campion I was then, but my husband died
of a fever out there and here I am, home again and married
now to Colonel Bob Beauchamp—you know him too, I believe.'

'We have met.' Ben's voice was dry. 'You will allow me
to present Miss Susanna Beverly to you. Miss Beverly,
Colonel and Mrs Beauchamp.'

'Ah,' said Mrs Beauchamp, at last acknowledging Susanna's existence. 'So you are the little heiress who has
recovered her lost fortune!'

She said this as though Susanna's carelessness had caused
this sad mishap through conduct on a par with her mislaying
her reticule or her kerchief.

'An heiress, true, but not little,' said Ben before Susanna
could answer—something, she thought crossly, which was
happening to her too often these days. She was perfectly
capable of defending herself, both Ben and *Madame* were
doing it a little too brown by deciding otherwise.

She was reduced to smiling vaguely at Mrs Beauchamp
whilst wondering if she had ever been Ben's mistress—or
even a passing lover. Her manner seemed to suggest so.

Colonel Beauchamp had produced a monocle which he

jammed in his right eye to enable him to survey Susanna more closely after a fashion for which she did not care.

'Must come to supper with us soon,' he offered. 'Eh, Charlie?'

'Oh, indeed. I can gossip about old times with Ben and you can tell Miss—Beverly, is it?—all about Waterloo, leaving out all the gory bits, of course.'

'Supposing I wanted to hear about the gory bits,' Susanna raged at Ben when the Beauchamps had departed after Mrs Beauchamp had hurled a few more poisoned darts at Susanna. 'What then? How well did you know her in India?'

To his inward horror, Ben realised that he was delighted to detect a note of jealousy in Susanna's response to Charlotte Beauchamp's overblown charms. He must be going mad. Worse, it was even madder of him to stoke the fire by saying confidentially, 'Very well. Every man in Indian society knew her very well.'

'How fortunate for them all,' said Susanna tartly, 'to find someone so obliging.'

'True,' said Ben naughtily. 'Particularly when there was such a dearth of females who were.'

He was highly entertained when Susanna closed her parasol, produced a fan and began to wave it vigorously in front of her, saying crossly, 'You really should not talk like this to me, you know. I am an unmarried female whose innocence ought to be protected.'

'I am taking my tone from you,' retorted Ben primly. 'If you wish to discuss something less…inflammatory…we can embark on some more respectable topic.'

'Oh, so you admit that the lady is not respectable.' The accusation shot out of Susanna without her willing it.

What on earth is the matter with me, she thought dismally, that every time I am with Mr Big Bad Wolfe I find myself saying the most dreadful things and behaving like Lady Caroline Lamb at her worst? I never do it with anyone else. Quite the contrary, I am usually as solemn as a parson or a judge—more, in fact. I really must compose myself.'

Ben watched the play of emotion on her face, guessing a little of what she was thinking.

'Cannot you think of anything suitable to discuss?' he offered helpfully. 'If you cannot, might I suggest we converse on the state of the King's health. I hear that it is declining rapidly.'

'I shall decline rapidly if you don't behave yourself,' retorted Susanna, watching another group of curious sightseers approaching their carriage. Among them were the Westerns and Amelia. Amelia was wearing a brilliant purple walking dress which did nothing for her complexion. Her mouth was turned down at the corners, too.

'Whatever can be the matter with her?' whispered Susanna to Ben. 'She is generally so high-spirited as to be unendurable.'

'Her marriage to Lord Darlington will not take place,' Ben whispered back. 'Yours is not the only sensation here today. The *on dit* is that Babbacombe's financial situation is so dire that the Westerns cried off shortly after learning of it. Apparently they concluded that even to gain a title was a game not worth the candle if by doing so they risked bankruptcy themselves in order to save Babbacombe. Smile at them; for the moment you are up and they are down.'

Susanna duly obeyed him when they finally reached the carriage. It appeared that the Westerns had decided that they might recognise Mr Wolfe and his companion after all.

Preliminaries over, Amelia said to Susanna, 'I suppose that I ought to congratulate you, so I will.'

'Thank you,' said Susanna, ignoring the graceless nature of this remark and wondering what to say in reply, but Amelia, joining the growing throng of those who never allowed her to finish a sentence, added immediately,

'I suppose that you have heard of my bad news?'

'Mr Wolfe has just informed me of it.'

'No doubt—he seems to know everything. Who would have thought that Lord Babbacombe would be so deceitful? M'lord told Papa a series of lies when the marriage settlement was being arranged. His estates were heavily mortgaged, he was deep in debt, the moneylenders were after him, and only an anonymous letter informing our lawyers of the true state of things prevented us from becoming part of his general ruin. I was sorry to lose George, of course, but I'm sure that you will agree that I could not marry him and end up a pauper.'

'But I thought that you shared a deathless love with him?'

Oh, dear, now she was beginning to sound exactly like Ben Wolfe himself, coolly sardonic!

Amelia stared at her. 'Deathless love would be hard to manage in a garret,' she said at last.

'Oh, indeed. On the other hand, I believe that deathless love is hard to manage anywhere.'

And now I've done it again. I must stop before I say something which I shall regret.

Ben, who had been conversing with the Westerns—on a respectable topic, Susanna hoped—overheard this and made his contribution to the wake for George and Amelia's marriage.

'If you believe in love, that is. In any case, outside of novels, it seems to me that love and marriage have little to do with one another.'

Well, one might have expected Ben Wolfe to say something like that. It killed the conversation dead. Amelia dabbed at her eyes with her handkerchief, but whether she was crying for George, or the loss of his title, was difficult to guess.

After that the conversation went even further downhill until at last the Westerns drifted away, leaving Ben and Susanna alone for a moment.

But not for long.

The next to approach them was, improbably, Jess Fitzroy,

riding a superb grey. He swept off his hat to Susanna and said cheerfully to Ben, 'Good afternoon, sir.'

'Very good for you,' returned Ben, 'if you have nothing better to do than ride in the Park.'

'Oh, all in the way of business,' replied Jess, not a whit disturbed. 'I not only have information for you which cannot wait, but I have also been gathering even more as I made my way around the Park.'

'Urgent or not, the business must wait until we return home,' replied Ben. He was quartering the Park with his eyes and, when he finished, said affably to Jess, who was smiling at Susanna, 'You could do me a service if you would, Jess. You could take Miss Beverly for a short walk, for I believe that I see another person who has urgent business with me approaching. She will not wish to listen to a dull recital of Stock Exchange prices, I am sure.'

Now how did she know that he was not telling the truth? Susanna had a mind to refuse him and see what he said to that. Forestalling her—as usual—Jess said cheerfully, 'Are you sure that Miss Beverly wishes to take a stroll around the Park?'

'Nothing would please me more,' said Susanna before Ben could answer. She was tired of having others anticipate her wishes for her.

'Very well,' said Jess, dismounting and throwing the reins of his horse to one of Ben's attendant grooms, before handing Susanna down from the carriage.

'Do you wish me to walk Bucephalus with us, Miss Beverly? Or would you rather take a turn without him?'

'Oh, let him walk with us,' said Susanna, gratified that someone had taken the trouble to ascertain her wishes. 'He is very beautiful, is he not? Have you had him long?'

Jess took the reins from the groom. 'Alas, he is not mine, Miss Beverly. He is Ben's…I mean, Mr Wolfe's. He allows me the use of him.'

Susanna noticed, as she had done before, that Jess Fitzroy

had the speech and manners of a gentleman, something which intrigued her. How had he come to be Ben Wolfe's faithful dogsbody?

'Where did you meet him?' she asked, apparently idly.

'In India,' Jess responded frankly. 'I was an officer in the regiment in which he was a sergeant. I was lucky to have him. I was a raw fool and he saved my bacon once or twice in several frontier skirmishes. He left the army shortly after that and set himself up in business.'

He paused, before adding, 'I respect you enough to be honest with you. I was a fool, do not ask me how. I was duped by others and ended by having to resign my commission. There I was, penniless, with no family, other than the knowledge that my grandfather had been the natural son of Frederick, Prince of Wales, and that I was his only descendant. I had no prospects, no near relatives, and nowhere to go. Ben found me, offered me work and I have been with him ever since. I owe him everything for he saved me from being a pauper.

'Do not be deceived by his manner. Oh, he is hard, I grant you, but he is true, as true as a new-minted golden guinea. On the other hand, if *you* are not true—then look out is all I can say!'

'You can say that, Mr Fitzroy, even after he tried to kidnap Miss Western?'

Jess smiled wryly. 'I did not say that he was virtuous, Miss Beverly. Virtue is quite another matter and is rarely found—even amongst those who claim most loudly that they possess it.'

Susanna said nothing for a moment. She honoured Mr Fitzroy for being frank with her so she asked him another question.

'You spoke almost dismissively of virtue, sir. Does that mean that neither you nor Mr Wolfe practise it?'

'On the contrary: but acts of kindness individually performed do not in themselves constitute virtue, as I am sure you understand. Mr Wolfe looks after people—but in doing so not all his acts are virtuous. The world in which we live is a cruel one, and the good do not survive in it if their only defence is their virtue—more than that is frequently necessary.'

Susanna did not ask him what 'more than that' might entail. Her own experience had taught her that much of what he had just said to her was true. She had been good and her goodness had not prevented Mr Mitchell from ruining her— quite the contrary, it had made it easy for him to do so.

A sudden thought struck her. A thought which she did not wish to share with anyone until she had examined it carefully. Her life had been growing increasingly difficult until she had met Mr Ben Wolfe. From that moment on everything had changed.

She had been introduced to *Madame* and all her fears for her immediate future had disappeared. And then, suddenly, mysteriously, her fortune had been restored to her, and she was again Miss Susanna Beverly, the heiress, no longer a poor dependant on the charity of others.

Jess Fitzroy had said that Mr Wolfe looked after people, and he had undoubtedly looked after Jess. Had he looked after her? Who else knew her who was powerful enough not only to discover Mr Mitchell's theft of her inheritance, but was also able to restore it to her?

And if her reasoning was correct, how did that affect her feelings for him? She must be grateful—but might he expect more from her than that? And if so, what? By helping Jess, Ben had gained a faithful servant and an honest henchman— what might he expect to gain from helping her?

A man who was not virtuous—even if true—might have a hidden reason for his charitable acts. She looked sideways at Mr Jess Fitzroy and half-thought of saying something on these lines to him.

Reason told her that might be foolish—he was Mr Wolfe's faithful servant, not hers. On the surface he was everything a gentleman ought to be, but she must not forget that he had kidnapped her on Mr Wolfe's orders and it was to him he owed allegiance.

'You are quiet,' Jess said at last. 'But then, I like a quiet woman.'

Susanna laughed, and her laughter drove away her darker thoughts. 'You did not think that I was quiet when you snatched me from the street—on the contrary.'

'Ah, but you were defending yourself, were you not? And that is what I meant by goodness not being enough. To have acted like a perfect lady would not have helped you in your dealings either with me or with Mr Wolfe. He admired the manner in which you stood up to him and refused to be put down. And then, when all was settled, you reverted to being a perfect lady and allowed yourself to be good again.'

'You tempt me, Mr Fitzroy, to ask you whether you learned your deviousness from Mr Wolfe—or did you always possess it?'

The look he gave her was an admiring one. 'And you tempt me, Miss Beverly, to remark that you needed no lessons in that line from Mr Wolfe since from the first moment you met him you also were deviousness itself. That is why he admires you.'

So Mr Wolfe admired her—and what was she to make of that? She was about to answer Jess—or, rather, ask him another question—when she saw that they had walked in a half-circle and were almost back to their starting point.

She could see Ben talking earnestly to a man in dark unfashionable clothing who was sitting beside him in his carriage. She thought suddenly that Jess's arrival in the Park might not have been accidental, even though Ben had twitted him on it.

'You have honoured me by giving me your confidence, Mr Fitzroy,' she said at last, discarding her question, 'and I will not betray it. I had, I must admit, wondered about your name. You do not have a great look of the Royal Family.'

'No, indeed, and that is a relief. I take after my grandfather's wife or so my father told me. And, yes, I would prefer it if you did not inform Mr Wolfe of what I have said of myself—or of him. And now that is enough of me.'

'Oh, I have learned to be close-mouthed in a bitter school,' Susanna told him, 'for if I did not look after myself, no one else would.'

Jess did not inform her that she, like himself, now had a benefactor in the unlikely person of Ben Wolfe, for he had been forbidden to do so. He would not be surprised, though, if Miss Susanna Beverly did not work that out for herself quite soon. He was not to know that she had already done so.

After that they talked idly until Jess, seeing that Ben's visitor had disappeared, walked Susanna back to his employer's carriage again, mounted his grey and bade them adieu.

His business apparently over—and Jess disappearing into the middle distance, doubtless to carry out more of his errands—Ben gave Susanna his full attention. His first sentence proved that, even when apparently conducting business, he still had time to watch what was going on about him.

'Jess had plenty to say to you,' he remarked drily as he drove slowly along, 'and you seemed to be equally loquacious. Was it the weather or the current *on dits* which occupied you?'

'Neither,' said Susanna briskly. 'The weather has been unchangingly temperate recently, and I know little of any *on dits*. Instead we enjoyed a short philosophical conversation on the nature of virtue.'

'Of which Jess knows a great deal, I am sure,' remarked Ben, a trifle ironically.

'Oh, one need not practise something in order to discuss

it,' retorted Susanna. 'Otherwise it would be difficult to discuss anything—paintings or poems, for example, seeing that
most of us are neither painters nor poets.'

Few men, and no women, ever spoke to Ben Wolfe in
such a downright fashion. He gave a short laugh and said,
'I shall make it my business, Miss Beverly, to choose my
words very carefully when I discuss anything with you. You
would have made a good career in the world of business
had you been a man.'

He had almost said 'been lucky enough to be a man,' but
had revised that statement before he made it for he was sure
that Miss Beverly would have had said something sharp in
reply. He thought that she was happy to be a woman even
if, in many ways, she possessed the kind of acuteness which
was commonly thought to be confined to men. Besides, he
had absolutely no wish for her to be a man!

'Is that intended to be a compliment, Mr Wolfe?' she
asked him gravely.

'Many would think it so.'

'But am *I* to think it so?'

The look she gave him as she said this set Ben groaning
inwardly. He wished that they were alone, not in a crowded
Park with idle, curious and malicious eyes upon them. He
would have kissed her for her impudence, there, at the corner of her smiling mouth. And then he would…he would…

Stop that, he commanded himself sternly. This is neither
the time nor the place…

And stop that, too. I have no wish to be any woman's
slave—even one as clever and desirable as Miss Susanna
Beverly.

'I meant it as such,' he came out with at last, Susanna
meanwhile wondering why it took him so long to answer
her.

'Then I will accept it as such.'

'And in the meantime,' he ground out, 'you will oblige
me by cutting that obnoxious puppy, George Darlington,'

for he had just seen George tipping his hat and smiling at Susanna for all the world as though he had not recently attempted to assault her in Lord Exford's study.

'You know, Mr Wolfe,' Susanna told him after doing as he wished, 'I don't really need a duenna when I am with you. You perform that service so admirably I wonder that you do not take it up as a profession!'

He replied to her in kind, 'I would if it paid as well as being a financier in the City.'

'I must remember that,' she said, 'if I lose my fortune again and need to find a well-rewarded occupation.'

'You did not lose your fortune, Miss Beverly, you had it stolen from you. Remember that if you begin to feel mercy towards those who robbed you.' His voice was both stern and forbidding.

'You surely do not mean that my mother—?'

'Your mother, from what you have said of her, turns a blind eye to her second husband's actions. I cannot believe that she was completely unaware of his misappropriation of your inheritance.'

In fact Ben, from his investigations, knew that what he was saying was true. Equally, Susanna, with a sinking heart, was sure that what he was telling her was the truth because he had been her unknown saviour.

For a moment she debated whether to tell him that she was aware of that, but decided against it. If he wished to keep his secret, then she would take no steps to make him aware that she had discovered it.

Jess Fitzroy is right. I am as devious as he is. Knowledge is power, as the old saying has it, and although I cannot yet conceive what power over him this knowledge gives me, I will continue to keep my secret—as he keeps his. Like it or not, what frightens me the most is the knowledge of the attraction he has for me so that simply sitting by him excites me strangely.

And the most exciting thing of all is that that is another of my secrets, from him and the world.

Thus, side by side, they drove back to Stanhope Street, chatting amiably together, neither of them giving the slightest sign that what was growing between them was slowly becoming so powerful that they would be unable to deny it—either to themselves or to the other.

Once back at *Madame*'s Ben refused an offer of early supper. 'Alas, I must decline,' he said, 'I have another engagement, made only this afternoon. What would please me is if you would both consent to dine with me on this coming Friday evening. Pray forgive me for asking you at such short notice.'

'Not only do we forgive you,' said *Madame*, 'but we shall be delighted to attend as we have no other engagements—is not that so, Miss Beverly?'

'Indeed,' said Susanna who, beneath her quiet acquiescence was all agog at the prospect of dinner with Mr Wolfe. If his country home was The Den, what was his London home called? The Lair, perhaps?

She hugged this gleeful thought to herself as *Madame* discreetly questioned her about her ride with Ben and she as discreetly answered, amused, as always, at the distance she had come from being the naïve girl whom Samuel Mitchell had cheated so easily.

Chapter Nine

'I say, Gronow, ain't that Ben Wolfe? Who let him in? All sorts of stories goin' around about him. No one knows who the devil he really is.'

'Best not let him hear you say so,' returned Captain Gronow, looking up from his game of whist to rebuke the speaker, his partner, James Erskine. 'He's a devil of a fellow for anything you care to name: rapier, sabre, pistols or fists. What's more, he's a member here. That Indian nabob, Wilson, put him up for membership and he was accepted before the *on dits* started their rounds. Whatever else, he's the dead-spit image of his supposed father, the late Charlie Wolfe, but on which side of the blanket...who knows or cares?

'In any case, your turn to play—you haven't forgotten that we *are* playing at whist and not at gossip.'

Since Gronow possessed all the athletic attributes which he claimed for Ben Wolfe, James Erskine flushed and played the card which he had been holding in the air. 'Only asking, old fellow, only asking,' he muttered.

Ben, watching them from where he was propped against the mantelpiece, a glass of rather inferior port in his hand, would not have been surprised to learn that he was the subject of their conversation. Only that morning Jess Fitzroy, as tactfully as he could, had told him of the unpleasant rumours about him circulating around London.

'So that was why I caused such a commotion in Hyde Park yesterday,' he had said. 'I might have thought that it was the splendour of my turnout, but no. Try to find out where this nonsense came from—who started it on its way.'

'Difficult, that,' said Jess, shrugging his shoulders. 'I'll do my best, though.'

Ben had said no more. He thought he knew who had started the lie on its way, but he wanted hard evidence before he took any action. He drank down the remains of his port and turned to speak to his friend, once his patron, Tom Wilson, who was standing near him.

He had only exchanged a few words with him when someone tapped him aggressively on his shoulder, causing him to turn in the opposite direction—to discover that he was facing George Darlington.

'You wish to speak to me?' he asked. He kept his voice low and his manner courteous. He had no wish to embarrass Tom Wilson to whom he owed a great deal, including his membership of White's.

George, however, was suffering from no such constraints. 'I have no *wish* to speak to you,' he said roughly, treading on the word wish. 'But I am compelled to do so in order to ask you what you are doing here in a club reserved for gentlemen. You, being neither a gentleman nor entitled to the name you pretend to, have no business here.'

'Steady now, young fellow,' exclaimed Tom before Ben could answer. 'He is here because he has been properly elected at my sponsorship and that of Lord Lowborough with whom we were both acquainted in India.'

'Oh, India,' jeered George, 'one might claim to be anyone in India, eh, Father?'

George's father, Lord Babbacombe, who had been a little way behind his son because of handing his hat and greatcoat to a footman, said approvingly, 'Indeed, that is so. We order matters differently in England as this fellow will soon discover. I shall make a complaint immediately to the committee and ask them to revoke his membership forthwith. To my certain knowledge he is an impostor. Charles Wolfe's only son, Benjamin, died in childhood.'

'A fate likely to overtake your son at a somewhat later stage in his life,' ground out Ben through his teeth, 'since I am giving him notice that I shall be sending my seconds to him to arrange for us to meet on the field of honour so that I may repay him for the insult which he has put upon me.'

'You may send as many seconds as you please,' returned m'lord, 'but no son of mine, nor any other gentleman, will soil his hands by engaging in an affair of honour with a cheat and impostor. Be warned, sir, I shall shortly be laying before the proper authorities evidence of your crimes. I say nothing of the fact that you have spent your time since you returned to England attempting to ruin me financially. That has nothing to do with the case, other than to prove that you have no shame and that the word honour on your lips demeans it.'

'Attempting to ruin you,' said Ben, his eyebrows rising. 'I believe that I have gone further than that—for a reason which you well know and which I shall not mention here.

'I take note that your son, having insulted me, is neither ready to take the consequences, nor to speak for himself. I wondered where the courage—which he so recently lacked—came from when he taunted me a moment ago, but I see that it was because he had no intention of proving either his courage or his honour. I don't find that surprising since he apparently possesses neither virtue.'

He swung round on George, who had stepped back to allow his father to fight his battles for him.

'Do you intend to allow me to insult you at will? I shall certainly do so if you don't remove yourself from my sight.'

His whole appearance was so threatening that George retreated even further backwards, his face paling, proving, if proof were needed, that Ben's impugning of his courage was no less than true.

Tom Wilson put a hand on Ben's arm. 'Come,' he said, 'you have made your point. If the young fellow won't fight, we all know what to think of him.'

Captain Gronow, who had abandoned his card game, came over to them. 'What's to do?' he asked, being very much a man who was sought after to pass judgement when such quarrels had reached *point non plus*.

Before Ben could answer Gronow's question, Tom Wilson put his oar in again. 'I am a third party here, albeit I am Mr Wolfe's friend. The matter lies so,' and he gave a brief and accurate account of what had passed.

'Hmm,' said Gronow, managing to make that mild exclamation sound magisterial. 'A serious business, I see. My own feeling is that Lord Darlington should not have gone as far as he did unless he intended to back his accusation with the force of arms. On the other hand, Lord Babbacombe has some right on his side when he argues that the accusation, if true, relieves his son of defending himself against someone whose own honour is dubious. The matter is at a stand-off until Mr Wolfe's claim to be who he is has been proven beyond doubt.'

Tom Wilson said indignantly, 'I have known Ben Wolfe since he was eighteen and he has borne no other name.'

'Which proves nothing, Tom,' said Ben savagely. 'You are but an India merchant, and who I claimed to be at eighteen is neither here nor there—as you well know. I thank you for your defence, but…' and he shrugged his shoulders.

Captain Gronow's reply was mild. 'Until matters are settled, all parties must agree to let them rest. No unproven accusations and insults should be exchanged, and consequently there should be no duelling, either provoked inside these walls or outside of them. I think that is clear, you will agree.'

He was one of society's arbiters, and most of the men who had clustered around Ben and his two accusers would consider what he had said to be fair and reasonable. Both parties could do nothing but accept what he had said.

'This is not the end of the affair,' exclaimed Lord Babbacombe. 'You heard what I said. I shall pursue you until I have broken you, as you are breaking me. I believe you to be the person behind the collapse of my son's marriage to Miss Western.'

'Come, come, m'lord,' said Gronow, the only person brave enough to say such a thing to a peer of the realm, 'you have no proof of that. No proof at all. Let us, as I advised, leave the matter where it stands.'

Even Babbacombe could not refuse to agree with him, especially when he was surrounded by nodding heads all agreeing with Gronow. There were those who hastened to put their name in White's famous betting book, wagering good money that Ben Wolfe and either Babbacombe or Darlington would meet one dawn at Putney to put the matter to the final test of a duel, even though they dare say nothing aloud.

His face furious, Lord Babbacombe walked away with his son, exclaiming vigorously that he had no mind to remain at White's while it was polluted by Ben Wolfe's presence. Ben himself made no effort to leave. He picked up his glass of port and coolly continued his conversation with Tom Wilson as though he had never been interrupted.

Tom heard him out before saying bluffly, 'Well, at least one thing that m'lord said was true. You are, I am reliably informed, responsible for his financial ruin.'

'Now where did you hear that?' Ben's reply was almost indifferent.

'Oh, you can't keep such matters secret.'

'I know. Every camp has its traitor. Be sure I shall find mine.'

Tom clapped him on the back. 'I wouldn't like to be in

his shoes. If you leave him the wherewithal to buy any, that is.'

'Are you referring to the traitor—or Lord Babbacombe?'

'Either or both,' said Tom with a grin. 'Take your pick.'

'Oh, I will. Another thing you may be sure of.'

His friend nodded. One thing he *was* sure of was that he would not like to have Ben Wolfe for an enemy.

'You would do well not to underrate Babbacombe, though. He has powerful friends, and it would be advisable to take his threats seriously.'

'Oh, Tom, I always take everything seriously. As you should know.'

They had been friends since Ben had left the Army in India and had used his savings and his winnings at cards to start up his own small business. By chance he had done Tom Wilson so great a favour that Tom had rewarded him not only with money, but with help and advice in his new career.

Later Tom was to think, a trifle ruefully, that the help and advice had been scarcely necessary, for Ben had soon carved out for himself an empire even greater and more prosperous than his own. But being Ben's friend, he had discovered, brought its own rewards. Jess Fitzroy had not lied when he had told Susanna that Ben looked after people. When ill luck overtook Tom, it was Ben who had bailed him out, and helped him to recover most of what he had lost and enabled him to make an even greater fortune.

And now they were both in London, enjoying their success, and building a new life in the land which they had left behind as very young men.

'Did you ever think, Ben, when you were a penniless private soldier, that one day you would be drinking with the nobs in the best gentleman's club in London?'

It was a question which invited 'no' for an answer, but Ben lifted his refilled glass and grinned at his old friend.

'Oh, yes. Even then I dreamed of a day like this. And what I should do when I achieved my dream.'

'You mean—about Babbacombe?' asked Tom shrewdly.

'Among other things, yes.'

His face when he came out with this was so grim that Tom shuddered. Ben had served under the Duke of Wellington when he had been what Napoleon had sneeringly called 'a mere Sepoy general', and he thought that, like Wellington, Ben had steel in his soul.

He pitied Babbacombe and his cowardly cub of a son from the bottom of his heart, but he also knew that if Ben Wolfe was pursuing them they deserved to be pursued.

'So,' said Susanna prettily to her host, 'you didn't name your home in London "The Lair" as I thought that you might. Croft House seems a pretty innocent place for a Wolfe to live in.'

Ben smiled at her. They were in the drawing room, waiting to go into dinner. 'I might have known,' he told her, 'that I would suffer the edge of your tongue. My London home is called Croft House because the Croft family lived here until they died out some fifty years ago. But now that you have mentioned it I shall probably change it to The Lair—it might frighten off housebreakers and scapegallows.'

'Scapegallows?' exclaimed Madame de Saulx. 'That is a new word for me. Pray, what does it mean?'

'Oh, you must ask Mr Fitzroy that—it is he who collects thieves' slang for me.'

Jess smiled and bowed to *Madame* before saying, 'A scapegallows is a criminal who has done exactly that. He has escaped hanging by some artful means and returns to prey on us again. At the moment, there is a new and violent crew of them—their word for gang—stopping honest citizens in the street at night and relieving them of their valu-

ables. The watch seems unable to protect us from their depredations.'

'Best not to go out alone at night,' said Tom Wilson
practically. 'I never do.'

'Wise advice,' drawled Lord Lowborough. 'Coming back
to it, I find that London is a paradise for rogues of all de-
grees. There are nearly as many swindlers in the City in the
day as there are pickpockets in the streets at night.'

'Oh, come, Lowborough,' exclaimed Tom. 'That's
stretching it a little, ain't it?'

'Hardly,' murmured Ben, smiling.

'And you should know.'

Lowborough smiled back at him. He had been young
Henry Forster, a poor lieutenant in Wellington's Indian
army, three lives from a title, when Ben had been his sergeant. As an almost penniless boy, he had been helped by
Ben Wolfe after Ben's rise to fortune nearly as much as Jess
Fitzroy, except that his unexpected accession to his title had
suddenly transformed him into a rich magnate who needed
no man's help.

Unlike many, he had been as grateful to Ben when he
was rich as he had been when he was poor, and their friendship had continued unabated. He had married into the Mil-
ner family and his pretty wife, Jane, was sitting next to
Susanna, listening in some astonishment to the lively conversation going on around her. The Milners were devout
Christians and discussions about swindling and thieves and
thief-taking were not the staple of their normal conversation.

She whispered to Susanna, 'Are Mr Wolfe's dinners always like this?'

'I don't know,' Susanna whispered back. 'This is the first
of his which I have attended.'

'Henry swears that Mr Wolfe is the cleverest man he
knows, and he always says and does the unexpected. Looking at him, I find that I can quite believe that to be true. He
frightens me a little. Doesn't he frighten you? If you will

forgive me saying so, you didn't seem frightened when you quizzed him about the name of his house.'

Does he frighten me? thought Susanna. I can't honestly say that he does. He didn't frighten me when we first met because I was too angry with him to be frightened of him, and he doesn't frighten me now. On the other hand, he does disturb me in the oddest way. If I were a character in a novel, I should probably believe that I was falling in love with him—although I can't imagine him falling in love with me.

'No,' she told Jane honestly. 'He doesn't frighten me, he intrigues me.'

She was watching him laughing at something Lord Lowborough had said, his head flung back, his strong white teeth gleaming, his eyes shining, looking for all the world like the wolf he was named after. She was surer than ever that he was her unknown saviour—and by what devious means he had saved her she did not yet care to know.

'You have heard, I suppose,' Jane said, 'that Lord Babbacombe, who is a distant relative of the Wolfes, swears that he is not a Wolfe at all and has no right to the name or to the house and the remnants of the Wolfe lands which he claimed when he returned from India. He says that he will go to law to prove it.'

Susanna swung her head around to stare at Jane. 'No, I had not heard that. Is it true—or is it idle gossip?'

'Oh, I overheard Henry telling a friend that Lord Babbacombe and Mr Wolfe had a set-to at White's the other night. He said that Mr Wolfe challenged Lord Darlington to a duel for insulting him and Lord Darlington refused on the grounds that he did not fight men who had no right to the name they bore. Even if that name was tarnished by the scandals around the late Mr Wolfe.'

'He would,' said Susanna curtly. 'He is too cowardly to face Mr Wolfe—or any other man in a duel.'

'Well, I'm glad that Henry is Mr Wolfe's friend,' said

Jane, 'for I can't imagine anyone wishing to face him in a duel. Henry says...' and she began to describe her husband's account of Ben's prowess as a swordsman, marksman and pugilist.

One thing was plain to Susanna—beside the proof of Ben Wolfe's many-sided talents—Jane Lowborough was so besotted with her husband that 'Henry says' prefaced most of her conversation.

What worried her, though, was Lord Babbacombe's reported attack on Ben. If Ben hated Lord Babbacombe—and her memory of what he had said of him at the time of his kidnapping told her that he did—then, equally, for whatever reason, Lord Babbacombe hated Ben. And what were the scandals which surrounded the late Mr Wolfe? They must be old ones, for she understood that Ben Wolfe's father had died when he was little more than a boy.

'Did your husband tell you, or have you any notion, why Lord Babbacombe dislikes Mr Wolfe so much?'

'Oh, the rumour is that it was Mr Wolfe who ruined him financially—which was why Lord Darlington's marriage with Miss Western was called off, and possibly why Lord Babbacombe is accusing him of impersonation now.'

She paused reflectively. 'I had no notion when I married Henry that life would be so exciting. Papa was a country Rector, you know, and the most excitement we ever had were the disputes among the men about who was the best shot and among the ladies about who should organise the flowers in church, or go first into dinner. One can scarcely imagine Mr Wolfe and Mr Wilson troubling themselves about such innocent matters.'

'Ah, Lady Lowborough,' said *Madame* on overhearing this, 'you intrigue me.'

She had been conversing with Mrs Wilson and Mrs Dickson. Mrs Dickson was the wife of another of Ben Wolfe's financial allies. She had been, before their respective marriages, the companion and friend of Lady Devereux, famous for her wit and her eccentricity.

'If you are discussing innocent matters with Miss Beverly, then I fear that you may be the only pair in the room who are. Mrs Dickson and I have discovered a common admiration for the late M. de la Rochefoucauld, who cannot in any circumstances be described as innocent. We have been shocking Mrs Wilson with his cynicism.

'As for the gentlemen of the party, their conversation is never innocent, and we must hope that dinner will be soon announced so that it becomes trivial again when they decide that they must spare the ladies' delicate feelings.'

Jane Lowborough gave a little gasp on hearing such frank heresy. Susanna, on the other hand, was as entertained as she always was when *Madame* spoke her mind.

Mrs Dickson remarked approvingly, 'Well said. I am sure that they will deal only with crinkum crankum in our presence.'

'Crinkum crankum?' queried *Madame*. 'Pray, what does that mean? My command of English does not extend to understanding that.'

'Women's nothings,' returned Mrs Dickson. 'Most of the men are not very good at it. Real crinkum crankum is dress and gossip and the latest Gothic novel—about which none of them know anything.'

'I wouldn't bet on Mr Ben Wolfe being ignorant of such matters,' offered Susanna, 'he seems to know everything.'

Privately she was amused at the turn the evening's conversation had taken with earnest discussion on thieves and society slang being intermingled with lofty discussions on French philosophers.

Dinner being announced had them all parading into the dining room. Susanna was led in by Jess Fitzroy; *Madame* was Ben's partner. Dinner-table conversation, as prophesied, was light in the extreme.

The only serious remark came from Tom Wilson, who

told Ben to watch his back and earned in response, a light-hearted, 'Don't worry, Tom, I always take more notice of my enemies than my friends.'

How typical of him, was Susanna's immediate reaction. He was sure to say the very opposite of what one might have expected! She said so to Jess. 'I shall take a deal of notice of your judgements in future, Mr Fitzroy, particularly to those concerning your employer.'

'Oh, all my judgements are worth heeding, Miss Beverly,' he told her, giving her his most dazzling smile. He really was the most handsome man, so why his golden beauty and regular features were unable to excite her in the same way that Ben Wolfe's harsh and craggy face did was a puzzle which Susanna was unable to solve.

In fact, she seemed to be surrounded by puzzles. Why had *Madame* been so eager to borrow Lord Exford's copy of La Rochefoucauld's *Maximes*? Did the inscription in it have any significance? What were the scandals about his father to which Jane Lowborough had referred? Was Ben Wolfe truly entitled to his name? Why did he wish to ruin Lord Babbacombe and his family? And why had he wanted to kidnap Amelia?

Were all these things connected in some way? It was difficult to see how her new friend and patroness Madame de Saulx was involved, other than that she was also the most unlikely friend and patron of Ben Wolfe.

'You are quiet tonight, Miss Beverly,' remarked Jess as they were served the next course. Ben Wolfe's dinners were organised after the Russian, not the English, fashion with footmen handing the food around rather than all the courses being put in the centre of the table.

Susanna's eyes were alight with mischief as she answered him. 'Does that mean that you usually find me noisy?'

'On the contrary, you have a low voice, which I assure you is what pleases men most in women, but you commonly use it well and wittily. Tonight, though, you are a trifle subdued. I trust that you are not feeling low.'

'Oh, no, I am in rude health, but...' For a moment Susanna considered asking Jess the nature of the scandal about Ben's father, but decided against it.

'But?' he prompted her.

'But I have been reading M. de la Rochefoucauld's *Maximes* and his cynicism has left me feeling a little melancholy.'

There was a certain amount of truth in that statement, but not much, Susanna reflected, but it was the best explanation which she could offer to satisfy Jess at such short notice.

'Then allow me to dispel your melancholy by regaling you with some of the more amusing rumours circulating about town at the moment.'

The greatest rumours, thought Susanna, as Jess was as good as his word, telling her of the Prince Regent's latest efforts to rid himself of his unwanted wife, were those concerning their host, which were hardly the subject for wit at his own dinner table! However, she laughed obligingly at Jess's spirited delivery, so much so, indeed that Ben leaned forward and remarked, 'You seem to be enjoying yourselves a great deal at your end of the table, Jess. May we all be allowed to share your jokes?'

The true reason for his intervention was his very real jealousy at the sight of another man entertaining Susanna and fixing admiring eyes on her.

He gained his reward when Jess looked away from her and turned towards him, saying, 'I was informing Miss Beverly of the Regent's remarking that he could not wait to rid himself of his elderly, plain and ill-dressed wife to his latest female favourite who is, if anything, even older, plainer and worse dressed.'

'An old Hanoverian custom, I understand,' remarked Lord Lowborough. 'Ever since the Royal family came over to rule England in 1714, their monarchs have always favoured plain women. I understand that, when the Regent becomes King, he will immediately press for an Act of Parliament to be passed to permit him to divorce his wife. Divorced or not, he will not allow her to be crowned with him.'

Ben was happy to notice that talk now became general, centred mostly on the Regent's affairs, with Jess's attention diverted from Susanna, who conversed instead with Lord Lowborough, who was recently and safely married to a wife whom he loved. No danger there from him: Susanna might talk to him as much as she wished.

Later, alone with the women, whilst back in the dining room the men drank port at their leisure, the conversation again turned to the Princess of Wales, the Regent's unhappy wife.

'One has to say,' remarked Madame de Saulx, 'that the poor woman has a certain amount of right on her side. Whilst we may not agree with the London mob that she is a totally wronged woman, nevertheless we must always remember that she was given in marriage to a man who treated her abominably from her wedding day onwards. She may have acted unwisely on occasion, but how has *he* behaved?'

It was plain that all the women agreed with her over the Regent's bad behaviour, even if they did not condone his wife's. 'Nevertheless,' said Jane Lowborough slowly, 'I am happy that she is rarely received in good society. None of our husbands would be safe, I understand, if she were.'

'True,' said *Madame*. 'And more's the pity. The greater the persecution which she suffers, the more she becomes a driven woman.'

After that the conversation took a lighter turn, ending with a discussion of the first Canto of Lord Byron's latest poem, *Don Juan*, which, among other things, contained an unkind portrait of the poet's estranged wife.

'But,' said *Madame*, when that subject was almost exhausted, 'we must confess that, as always, he mingles his satire with the most divine poetry. Who can disagree with him when he writes,

Man's love is of man's life a thing apart,
Tis woman's whole existence...

For do not men have many worlds to range to which we are not admitted? We are but wives or daughters: but they are not only husbands or sons.'

Susanna clapped her hands together and exclaimed impulsively. 'How true—and how ironic that a man like Lord Byron, who has always behaved so badly towards women, should at the same time be aware of how circumscribed we are.'

She was thinking of the ruin which had almost overcome her when she was neither wife nor daughter, just an unconsidered and unwanted spinster with no profession, and no occupation. Even the meanest of younger sons had more than that to expect from life.

No time to revisit the unhappy past, though, for the men were returning and the present became all-consuming again. Ben made his way to where Susanna and Jane were and took a seat between them.

'Lowborough has proposed a game of whist,' he told them, 'and, since the party is large enough to make up three tables, I hope that the ladies will all consent to play.'

Jane said, a trifle agitatedly, 'I'm afraid that my card-playing skills are not good enough to allow me to take part. We rarely played at home, and Henry has been trying to teach me.'

'And I am in a similar situation,' added Susanna.

As might have been expected, this did not deter Ben Wolfe at all. 'Splendid,' he exclaimed, lying in his teeth. 'I can think of nothing better than spending an evening trying to teach my partner how to play. Now, if you partner your husband, and Miss Beverly agrees to partner me, we can have a happy hour enjoying ourselves and leave such experts as Madame de Saulx and Tom Wilson to play the game with those others who share their grim determination to win. They can play for money; I propose that we play for bonbons, eh, Henry?'

Madame said, 'That's the most remarkable proposal I've ever heard, seeing that it comes from a man who once earned his living playing every card game ever invented!'

'Did you?' asked Susanna, fascinated by this new revelation about Ben's past. 'Earn your living by playing cards, I mean. Oh, forgive me, I shouldn't really question you about such matters—or so I used to tell my charges.'

'*You* may question me about anything, Miss Beverly,' said Ben. 'And yes, I did. But I have forgotten everything I ever knew.'

'And that's a Banbury tale if ever I heard one,' drawled Lord Lowborough. 'Seeing that you emptied everyone's pockets playing whist the other night at White's.'

'Oh, I only forget everything I know about cards when I play with those innocents who genuinely know nothing—other than anything necessary to teach them the rules of the game, that is.'

'You should have been a lawyer, Ben,' laughed Tom Wilson, 'or a member of Parliament, you play with words so well. I propose that we play cards immediately so that we may have the pleasure of watching you join with Lowborough in playing for nothing rather than for something. I cannot believe that you ever did such a thing before.'

'I agree,' said Ben, rising. 'Let us begin, if only to stop these unwarranted attacks on my reputation. Before we do, however, I hope my two pupils already know that there are fifty-two cards in a pack.'

'Really?' exclaimed Susanna, putting on what Ben recognised as her teasing face. 'I thought that there were only twelve.'

Before Ben could tease her back, Jane Lowborough said mournfully, 'Oh, are there? I had thought that the number was fifty-two—but I suppose that I am wrong. I am usually wrong about figures.'

'Nonsense,' said Ben firmly. 'Miss Beverly knows exactly how many cards there are in a pack. She is teasing us so that when we begin to play we shall underrate her and thus enable her to win more bonbons than she ought.'

'Exactly,' said Lord Lowborough. 'Jane, you may sit opposite to me, and I shall endeavour to explain the game as we go along. Wolfe, you may do the same for Miss Beverly—but none of your tricks, mind.'

'As though I would,' returned Ben, putting on a mournful face. 'The footmen have finished setting out the tables, so let us begin. The rest of the party may arrange themselves as they please.'

Afterwards, Susanna was to remember that evening as one of the last for some time that she and the rest of the party spent in innocent pleasure. Ben used his tutoring of her as an excuse to tease her. He also whispered confidentially to her while he taught her—despite Lord Lowborough's warning—some of the tricks of the game. For the last few years Susanna had been outside the magic circle of fun and laughter at such parties, condemned to watch others enjoy themselves, and now she was inside that circle again.

The evening passed so quickly that she could scarcely believe that it was over when *Madame* whispered to her that it was time to leave and their carriage was waiting for them.

'Oh, I have enjoyed myself tonight,' she told Ben before they left.

'So you will come again soon?' he asked, taking her hand and pressing it gently.

'Of course, if you invite me,' she told him, a little breathlessly, her eyes shining as her whole body vibrated at his touch, telling her that for good or ill she had fallen in love with Ben Wolfe.

'Never fear,' he said. 'You will always be at the top of my guest list.' He relinquished her hand reluctantly.

Jess Fitzroy, watching them, knew that he had lost her, but then, he had never possessed her and now never would. Damn you, Ben Wolfe, he thought, if you mistreat her, however loyal I have been to you in the past, my loyalty would not survive that!

He was not the only one who had guessed Susanna's secret. Madame de Saulx, seated opposite her glowing protégé on the drive home, was also aware of it and was making Ben a similar promise to that of Jess's.

If Ben could not see what a suitable wife Susanna would make for him, seeing that she was one of the few women who would stand up to him, then he was less shrewd than she had always thought him.

Despite the success of his dinner party, Ben found it difficult to sleep that night. It was not only the memory of Susanna's face which haunted him, but something which Lowborough had told him: that, as well as the rumours which Babbacombe was spreading about his legitimacy, he was also resurrecting the old scandal about his father and mother.

He thought grimly that, whilst he was redressing other people's wrongs, he ought to find time to right some of his own.

Morning found him tired but resolute. He had business to attend to at his counting house in the City of London before he talked in the afternoon with the Rothschild brothers, with whom he was engaged in discussions about enlarging trade with the United States as well with the East. He acknowledged that his ambitions were limitless—but then, they always had been, even when he had been a private soldier.

Yet, to his surprise, he found that memories of Susanna's face laughing up at him whilst he was teaching her to play

whist came between him and the papers which he was
studying—something which had never happened to him before.

He smiled ruefully to himself before attending carefully
to what Mr Leopold Rothschild was saying to him in his
beautifully furnished office.

'My brothers and I will be happy to do business with
you, sir. Your reputation as a man of your word is good,
your honesty as a man of business is unimpeached, and our
investigation of your financial situation shows that the
claims you make in your propositions to us are accurate.

'You will forgive my plain speaking, I hope, but our reputation has been built on taking only those risks which are
unavoidable—we see little danger of them occurring in our
future dealings with you.'

Ben inclined his head. Mr Leopold was a man after his
own heart, downright and straightforward—in speech, if nowhere else.

'I prefer plain speaking myself to the other kind,' he told
them. 'I take it, then, that our lawyers will draw up the
necessary papers between them, ready for us to sign as soon
as possible.'

'Indeed, and in the meantime, let us shake hands upon
the bargain we have made as surety of our respective goodwill.'

It was done. All that remained was for him to return to
his office and alert Jess and his clerks, inform the lawyers
and complete the deal.

It was well into the dusk of the evening by the time that
Ben had finished working. He had sent Jess off in the gig
to carry out some necessary errands relating to the business
with the Rothschilds, telling him that he need not return to
collect him. He would walk home.

Jess demurred. 'You heard what was said last night—
about it being unsafe at present to walk London's streets

unaccompanied after dark. Let me call for you when I have finished.'

'I thank you for reminding me, but the journey home is not long and I have been cooped up all day. I have a stout stick with me. Do you go straight home when your work is over. You may report to me there later tonight.'

There was no arguing with him. Jess shrugged his shoulders and drove off. Later, Ben wished that he had listened to him for he was tired and impatient: the day had been harder than he had expected and the walk home seemed less attractive than he had earlier thought.

He took tight hold of his stick—it was almost a cudgel— and set off through the City's maze of streets. He was almost out of it when disaster struck.

A group of men, armed with bludgeons, sprang out of an alley to attack him on a deserted street. He was fortunate enough to glimpse them coming and guess that their purpose was to attack him. Rather than try to defend himself he began to run at top speed, away from them. Only to find himself faced by two more men who had been hiding in a doorway, one of them being armed with a pistol, the other with a cudgel.

Nothing for it but to try to tackle them. He raised his own cudgel to strike the pistol out of the fellow's hand and send it skittering into the gutter, although concentrating on him meant that he took a blow on the shoulder from his pal.

Ben, reeling from the blow, was sent backwards and to the ground, to come up holding the first robber's pistol which he fired at the man with the cudgel, hitting him in the shoulder. Clutching it, and dropping his cudgel, the robber staggered off to escape further punishment. The man whose pistol Ben had snatched from the gutter picked up the cudgel, raised it, and ran at him.

By this time the first group of robbers had caught up with him, ready to finish him off, but the noise of the pistol shot had brought workmen from a nearby yard into the street where, after watching the struggle for a few moments they took Ben's part and a general mêlée broke out. At the same time two watchmen, just beginning their rounds, arrived to join in the battle.

The thieves, now heavily outnumbered, began to run off, pursued by those men who were armed with the hammers with which they had been working.

Ben, who had taken several more blows and was now unsteady on his feet, sat down on a nearby wall, still clutching the pistol. Now that the fracas was over, men and women who had been watching from windows and doorways began to emerge from the houses and workshops which lined the street.

The man who had been in charge of the rescuing workmen came up to Ben to offer him further assistance. On reaching him, he exclaimed, 'Ben! It is Ben Wolfe, isn't it? I couldn't see who you were in the mêlée. Are you hurt? Should we send for an apothecary?'

It was George Dickson, his friend, business acquaintance and recent dinner guest who owned the saddler's yard from which the workmen had come.

Ben shook his dizzy head. 'Bruised,' he said briefly. 'Nothing serious, thank God—and I owe my safety to you and your men. I can't thank you enough. Without your timely help I should probably be lying dead in the road. One of the ruffians attacking me had a pistol. I shot him with it, but he wasn't mortally wounded, just ran off. That's my cudgel over there. I lost it in what followed.'

'Trust you to shoot a man with his own weapon,' said George, who was himself an old soldier. 'Come in and let us look after you. Emma can make you a cup of tea—or you can have some brandy if you prefer it.'

Still talking, he led the dazed Ben into his living quarters which were above his shop and office. The watch, who had failed to catch any of the ruffians, resumed their rounds and, the excitement over, the spectators went indoors again.

'The streets are no longer safe,' mourned Emma Dickson as she applied salve to Ben's bruised face. 'But I haven't often seen such a large number of men attack one person before. I saw everything from the window, including George's men rush out to discover what was what when the shot was fired. It was lucky that they were working late on a commission tonight, or you would have had the worst of it.'

'Yes,' said Ben, drinking first the tea and then the brandy. 'My thanks to them, and to Dickie are heartfelt.' Dickie had been George Dickson's nickname ever since he had been a trooper in the army: his friends still used it.

What the worst of it was he did not tell them immediately. The pistol which he had scooped up from the gutter was an expensive piece, and he was sure had been meant to finish him off. That, and the large number of men involved, convinced him that this had been no chance attack. It had been planned and he had been followed, almost certainly from his counting house.

How many nights had they been watching him—and who had paid them to kill him? The pity was that they had all escaped in the confusion which had followed Dickie Dickson's intervention, thus preventing any hope of questioning any of them.

Useless to repine. Tomorrow he would set men on their trail. He knew that he had enemies—no man in his line of business could escape them—but an enemy who wanted to kill him—now, that was quite another thing!

As Dickie Dickson said in his quiet way when he offered to drive Ben home in his gig, 'You ought not to leave unescorted, they might still be waiting for you. That was a hardened crew of bludgeoneers with an upright man in charge—the one with the pistol, I suppose. Who dislikes you enough to want to half-kill you, Ben?'

He didn't need to tell Ben that an upright man was the

captain of a crew or the leader of a gang: like him, Ben was
au fait with thieves' slang.

'And a good pistol, too,' said Ben, thinking that Dickie
might prove a useful ally. 'One of Manton's best with a hair
trigger.'

He showed it to him, saying, 'Either stolen or given to
him to finish me off when the bludgeons had done their
work. You might as well know that I think that murder was
their aim—theft would have been a bonus. I'll accept your
kind offer of a ride home.'

Dickie nodded thoughtfully. 'I thought murder was on
their mind—and wondered if you did. Would you like me
to make some enquiries? I promise to be discreet.'

'Only if you let me pay you.'

When Dickie raised his hand and made protesting noises,
he said, gently enough, 'You have a business to run and a
young family to look after—I know I'm a friend, but I'm
not going to trade on that.'

Later that night Emma Dickson said briskly to Dickie, 'I
thought more highly of Ben Wolfe tonight, George, than I
did when I first met him in his drawing room last night. His
bark is worse than his bite and his courage is undoubted. I
wouldn't like to be on the wrong side of him, though.'

'Nor I,' said Dickie, 'but he ought to guard his back. I've
offered him the service of a bruiser I know to act as a bodyguard and he's almost agreed. He doesn't like to depend on
others, but there are times when one has to.'

'Like Dev and Dickie were,' said Emma sleepily, referring to her husband's David and Jonathan-like friendship
with Jack, Earl Devereux, when they had been soldiers together.

'Exactly,' said Dickie, 'and now, do your duty to me,
wife.'

'That's what Ben Wolfe needs,' murmured Emma, turning happily into her husband's arms. 'A wife.'

Chapter Ten

Ben said nothing of the attack on him, and the only others who had immediate knowledge of it were Dickie and his wife, and Jess Fitzroy, whom he told when he reached home, so it was surprising that, by the next afternoon news of it was circulating in the *ton*. Since Dickie never mixed with the *ton* and Jess had been sworn to secrecy, it told Ben that the only person who could have set the story on its way was the person who had ordered the attack.

He puzzled over the motive for such an odd action and concluded that the notion was that it proved Ben Wolfe to be a shady character if someone was determined to maim or kill him.

He passed a restless night pondering on who his enemy might be. He finally determined on three names: Samuel Mitchell, Lord Babbacombe and Herbert Jamison, with whom he had had some dealings which ended in acrimony as a result of Jamison's dishonesty. The result for Jamison had been bankruptcy, but Ben did not honestly believe that he could have behaved otherwise. Babbacombe and Mitchell had reason to hate him, but would they kill him? For what purpose?

When morning came he decided against going to his

counting house—his face was heavily bruised and he did
not wish the sight of it to encourage gossip. Instead he sent
for Jess, on whom he could rely, with instructions, not only
for him, but for his clerks, regarding both the business with
the Rothschilds and the attack of the previous night. He also
complainingly agreed with the doctor whom Jess had called
in that he should rest for two or three days before returning
to work.

By mid-morning on the second one he was already feeling
better and ready for action again, but he also felt regretfully
compelled to keep his promise to Jess that he would obey
doctor's orders.

That afternoon *Madame* and Susanna were enjoying
themselves at the piano. *Madame* was playing and Susanna
was singing, when Lord and Lady Exford were announced.
Both of them looked exceedingly grave. *Madame* rose to
greet them and offered them refreshments. Lady Exford settled for tea but Lord Exford, usually an abstemious young
man, asked for sherry.

'For,' he said, 'I have just heard some unwelcome gossip.
It appears that Mr Wolfe was attacked three nights ago when
he was walking home from his counting house in the City.
Report has it that he was only saved from being injured by
the intervention of a group of workmen. Report also says
that he is confined to his home until his injuries improve.'

He looked at *Madame*, and said heavily, 'As if that were
not enough, someone has also revived the old scandal about
his father. This, as you must know, *Madame*, affects me
since my late mother, as well as Charles Wolfe's wife, was
involved, and the last thing which Lady Exford and I wish
is that it shall become the commonplace of gossip again.'

Susanna, drinking her tea, now had an explanation for the
inscription in the *Maximes*—the Wolfes and the Exfords had
been friends—but none for the nature of the scandal.

She would not have been human if she were not curious,

but she said nothing. *Madame* commiserated with the Exfords without giving anything away, but the effect of their news was to throw a cloud of melancholy over the afternoon.

After they had departed, *Madame* did not take her seat at the piano again, but instead came and sat near Susanna, saying, 'I did not like to speak of the matter with the Exfords present, but it seems to me that, since the rumour is going the rounds, you ought to know the truth of it lest you unwittingly say something untoward. The truth being almost certainly different from the rumour. I must warn you that it is not a pretty story and will be painful for me to relate.

'When Ben Wolfe was but a boy his mother and father were bosom bows with the late Lord Exford and his wife, all of them being of a similar age. I am speaking of some twenty-five years ago. The Exfords were staying with the Wolfes at The Den when, one afternoon, Lord Exford went shooting with some local gentry and Charles Wolfe was engaged in business with the then Lord Lieutenant of Buckinghamshire at his seat, Beauval, nearby.

'The two women decided to go for a walk in the grounds without taking an attendant footman. Mrs Wolfe was a skilled amateur painter and Lady Exford was carrying a book: the *Maximes* of M. de la Rochefoucauld. Both the men returned home in the early evening to find the servants in an uproar. Their wives had not returned although they had been gone for over three hours and a search party was being prepared by Mr Wolfe's agent, one Thomas Linacre.

'They were not in the spot by a small stream where they had told their lady's maids that they were going: Mrs Wolfe to sketch, Lady Exford to read, although her book—the one I have borrowed from Lord Exford—was found thrown down nearby, together with the shawl she was wearing. There was no sign of Mrs Wolfe and she has never been seen since that fatal afternoon. Her sketching equipment was found floating downstream later that evening. Lady Exford was eventually discovered some distance away from her book and shawl. She had been dragged into a copse and left for dead after being criminally assaulted.

'When she recovered consciousness her memory had gone. The last thing which she could recall was being in the drawing room after nuncheon. She remembered nothing about her and Mrs Wolfe's decision to go for a walk and what had occurred during it. Consequently she had no notion of what might have happened to Mrs Wolfe. One might have said that nature was merciful to her, given what she must have suffered, except that that mercy left such a dreadful mystery unsolved. She never recovered her full health and died within the year…' *Madame* paused.

Susanna was puzzled. 'But why did that create a scandal involving Mr Wolfe? From what you have told me he was far away at the time.'

Madame sighed. 'As soon as the matter was investigated a number of contradictions came to light. It turned out that no one could say with any certainty that the two women *had* left together. The stories of the servants differed. And although there were plenty of witnesses to testify that Lord Exford was with a group of gentlemen all afternoon, it turned out that Mr Wolfe had left the Lord Lieutenant's home after spending only an hour with him. Yet he did not arrive back at The Den until two hours later, although the journey from Beauval should have taken him no more than half an hour.

'Lord Babbacombe's agent testified to having seen him not far from the spot where Lady Exford was found around forty minutes after he had left Beauval. As though that were not enough, Lord Babbacombe, who lived nearby, testified that, at a dinner he gave the night before, Lord Exford and Mr Wolfe had had a fierce argument, although Lord Exford later said that what had passed was of little import since each had been joking with the other.

'He would never hear a word said against Mr Wolfe although gossip began immediately that Mr Wolfe had come across Lady Exford alone, had made advances to her which she had refused, that he then overcame and mistakenly left her for dead, but was interrupted by the arrival of his wife—whom he then killed in her turn. All this despite the fact that both couples, until then, were famous for their happy marriages and for their friendship, and with no evidence to support such a theory.

'But an *on dit*, although supported by no real evidence, once started on its way is hard to refute. No action was taken against Mr Wolfe because the evidence that he might have been involved was so tenuous. At the same time his financial situation became difficult—some said because either grief, or guilt, had caused him to become careless. He never ceased to search for his wife. Eighteen months later he was found dead, again in odd circumstances, and it was assumed that he had committed suicide. His death proved that his ruin was absolute and he left his son penniless. Young Ben was sent to an elderly relative who turned him out when he reached sixteen, giving him only enough money for a passage to India where he enlisted as a private soldier.

'The rest you know.'

Susanna sat transfixed.

'So it was Lord Babbacombe who started the rumours on their way—which explains why Mr Wolfe hates him so.'

Madame nodded. 'Exactly—and there is another twist to the story. Ben Wolfe was his father's only male heir. If he were proved to be not the late Charles Wolfe's son, then the Wolfe estates would revert by a female entail to Lord Babbacombe—since his mother was Charles Wolfe's father's only sister.'

'And were Lord Babbacombe and Charles Wolfe friends?'

'Not particularly. Charles Wolfe and m'lord both wished to marry the same young woman, who later became Charles's wife and Ben's mother. Lord Babbacombe was particularly eager, he said, to discover Mrs Wolfe's fate, for he claimed to be still in love with her and disappointment at losing her had prevented him from marrying another. What *is* true was that he did not marry George Darlington's mother until some years after Mrs Wolfe's disappearance.'

Susanna said shrewdly, 'So you are hinting that Lord Babbacombe has a direct interest in trying to prove Ben Wolfe an impostor? But surely he would gain very little in inheriting what is left of the Wolfe estates, seeing that the majority of them were sold after Mr Wolfe's suicide to pay off his debts, leaving him only The Den and its immediate surroundings?'

'I warned you that I was not about to tell you a pretty tale and where the truth lies is unknown, and may, indeed, never be known. After all, this happened twenty-five years ago. There is another problem: the agent who reported seeing Mr Wolfe near the spot where Lady Exford was found himself disappeared shortly after telling his story to the magistrates. That was one reason why Mr Charles Wolfe was never arrested.'

She fell silent, but not before adding, 'Now you know why Mr Ben Wolfe is such a strong and stern man: he has had much to overcome. It is to his credit that he has carved himself a fortune and been able to restore his family home to its former glory. But his misfortunes have inevitably left their mark on him.'

'You have spoken of his family home,' said Susanna slowly. 'Does that mean that you do not believe him to be an impostor?'

'Oh, yes,' said *Madame*, 'I am sure that he is not. As sure as I am of anything. Lord Exford must think that he is not, too, and he must believe that Ben's father was innocent of wrong doing or he would not receive Ben in his home. As for what Lord Babbacombe has to gain, it is possible that if a Writ of Ejectment were to be served on Ben by Lord Babbacombe and the courts found against him, they might rule that Ben should pay heavy damages to m'lord for having cheated him of his inheritance.'

Seeing Susanna looking puzzled, she said, 'If someone thinks that their rightful inheritance, or their property, has been stolen by an impostor they take out this Writ to compel them to come to the Law Courts in order to prove that they are the rightful owner. If the person on whom the Writ is served loses his case, he is ejected from his property and it is restored to the complainant. It is a long, complicated and expensive procedure as those who have used it have often found. Some seventy years ago James Annesley regained his home and his title through such a Writ.'

Susanna made up her mind. 'You will not think me forward, I hope, if I ask that we may visit Mr Wolfe as soon as possible to show that we, at least, believe that the rumour about him being an impostor is a lie. Of what happened to his mother and Lady Exford twenty-five years ago I cannot speak. Time, perhaps, may yet tell.'

'Of course I do not think you forward, and I heartily agree with your suggestion. I shall ask John Coachman to drive us there this afternoon instead of to our usual rendezvous in Hyde Park. We must assure Ben that he still has loyal friends who will rally around him in his time of need.'

'If he is well enough to receive us,' qualified Susanna.

'True, if he is not we may put off our visit until he is, and grace the Park instead.'

Ben *was* well enough to receive them and they found him in his drawing room before his escritoire where a pile of papers and ledgers betrayed that he had been working. He rose to meet them, pleasure written on his stern face.

'I never knew who my true friends were,' he told them, 'until I was attacked. There has been a small procession of them here over the last two days. Lord and Lady Exford have just left. They told me that they had visited you and informed you of what happened three nights ago. What no

one has told me is who informed society of it, seeing that
I have said nothing, nor, I am sure, has my rescuer, or Jess,
who is busy doing my work for me.'

'Not all of it,' said *Madame*, gesturing towards the laden
escritoire. 'Perhaps your servants started the story on its
way.'

'Oh, that!' he exclaimed of his pile of papers. 'That's
some small nothings. And you may be right about the servants.'

Susanna, who had been relieved to see that although his
left eye was black, and that side of his face was bruised, he
was not, as she had feared, so badly injured that he was
crippled in any way.

'Lord Exford told us that you were walking home on your
own—which surprised us after all the warnings we have
been given about not going out alone at night.'

Ben smiled ruefully. 'Foolish of me, wasn't it? It served
me right for being conceited, I suppose. I had imagined that
I could fight off one or two men, but it was a small army
who attacked me. It was fortunate that by chance the attack
occurred outside George Dickson's place of business. He
and his men rescued me or I should have been cats' meat
by now.'

Susanna shuddered. 'Never say so! You will take more
care in future, I hope.'

'If you agree to order me to do so, then I will, Miss
Beverly. I only exist to oblige you.'

He had bent forward a little to answer her, and his voice
was teasing her, but his eyes told her a different tale. Madame de Saulx, watching them, thought that Ben Wolfe's
hard heart was at last being touched by a woman—something which she had thought she would never see.

'I wish I could believe that,' Susanna told Ben, forgetting
that they were not alone, intent only on answering the un-
spoken message of his eyes.

'Believe it,' he said, astonished to discover that his gratitude for his salvation lay partly in his barely conscious desire to know more of the woman who intrigued him so. He suddenly knew that he did not want to go to his grave unloved and unmourned. More than that—since he had met Susanna he had become aware of how lonely he was and, what was worse, was likely to remain, if he let no one into his life.

For a long moment they looked into one another's eyes before Susanna half-whispered, 'I think that I will, Mr Wolfe.'

'Good,' he said, straightening up again and resuming all his usual arrogance, 'for you must understand that my word is my bond, and what I promise, I always fulfil.'

She could believe that of him, and it almost frightened her, for it told her what a dreadful enemy he would make. On the other hand, it meant that he would also make a staunch friend—as Jess Fitzroy had once assured her.

She told him so—that she would sooner have him for a friend than an enemy.

'Which shows your good sense,' he said, smiling at *Madame* as he spoke. 'And now, may I offer you some refreshment? Ladies usually require tea, and I can ring for some immediately. My cook has, I am told, a nice line in Sally Lunns; perhaps you would care to sample them.'

Susanna laughed. 'I always associate you with food, Mr Wolfe. May I remind you that from the very first moment that we met you have been plying me with it. Yes, pray bring on the Sally Lunns and the tea.'

Ben smiled, not something which he often did. 'You also remind me that I once asked you to call me Ben. Pray oblige me on that. There can be nothing improper in it when Madame de Saulx is happy to humour me by doing so.'

Susanna cast her eyes down primly and muttered. 'Yes, Ben. Certainly, Ben. By all means, Ben.'

Ben could not help himself. He bent down, caught her chin in his hand and tipped her face towards him—to find that she was quietly laughing at him while teasing him with a show of grudging agreement. Had *Madame* not been there he would have swept her into his arms and taught her what was what in double quick time. As it was, he released her, muttering softly, 'Minx,' and nothing more.

The rest of the afternoon passed like lightning. Tea was brought in and after it Ben asked *Madame* and Susanna to play and sing for him on his new Broadwood piano.

'I cannot play myself,' he said, 'but one of my happiest memories is of my mother playing and singing nursery rhymes to me when I was a little boy. I must hope that my visitors will oblige me by performing on it.'

Of course, they promptly did and Ben had the pleasure not only of hearing Susanna sing some old Scottish airs, but of watching her mobile face as she did so. Her voice was light but true, and delighted him more than those of the most celebrated Grand Opera divas.

On the way home *Madame* said thoughtfully, 'In all the years I have known him I have never before heard Ben Wolfe speak of his mother. I believe that to be your influence, my dear. You know how to talk to him without being either frightened of him or flirtatiously forward—he must feel safe with you.'

'If so, I wish my influence over him would extend to compelling him not to take unnecessary risks as he did the other night,' sighed Susanna, thus revealing to *Madame*—if such a revelation were needed—how much she was beginning to care for Ben.

She need not have worried. Grumblingly Ben consented to Dickie Dickson finding a reliable bruiser for him to act as bodyguard. He was provided with a former soldier who was a useful hand with a pistol and who would keep an eye on Ben as discreetly as his duties would allow.

'I feel a rare old woman,' he told Dickie and his guest in

Dickie's snug little parlour on his way to the counting house on the first day that his physician thought it wise for him to go out again. 'A fine milksop you have been making of me!'

Dickie's guest—who looked something like the bruiser who was sitting outside in Ben's landau, keeping watch—smiled. 'No one looking at you, sir, would think that.'

'I should have introduced you when you came in,' said Dickie apologetically. 'Allow me to present to you my friend and patron, m'lord Devereux, here on one of his rare visits to town.'

Earl Devereux stood up and extended his hand. 'Jack, please. I was Jack long before I became Earl Devereux and I still think people are referring to my father when the name Lord Devereux is mentioned. And as to a bodyguard for you, I would have offered myself, only I am too busy these days to find the time, but Jem Walters is a good fellow, as we both have reason to know, eh, Dickie—I mean, George!'

Dickie nodded soberly. 'Oh, we are all respectable, these days, so I suppose that you must call me George. But speaking of the attack on you, Mr Wolfe, I have had some of my men on the *qui vive* for any information they can gather, and one of them says that the word is out that a deal of money awaits anyone who can do you an injury, preferably a mortal one. Where the money is coming from is unknown—but the other rumour is that a gentleman is behind it.'

Ben nodded. This was similar to information that Jess had gathered for him, and which had made him grudgingly agree to a bodyguard, since an attack might come at any time, and always from persons unknown to him.

What he did not know was that Jess Fitzroy had already carelessly let slip to Susanna and *Madame* that someone was out to injure him. Or had he been careless, Susanna thought afterwards? Had his slip been intentional?

In any case the information started her busy brain working. Someone must hate Ben very much to want to do such
a thing. She knew that a man in his way of business must
make enemies, but that someone should wish to kill him
seemed an excessive reaction.

On the other hand, supposing he had virtually ruined
someone? Would not they want revenge?

An icy hand clutched her heart, for she knew what Ben
must have done to Sam Mitchell to make him disgorge her
fortune. Was Sam his mysterious assailant? And if he were,
was she not in some measure responsible?

The thought was unendurable. She sprang to her feet and
went to the little study where *Madame* was writing letters
and said, 'May I borrow the carriage this afternoon? I should
like to visit my mother.'

Like to visit her mother, indeed! She had not the slightest
wish to see her, or her stepfather, but if she visited them
she might learn something which would either bolster her
sudden suspicion—or dismiss it.

'Of course, my dear. You share in the expense of living
here, so you have only to ask.' Susanna, indeed, had made
it plain from the moment that she recovered her fortune that
now she was no longer a paid attendant she was as responsible as *Madame* for the upkeep of the house in which they
resided.

She knew where the Mitchells were living; her mother
had sent her a bitter letter giving her the address in Islington
where they were renting a house, ending with the words,
'You see to what straits you have reduced us.'

They were, indeed, settled in the wrong end of Islington
when she reached there in her modest carriage, grateful that
Madame's taste did not lend itself to a chariot emblazoned
with a lozenge showing the arms to which she was entitled.
Such an equipage might have caused commotion in the
humble street.

A woman's face appeared—and then hastily disappeared—at the tiny bow window when the footman travelling behind handed her down and followed her to knock on the door before he returned to the carriage.

The face belonged to a slatternly servant girl who drawled, 'Yus?' at her after she opened the door just enough to show Susanna a tiny hallway with a steep flight of stairs facing the door. There was another door to her right, and a half-open one at the end of the hall. There was no carpeting on the worn boards of the hall or staircase.

Susanna swallowed. Her mother had not exaggerated the depths to which she and her family had sunk. She clutched at her reticule and offered the sullen girl—little more than a child—a watery smile.

'Please inform Mrs Mitchell that her daughter is here to see her.'

Before the girl could as much as move the door to the front room opened and her mother appeared.

'I thought when I saw the carriage that it might be you. What do you want?'

Her voice was as cold as she could make it, and she did not invite Susanna into the house.

'I would like to speak to you, Mother—if you will invite me in, that is.'

'Certainly not. Say what you have to say to me now— and go.'

'Very well, but I think that you would prefer to hear me out in private, rather than in the street.'

'Go to the kitchen, Polly,' was all that that earned her.

'Yessum,' drawled Polly.

'Yes?' said her mother to Susanna, motioning her just inside the front door after the girl had left them, exactly as she might have asked a disobedient servant to explain herself.

'Mother, I want you to know that I had no notion of what was being done for me when my inheritance was being recovered. I am certainly not happy to see you and the girls in such reduced circumstances. I only ask you to remember that it was Mr Mitchell's actions which have brought you here, not mine.'

'Oh, yes?' sneered her mother. 'You expect me to believe such a Banbury tale as that when it was that man with whom you and that Frenchwoman are so friendly who brought this upon us? If that is all you have to say to me, you may leave at once.'

So it *had* been Ben Wolfe who had found out the truth about her fortune and had returned it to her.

'You must believe me, for I would not lie to you.'

'And did you also tell him to make sure that Mr Mitchell can find no employment after being branded an embezzler by him, and that we live on the edge of starvation?'

'If that is so, I am sorry—although I do not believe Ben Wolfe to be as vindictive as that.'

'Oh, it's Ben Wolfe, is it? What did you pay him with? Your money—or your person?'

She walked to the street door to fling it open, saying, 'Please leave, I have nothing more to say to you.'

Susanna stood in the open doorway, her face agonised, but determined to say what she had to, whatever her mother might think or do.

'But I have something to say to you, Mother, and in saying it I mean to help you. Please tell Mr Mitchell that if it is he who is employing men to injure or kill Mr Wolfe he is risking death or transportation, for Mr Wolfe is not only determined to track him down but he also has powerful friends who will see that he is suitably punished.'

She had barely finished speaking when the door at the far end of the little hall opened and Sam Mitchell stood there. He was so changed from the man she had once known that he was barely recognisable. He had not shaved for some days, his linen was filthy, his clothes dishevelled and he was clutching a bottle in his hand. He must have been listening to their conversation through the half-open door.

'What the devil's that you're threatening me with, girl? Do I look as though I've the dibs to pay a crew to nobble the swine who nobbled me? If I had, I would, but I haven't, and that's flat. You've brought me nothing but bad luck and now you promise to hand me over to the Runners.'

He took another swig at the bottle. 'Tell your bully boy that. And if I did know who was after him, I wouldn't peach on him, that I wouldn't, but I don't—and if I did, I'd help him if I'd so much as tuppence.'

A final swig and he was staggering back into the room. Mrs Mitchell finally gave way and began to cry bitterly.

Her bravado had not moved Susanna, but her despair did. She stepped forward and took the sobbing woman in her arms. Her mother made no effort to throw her off.

'Oh, Mama, don't. It's not your fault. Oh, this is terrible. Here.' She pulled her handkerchief from her reticule and began to wipe her mother's eyes with it. Her mother lay unresisting against her so Susanna walked her gently into the small front room and sat her on a greasy sofa.

After a time her mother subsided into weak snuffles, finally wailing, 'You see how he is. Nothing which I can say or do will move him.'

How to comfort her? Susanna opened her reticule and pulled out the handful of guineas which she had put there before she had left *Madame*'s.

'Oh, Mama,' and it was the childish name for her mother which was wrenched from her again. 'There is so little I can do to help you. The trustees who administer my money are firm with me because of their previous breach of trust. They don't want to make another mistake. I can settle nothing on you, but take this.'

She thrust the guineas into her mother's lax hands. 'Use it to make life for yourself easier. Don't let him know you have it or it will go on drink. I will try to send you a little when I can—but I fear it won't be very much.'

All her mother's defiance had leached out of her. She

clutched the guineas to her bosom before putting them into the deep pocket of the apron which she was wearing.

'I can't forgive you,' she said pathetically, 'but I can't forgive him, either. Which leaves me with nothing. Go now, before he comes out again. He hasn't mistreated me or the girls yet, but I fear that one day he might when the drink is in him. I hope you believe him when he says he knows nothing of any wrong doing.'

Susanna thought that she did believe Samuel Mitchell's denials. 'When the drink's in, the truth comes out', was a saying she had heard as a child and she thought that in this case it might be true.

She kissed her mother on her withered cheek—for she seemed to have aged twenty years since she had last seen her—and took her sad way home to Stanhope Street.

Ben Wolfe's carriage with its silver trimmings was outside. A large man was standing beside it, talking to the driver who was holding the horses. Susanna hoped that he was the bodyguard of whom Jess had spoken. Inside she found Ben talking to *Madame*. His face lit up when he saw her.

His greeting of her was, however, prosaic. 'I thought that I might have missed you. *Madame* tells me that you have been visiting your mother.'

Susanna thought for a moment before she answered him, considering whether or not to tell him the truth about her errand. She concluded that truth might be the best.

'Yes. She is living in poverty in a back street in Islington. I had an important question to ask of her and my stepfather.'

She concluded that Ben Wolfe must possess some sort of ability to divine what it was that those around him were truly thinking of or doing before they had told him, for he said immediately after she paused for breath, 'Why do I believe that your question had something to do with me?'

A little gasp of surprise was forced from her. 'Now, how did you know that? It is precisely why I went.'

'Nothing, something,' he said softly, aware that *Madame*'s shrewd eyes were on them both. 'Something in your expression, or your posture, I must suppose. It's an odd gift I possess which has sometimes proved useful, not only with men, but with animals. I can always tell a wicked horse from a good one.'

'And which do I qualify as,' Susanna could not help retorting, 'a wicked one? Or a good one?'

'Mixed a little, I should say,' he told her, keeping his face straight.

Susanna began to laugh. 'I asked for that,' she admitted. And then, growing sober again, she continued with, 'It was not an amusing question I had to ask her, nor was her behaviour to me amusing, either. On the contrary.'

She hesitated, for now she must tell him that she had guessed of his intervention over the matter of her fortune.

'You see,' she said, as quietly and calmly as she could, 'I guessed that it was you who had pursued Mr Mitchell in order to recover my inheritance, and since it must be supposed that you are being attacked by someone who considered that you had wronged him, it occurred to me that your unknown enemy might be him.'

Fascinated, Ben stared at her. 'May I ask how long you have known about my part in your recovered inheritance?'

'Almost from the day it was restored to me,' she confessed, 'for who else did I know who was powerful enough to right my wrongs?'

'And you said nothing,' he marvelled. 'Most women would have been chattering about it for evermore.'

'Well,' said Susanna, 'I supposed that had you wished me to know, you would have told me. Only the notion that Mr Mitchell might be your enemy caused me to use my knowledge and then to tell you what I think I may have learned.'

Both *Madame* and Ben were staring at her in astonishment.

Ben said at last, 'Never tell me you went there and asked him point-blank?'

'Not quite.' Susanna was a trifle uncomfortable over admitting what she had done when they were both looking at her as though she were an odd specimen in a case in a museum. 'But when my mother was so unkind to me and blamed me for her penury, I felt free to warn her what Mr Mitchell's fate might be if he were your attacker... Why are you both looking at me like that?'

Ben answered before *Madame* could. 'Well, if you must know, I was thinking of how you behaved when we first met, which should have told me that little was beyond you in terms of daring. But do go on. I am sure, again by your expression, that you have not concluded this remarkable narrative.'

'Nor I have,' said Susanna, smiling at him now she understood that his surprise at her forward conduct was laced with admiration. 'The moment I finished warning her, Mr Mitchell suddenly appeared from the back room. He was most unlike himself,' she finished thoughtfully.

'May one ask in what way?' intoned Ben sweetly.

'He was dirty, badly dressed and quite drunk. Not falling down drunk, you understand, just tipsy and still able to converse—'

'We both thank you for the definition, most helpful,' interrupted Ben. 'Do go on. What next?'

'Well, between swigs from the bottle he was carrying, he said that he had had nothing to do with the attack on you because he couldn't afford it, but he applauded it all the same. He said that I had brought him bad luck. I am inclined to think that he was telling the truth.'

'He's right about the bad-luck bit,' offered Ben, grinning. 'What makes you think that he wasn't lying about the attack on me?'

'They are most desperately poor,' said Susanna earnestly.

'I'm sure that he couldn't afford to hire bully boys, although he might like to.'

Ben thought for a moment. 'I'm almost certain that you are right. But, Susanna, I want you to promise me something. That you'll never do such a thing on your own again. It might be dangerous. You should have told me, and I would have gone to interview him.'

'Oh, I couldn't have done that. You see, if I hadn't received any kind of assurance, I didn't want you to know that I had guessed that you were my benefactor. Surely you can understand that?'

His eyes on her were assessing. 'Yes, we are more alike than anyone might think. It gave you a kind of power over me, didn't it?'

Susanna flushed scarlet. 'I suppose so, yes. I have to keep my end up you see, and you are such a superior creature in so many ways. Being a man to begin with... It doesn't leave a poor girl much in the way of feeling that she is in control of her life. Keeping from you the knowledge that I was aware that you were my benefactor was a small victory.'

Silence fell. Ben said at last, 'I see.'

He couldn't say, Thank God you're not a man because I want to take you in my arms and do with you all those exciting things which men and women can do together—particularly because you are such a gallant creature. I have a feeling you'd be gallant in bed, too.

So he said nothing.

Mistaking his silence—and the slightly strained expression on his face—for disapproval, Susanna said earnestly. 'It was also a way of thanking you for your kindness—to be able to find out whether or not Mr Mitchell was guilty. The only sad thing is my poor mother. She is being punished, too. I know you won't approve, but I gave her some ready money and I intend to give her more. On condition that she doesn't give it to him to buy drink.'

'Dear girl,' said Ben fondly, 'if she loves the wretch, and

from everything you tell me she does, of course, she'll give it to him to buy drink. But if it makes you happy to throw your money away on them, don't let me dissuade you.'

Madame spoke at last. 'Everything you have told us does you credit, my dear, and I'm sure that Ben knows that. He's only worried about your safety.'

'Well, I'm worried about his, so that makes us quits,' said Susanna cheerfully. 'May we talk about something else?'

'Not before I have thanked you,' Ben said. 'You understand that I must ask Jess to try to confirm what you have told me—but that is merely a precaution. A wise man always checks any information which he is given, he never merely takes it on trust.'

Susanna nodded. 'I can see that,' she told him, her face so earnest and confiding that it nearly unmanned him.

'But if Mr Mitchell proves not to be your enemy, then it narrows your search, does it not?'

'Exactly,' said Ben. 'You would be a most useful addition to my staff, Miss Beverly, if you can understand that without me telling you.'

'Susanna,' she said. 'I insist that you call me Susanna. We are friends now, are we not?'

'Friends!' Ben almost snorted. 'Yes, I suppose you may say so.'

Judging by their expressions during this interchange, *Madame* thought that friendship was far too mild a word to describe what existed between Ben and Susanna. The only problem was why it was taking so long for them to understand that. On second thoughts, though, it was possible that their difficult past lives had made it impossible for them to trust another completely. It was easy to detect how powerfully Ben was attracted to Susanna, but Susanna, for all her charming artlessness, was a far more difficult person to read.

That she liked Ben was plain—but was liking all that she felt for him? If so, it was a pity, for they were so well suited to one another that, for a moment, *Madame* was tempted to play matchmaker. Only for a moment, though. Ben and Susanna were both so strong-minded that they would strongly resent feeling that she might be manipulating them, and she liked and respected them both too much to risk losing their friendship.

Best simply to wait and see, however much that might exhaust her patience while she watched them refuse to admit what was before their very eyes—that theirs would be a marriage made in heaven!

Chapter Eleven

'Whoever is after you, it's not Sam Mitchell,' Jess told Ben later that week. 'He's neither the money nor the determination to plot to murder you. He's either sitting at home drinking, or sitting in the nearest dirty tavern drinking—take your pick. From a man who was once something of a thruster, he's turned into a maudlin sot. The way he's going on, he and his family will shortly be reduced to lodging in the nearest workhouse—he's heavily in debt with no way of honouring any of it.'

Ben groaned. 'Never say so, and his poor wife is Susanna's mother and the two girls are her half-sisters. If I know her, she'll find some way of squandering her little fortune on them.'

Jess forbore to say that only someone as rich as Ben would describe Susanna's fortune as little—instead he waited for the instructions which he knew from of old would shortly be forthcoming.

'I want an assistant to Dawes, the Clerk of Works down at the docks,' Ben said at last after staring glumly into space for some time. 'The man I've got there at the moment isn't up to snuff. Mitchell was a clever fellow—if dishonest. There's not much he could get up to with Dawes's eagle eye on him, and he'd earn just enough to keep his family in reasonable comfort. Send Tozzy to the inn he's frequenting, get to know him, and then offer him the post—telling him it's a chance to earn an honest living. Susanna Beverly was right, I've made his name mud—so, if I'm to stop her from trying to rescue him, it is I who must give him something to enable him to haul himself out of the mire.

'Tell Tozzy to warn him that if he gets up to his old tricks he'll soon be rotting in Newgate Prison. My mercy for him only extends so far.'

'Will he consent to work for you?' asked Jess, a trifle artlessly.

'Now, Jess, you know better than that. No one knows that Marsden and Sons is part of my empire. And Tozzy's not to tell him who owns Marsden's, of course. Just that Marsden's wants a competent man, and he was that—once.'

Jess gone, Ben stared at the opposite wall dispiritedly as he contemplated what his affection for the clever little hussy he had fallen in love with had let him in for. No less than rescuing the rogue who had swindled her in order to prevent her from being so unhappy at her mother and sisters' fate that—in a ridiculous act of charity—she would throw away the inheritance he had rescued for her.

And if Mitchell was sensible enough to accept this lifeline, neither he nor Susanna was to be told that it was Ben Wolfe who had thrown it to him—although, knowing her, it was quite possible that she would twig what he had been up to!

He smiled. It would add spice to his life, watching and waiting to discover whether she would. He might even have a little bet with himself about how long it would take her.

In the meantime, he would take himself to Louis Fronsac's fencing salon where Jack Devereux had promised to give him a lesson with the rapier and where he might learn whether there was any current gossip which might give him some clue as to the identity of his enemy.

* * *

Fronsac's was busy when he reached it. Jack was already dressed in formal clothing for fencing: black silk knee-breeches and a white silk shirt. Before his accession to the Earldom, he had been one of the salon's instructors and still kept his talent honed by practising there whenever he was in town.

Ben had been first rate when using both a sabre and a foil as well as a pistol when he had been in India. He was, though, astonished at Jack's expertise, which was beyond anything which he had ever previously encountered in an amateur.

He told Jack so.

Jack laughed wryly. 'I had to earn my living teaching others after I left the Army, and I soon discovered that fencing is an art as well as a science. Most people's problem is that they see fencing purely as a science. What they don't understand is that you are facing a man whose character, physique and personality must be taken into account when you fight him, as well as his skill. That is where the art of it comes in.'

So saying, he disengaged before starting the bout again— and promptly slid through Ben's guard for the fifth time. This time Ben stepped back, raised his foil in a gesture of submission and remarked thoughtfully, 'You are telling me that I am going at you like a bull at a gate, no subtlety, just using my strength.'

'Exactly, and most of the time you will succeed by doing that, but not when you meet a master,' was Jack's reply. 'However, because you can say that, there is hope for you. You have a chance to improve. For the moment, though, take a rest,' and he gestured at a row of benches on the side wall.

Blowing hard, his own shirt clinging to his back, Ben sat down, lifting the protective mask from his face, causing a young sprig who had just entered to exclaim, 'Good God, is there nowhere safe these days? Nowhere one can be certain of not meeting the riff-raff!'

It was George Darlington who had arrived while Ben and Jack were fencing and had not recognised Ben until he had unmasked.

Ben sighed. Jack said quietly, 'Ignore the young fool. He's a spoilt boy, the unpleasant sprig of an unpleasant sire.'

He had not needed Jack to advise him but, knowing that Jack was a hot-tempered man who did not suffer fools gladly, he also knew that he must have good reason to suggest that he did not rise to young Darlington's bait.

Young Darlington, however, had no mind to let the matter rest. Secure in his rank and surrounded by a group of his friends, he was foolish enough to forget the lesson Ben had taught him at the Leominsters' ball and continued to insult him.

'I had thought,' he said, 'Mr What-ever-your-name-is, that the attack on you the other evening would have convinced you that you are not wanted in London. One supposes that you find it impossible to take a hint—else you would not attend a place where gentlemen congregate.'

On hearing these words, Jack Devereux gave a low moan. Small chance now that Ben Wolfe would restrain himself after being offered such an insult.

He wronged Ben, though. Suppressing his very real desire to seize young Darlington by the throat and throttle the life out of him, Ben merely looked coolly around while saying politely, 'Are you referring to me? Or is some other unfortunate the victim of your bile?'

Several of George's companions tittered at this. George himself flushed scarlet, and answered in a high voice, 'You know perfectly well that my remarks were addressed to you. Who else in this room is so patently not a gentleman? Who else uses his hands to hump loads in the port of London?'

'Why, no one,' riposted Ben. 'Looking around me, I can't see anyone other than myself, or Devereux perhaps, who is in sufficiently good condition to do any such thing. Lifting a lady's fan—or her skirts—looks beyond most of you.'

Jack Devereux did not help matters by laughing loudly at this sally, and saying, 'Oh, come, Darlington. Give over, do. Neither Wolfe nor I intend to be provoked into folly by your lack of manners. Go and insult someone who punches your own weight—I commend you to the dwarf at Greenwich Fair.'

'My quarrel is not with you, Devereux,' said George, a trifle fearfully, for everyone in the room knew that Jack was a master of weaponry and was not to be trifled with by anyone. 'My quarrel is with *him*—and his presence here.'

'And with Louis Fronsac who runs this salon,' said a new voice, that of Fronsac himself, who, attracted by the noise, had left the private room where he had been instructing a personage so grand that he never used the public rooms. 'It is I who determines who practises here, not some young gentleman with his mother's milk still on his lips. If you have a quarrel with Mr Wolfe, then pursue it somewhere else.'

Furious, George said unwisely, 'I would have thought that since we pay you highly we have a right to say with whom we might mix.'

'Then you thought wrongly. Indeed, since you are here and have chosen to pick a quarrel with Mr Wolfe and Lord Devereux, then you must settle your difference with one of them in a practice bout with the foils, or suffer banishment from my salon in future. The choice is yours.'

George looked wildly around him. His supporters remained silent. Louis Fronsac was held in high esteem, not only by the Grand Personage who stood in the doorway of the private room, but by most of society. He had hoped to bait Ben, secure in the knowledge that if Ben challenged him he could always refuse to fight someone so patently not a gentleman. Louis Fronsac had taken that choice away from him.

Louis stared at George, raising high-arched brows. He was a handsome man in early middle age who had been an *émigré* from France during the late Revolution there: a member of a noble family who had chosen—like many— not to return to his native land.

'You have not answered me, *Monseigneur*. Either agree to a practice bout—or leave. Have no fear, you will only be fighting with buttoned foils. Whether Mr Wolfe or m'lord will insist on meeting you at dawn tomorrow for a more serious bout is their choice to make once they leave my rooms.'

Neither Ben nor Jack spoke while Louis was laying down the law. There was no need. He was doing their work for them. Desperate, and aware that he was about to be humil- iated, George ground out, 'I'll fight him,' pointing at Ben.

Louis Fronsac smiled thinly. 'Not like that,' he told him. 'What Mr Wolfe is, is neither here nor there. *You* pretend to be a nobleman—and a gentleman. That being so, chal- lenge him in proper form or forfeit those titles yourself.'

'Bravo,' said the Grand Personage from the doorway, leaving George no choice but to do as he was bid.

He bowed, lifted a tormented face and said through grit- ted teeth, 'I would be honoured, Mr Wolfe, if you would agree to a practice bout with the foils.' He added conciliat- ingly, 'M. le Marquis de Fronsac, to give him his proper title, will agree to adjudicate between us, I am sure.'

Ben, his face a polite mask, bowed back. 'It will be a great pleasure, m'lord, to oblige you. A very great pleasure.'

Jack Devereux choked back a laugh at this two-edged reply. Ben might not be his equal with the foils, but he was more than a match for anyone he had ever tutored at Fron- sac's: the Grand Personage included.

'Very well,' said Louis. 'I will give you ten minutes to prepare yourself whilst I clear the room and ask his Royal Highness to be good enough to allow me to conclude his lesson later—or resume it at another time. You will excuse me while I consult him.'

His Royal Highness, it appeared, was more than happy to abandon his lesson in order to watch a practice bout which promised more fun than most. A chair was fetched for him by one of the courtiers who had been attending him in the private room, and was placed in a most favourable position.

'Haven't enjoyed myself so much at Fronsac's for years, what!' he exclaimed loudly. 'Nor since I was last on a man-of-war.'

'You must understand,' Jack whispered to Ben while they waited, 'that HRH's presence made it impossible for the young idiot to back down. The Duke of Clarence suffers neither fools nor cowards gladly.'

Ben nodded a trifle glumly. This piece of flummery—for such he thought it—was not of his making, nor to his liking. 'You can say that,' he whispered back, 'since no one is asking you to make a raree show of yourself.'

'Oh, come,' riposted Jack briskly, 'the only person in this room who answers to that description is young Darlington. All you need to do is make sure that he learns his lesson: not to taunt those who are in a position to make him pay for his folly. It's a great pity this bout is only a practice one. A bit of bloodletting would do him no harm at all.'

Ben privately agreed with him, but said no more, simply moved into the middle of the room to wait for his enemy—wishing that it was the father, not the son, he was about to face. Jess Fitzroy's enquiries were making it more and more likely that Babbacombe was behind the attack on him.

Fronsac was pitiless. He made young George go through all the lengthy formalities required of one who was fighting another gentleman and George could do nothing about it. At this late stage, to withdraw under any pretext would place his own reputation for courage and fair play at risk. After all, most would ask where was the harm in a bloodless bout.

'Three hits or three disarmings and the bout is over,' declared Fronsac, immediately before the antagonists assumed the *en garde* position, both stripped to their shirts and breeches. Ben was fighting barefoot and George was wearing light shoes. The spectators lined the walls, standing: None could be seated now that the Duke was—unless he gave the word, and he was not doing that.

The contrast between the two men could not have been greater. On the face of it George, tall and slim, ought to have the advantage over Ben who was also tall but built like a bruiser—their skills being equal, that was.

The younger and less experienced men were betting on George. Most of them knew that Ben had served in the ranks and would therefore, in their opinion, be less skilled with a small sword, always considered to be a gentleman's weapon. Older heads were betting differently. Some of them had been watching Ben and Jack Devereux fence and had noted that Jack's superiority was not all that great.

Clarence did not bet at all, but kept up a loud running commentary on the bout which began slowly, both participants being wary of the other.

Ben was keenly aware that he was the outsider here—even though it was plain that George was not greatly liked. He soon knew that George was in no way his equal and that he could therefore do one of two things. He could either restrain himself and fight a tame draw, or he could throw tact and caution to the winds and teach George a shameful and humiliating lesson.

He had just decided on the former—which would save everyone's face—when, in a lull in the bout with the pair of them warily circling around one another, he heard a voice behind him drawl, 'The big fellow's all wind and importance, ain't he? No finesse there—ought to be in his proper place, the prize ring, not pretending to equal his betters. Glad my tin is on Darlington.'

Red rage roared through him: the rage which he had known from childhood but which he usually kept under strict control as a wise man would keep a fierce dog on a leash. Occasionally, though, the rage, like that of the dog's, would be so strong that it would snap the leash and run riot.

The world around him disappeared. All that was left in it was George opposite to him and the fierce desire to show those who secretly mocked him that he was not to be trifled with, for, although the rage was red, inside it he was icy calm.

In a moment he was through George's weak guard like a knife slicing through butter to catch George's foil near the hilt with his own. Then, he fiercely twisted his wrist with such force that George's foil was first thrown into the air before falling to the floor.

Both men stepped back, consternation written on George's face and cold savage glee on Ben's as they unmasked.

Clarence clapped his hands together, his florid face on fire. 'Bravo, Wolfe, never seen that better done.'

Ben inclined his head in acknowledgement. Louis Fronsac stepped forward and said, 'First point to Mr Wolfe. Pick up your foil, m'lord, and the bout may start again.'

Again they circled around one another while Ben debated what to do next. He made up his mind quickly, presented his whole left side, apparently unguarded, to George and as George gleefully went in for the touch, he side-stepped, and on the turn wrapped George square on the breast.

'A hit,' someone shouted, as Louis Fronsac separated them again.

'You tricked me,' muttered George through his teeth before they resumed their masks.

'So I did,' rasped Ben. 'I'll show you another ploy in a minute, if you'll only be patient.'

The room had fallen silent. The duel was turning into a massacre, as Ben disarmed George again, and for good measure rapped him on the breast having done so. The rage had begun to diminish and for a few moments he allowed

George a respite, dancing around him, apparently offering him the chance of a hit, almost inviting him to try one.

George, though, was beginning to learn his lesson. He would not be caught again by such an obvious trick, but alas, the third hit which finished the bout was accomplished by a reverse thrust on high which came as such a surprise that George lost his balance and sprawled on the ground so that all Ben had to do was to stand over him and touch his breast lightly again.

The voice which had mocked Ben now mocked George. 'The young cub should be grateful he didn't provoke Wolfe into a real duel,' it said. 'He would have been dog's food by now.'

His rage's appetite satisfied, Ben found his triumph to be an empty one—a common aftertaste, for he disliked not being in total command of himself. He swung round on the mocker and said through his teeth, 'Since you are such an authority, sir, would you care to engage me, and make a better fist of it than Darlington?'

He did not wait for an answer, but swung away, intent on changing into his street clothes and leaving, but he was stopped by the Duke who had risen from his chair, exclaiming peremptorily, 'Come here, Wolfe, I wish to speak to you.'

Ben did as he was bid, bowing as he approached Royalty. The Duke said genially, 'They tell me that you were a soldier in the army in India—and in the ranks at that. You are a gentleman—why in the ranks?'

'I had no money, Your Highness, and no real home. To enlist as a private soldier gave me both. I feel—and felt—no shame at earning my living in the only way I could.'

He was aware that he sounded defiant and wondered for a moment whether he had been wise.

The Duke suddenly gave a great bellow of laughter. 'You are an honest man, Wolfe, and have given me an honest answer. You have also provided me with amusement in the way in which you disciplined Babbacombe's young puppy. My gratitude is such that should you need a favour, you may call on Clarence to provide you with one. What do you say to that, hey?'

What could Ben say? He was well aware of the caprices of the Royal Family, from those of the mad King George III downwards. Clarence was brave, choleric—and irresponsible. He might forget immediately what he had promised—but he might not. Everything and nothing was possible.

So he bowed, and murmured, 'I shall not forget your kindness, sir.'

'See that you do not, what? See that you do not! And hello to you, Devereux,' he said to Jack. who was standing beside Ben, before calling to his equerry who had been standing at a respectful distance. 'Time to leave, I have had my fun. Fronsac may give me another lesson on another day.'

Jack murmured in Ben's ear, 'Put not your trust in princes, Ben. He'll probably forget you before he climbs into his coach. On the other hand, Clarence is the best of a bad lot. And before I forget, why did you trick me into believing you a relative novice with the foils? Fronsac tells me that one of your moves was a favourite of his old master Jean Dupuy, and that if he taught it to you he thought you were something of a master, too, because only a master could perform it. Is Fronsac right?'

Ben shrugged a little shamefacedly. 'A man does not confess to everything he knows—or can do—if he is wise. You should know that, Jack. As for Dupuy, he ended up in India teaching anyone who would learn. I was one of those who wished to.'

'I'll remember that the next time we practise together—for I shall give you no leeway at all. I was easy with you—but never no more—that I promise.'

'I shan't come to Fronsac's again,' said Ben dourly. 'I

lost my temper, and I don't care to put myself in the way of doing so again.'

'Fool's talk,' said Jack rudely. 'Don't let the smug swine who run London society drive you away. Take no notice of them. I never do.'

This was so patently true and was said in Jack's most aggressive manner, which drove Ben's megrims away and set him laughing.

'Well, I see that I cannot play the coward when you do not, so I'll withdraw my resolution.'

'Then we may still be friends. I see that that cub you've just thrashed is sulking in a corner. He grows more like his father every day. A word of warning, Ben, Babbacombe is dangerous because he is stupid. Guard your back against the bludgeoneers.'

'You have heard something?' asked Ben quickly, thinking of the recent attack on him.

Jack shook his head. 'No, I only have my hard-earned knowledge of the world and the fools and knaves who live in it to guide me. I see that you have agreed to employ a bodyguard—most wise of you. But remember, a man may be attacked in other ways than the physical.'

Jack Devereux was a good friend, and would also be a dangerous enemy, thought Ben as he was driven to *Madame*'s once his session at Fronsac's was over. He had tickets for a performance at Astley's Amphitheatre and thought that Susanna—and *Madame*—might be pleased to accompany him. These days it was always Susanna he thought of first.

In fact, if he were truthful he thought of her first, last and always—a new thing for him.

Madame, the butler informed him, was not at home, but Miss Beverly was, and he would ask if she were prepared to receive him.

Ben stood in the grand hallway with its black and white flagged tiles and its vases of flowers on tall occasional tables, hoping against hope that Susanna would break all the rules of conduct and entertain a single gentleman on her own. The expression on the butler's face when he returned gave nothing away.

He put out a hand for the hat which Ben was holding and enunciated clearly and disapprovingly, 'Miss Beverly will receive you, sir, in the small drawing room. Please follow me.'

His heart beating violently, Ben allowed himself to be ushered into the room where Susanna rose from her chair after putting down the book which she had been reading. She looked so enchanting that Ben could barely wait for the butler to leave before he told her so.

Susanna, her own heart bumping in the most alarming way—for was she not breaking every rule by which she had lived all her life?—said as soberly as she could when he had finished, 'You need not flatter me, Ben. I am dressed quite simply because I did not foresee that I should have company this afternoon—*Madame* has gone to the French Embassy to visit an old friend.'

'Then you should always dress simply,' declared Ben in his usual downright fashion, 'for it suits you even more than dressing grandly does—and I must thank you for receiving me when you are on your own.'

'More flattery—' Susanna smiled, '—and, seeing that we are now old friends, I have allowed myself the luxury of your presence.'

Ben could not help himself. The sight of her in her plain white muslin gown with its pale blue ribbons and its modest high neck, her hair dressed simply, so that one curl was allowed to coil around her graceful neck, was having the most disturbing effect on him, so that he blurted out, 'Friends! I should hope that we are more than that!'

And then, as she offered him a dazzling smile, he continued, the words pouring from him like water cascading downwards, out of control, 'Marry me, Susanna, at once, or

I shall immediately expire, or dissolve spontaneously into a flaming pyre like the ones on to which Indian ladies fling themselves after their husbands' death.'

This extraordinary proposal, totally unlike anything which a young gentlewoman of quality ought to expect, might have overset many young women, but it was so like the man making it in its downright extravagance, that it had no such effect on Susanna.

'Do but consider what you are saying, Ben! Did you really come here this afternoon to propose to me?'

'No,' he said, all sense deserting him, aware only that he would go mad if somehow or other he did not get her into his bed. 'Not at all, but the sight of you provoked me to it. Have you no notion of the effect which you have on me? Have had since I first clapped eyes on you. Only the presence of *Madame* in the past and now the conventions which bind us both in the present are preventing me from falling on you and physically demonstrating the passion which I have come to feel for you. It is highly inconvenient—particularly since you are not at all the kind of young person whom I have always thought of marrying!'

As soon as he had finished speaking, Ben knew that he must have dished himself by being so tactlessly truthful. Yes, he had thought that he would marry a biddable, pampered young woman whom he could shape and mould to his heart's desire, not someone like Susanna whose character and temperament had been sharpened and strengthened by the troubles through which she had passed—but he shouldn't have said so.

Before she could answer him he apologised humbly, 'Forgive me, that was no way to speak to the lady whom I have come to desire beyond reason, but I have a blunt man all my life, and it is difficult for me to change now.'

Susanna, her whole body singing a triumphant song, yet could not contain her amusement at her suitor's bluff and brusque proposal.

'Why should I wish you to change?' she enquired sweetly. 'I like you as you are. I admit that you could have made me a more elegant proposal. There are women who might be offended on learning that their suitor thought his passion for them to be inconvenient, but I am not one of them. In return, may I inform you that you are the last man I could ever have imagined either proposing to me at all, or to whom I could consider giving a favourable answer—which makes the fact that I am about to say "yes" to you even more remarkable. I once thought Francis Sylvester to be the kind of paragon whom I would wish to marry—and I cannot imagine anyone more unlike you than he is!'

Ben stood dazed, trying to work out exactly what she was saying to him. 'Do I infer that you are accepting me?' he came out with. 'If so, your answer is a good match for mine in its crossgrainedness!'

'True,' replied Susanna, 'but that is probably why we shall deal well together. Who else would wish to marry either of us? Seeing what an unlikely pair we are.'

He exploded into laughter, throwing his head back, behaving as usual totally against all the rules of polite society which demanded that a gentleman should never display strong emotions in public: a laugh should always be a pleasantly controlled thing—if one had to laugh at all, that was. Susanna's amusement at his frank enjoyment of her saucy sally set her laughing, too.

Wiping the tears from her eyes, she said, 'Oh, dear, now you have set me off as well. The late Lord Chesterfield would have been most ashamed of us.'

'Why so?' asked Ben curiously, his life not having been spent in reading elegantly phrased letters by elegantly living peers.

'He wrote letters to his son on how a gentleman ought to behave in which, among other things, he said that no true gentleman—and presumably gentlewoman—ever laughs aloud. The letters were published because it was believed that his advice on etiquette was so wise that all the world ought to know of it.'

Ben thought for a moment before answering her. Then, 'You really ought to marry me, if only because you know so much of these matters and I know so little. Between us you could turn me into a paragon who would know everything about Prince Hamlet and when to simper rather than laugh aloud.'

Susanna shook her head. 'Not at all. I much prefer you as you are. If I had wanted to marry a simpering gentleman, I should have accepted Francis Sylvester's second proposal.'

'Does that mean that you have accepted *my* second proposal?'

'I think so.'

'That is not an answer which a man of business like myself understands.'

'Which is precisely why I made it.'

Her face on throwing this conversational titbit at him was so *piquante* and alight with mischief that Ben's self-control flew away. He gave a little groan—and swept her into his arms.

His little groan was matched by her little cry on finding herself brought smack up against his broad chest.

He brought his mouth down on hers with a movement so swift that there was no stopping him. Susanna's heart beat rapidly as a consequence of fear as well as of passion. He was so big and strong, such a bear of a man, that she was momentarily afraid that his lovemaking would be as fierce as his name and appearance.

But no such thing. His mouth on hers was so tender and gentle, the big hands which rose to cup her face were so delicate in their handling of it that fright flew away and only passion reigned supreme. She moaned again and raised her own hand to stroke his face, letting her fingers run along his jaw in line with the shadow of his beard which grew so rapidly that by evening he was compelled to shave again.

And then delicately, oh so delicately, his mouth teased hers open and Susanna was ready to swoon when his tongue met hers and made it dance in unison with his. Only the right hand that he had taken from her face in order to cup her head kept her on her feet.

Francis's few kisses, perfunctorily snatched whenever, for a few moments, they were left alone, had not prepared her either for Ben's lovemaking or the strength of the passion with which she responded to it.

'Please, yes, please,' she muttered hoarsely and knew not for what she was asking, only that there was something more to come and that by contrast with what she had already enjoyed, it would be even more powerful and fulfilling.

He dropped his mouth to the hollows of her neck and began to celebrate them; at the same time his hand began to rove down her back to the base of her spine to cup her buttocks, creating a sensation which made her writhe and twist against him.

This, in turn, had such a powerful effect on Ben that his rapidly slipping control nearly disappeared altogether, so that it was fortunate that—as though they were taking part in a bad French farce, by Marivaux, perhaps—the drawing door opened to reveal to Madame de Saulx that her two protégés were so closely entwined that they might as well have been one.

The sound of her entry and her muttered, 'Ahem', set them springing apart, rosy-face, dishevelled—and guilty.

Ben, who, for obvious reasons, remained half-turned away, said with great joviality as soon as he had physically recovered and had rearranged his clothing, 'My dear *Madame*, you will be delighted to learn that Miss Beverly has agreed to marry me—and as soon as I can acquire a special licence—and with as little flummery as possible.'

Susanna, who had been carrying out some rearrangement herself, to *Madame*'s amusement riposted with, 'Oh, I'm sure I never agreed to any of that.'

'Indeed, but you did,' replied Ben. 'I distinctly remember that you said "yes". You did qualify it by remarking that, in effect, no one else would marry either of us—but that does not affect your agreement, as I am sure *Madame* understands.'

'And *Madame* will offer you both her congratulations,' said that lady calmly, secretly delighted that one of her fondest wishes was coming true. 'On mature reflection, Ben, I think that you will agree that your marriage must be no hole-in-the-corner affair, for that would reflect, not only on yourself, but on your bride. That does not mean that you must carry on as though you were one of the Royal Dukes tying the knot, simply that you must fulfil the duties which you owe to your station.'

Ben, busy thinking that hard though it might be to propose, the act of marriage itself seemed to be even harder, nodded a reluctant agreement.

'More particularly,' continued *Madame*, ignoring his reluctance, 'since, given your present situation of being under attack from Lord Babbacombe's spiteful accusations, you must not be seen to be afraid to appear in public.'

Susanna stifled a giggle at the expression on Ben's face indicating that to suggest that he was afraid of anything was a statement so monstrous that it was not worth contradicting.

Madame, seeing that Susanna was now composed again, moved over to her to kiss her on the cheek and whisper congratulations to her.

'He is a good man,' she said, 'and you have made a wise choice—as he has. I wish you well. You will, of course, be married from here.'

Somehow, until *Madame* uttered that last sentence, Susanna had not fully grasped what she had done in accepting Ben so lightly. It was as though they had been jousting with words quite bloodlessly and suddenly that joust had become a real, and not an imaginary, one and both of them had been laid low! So low that the carpet had nearly become their bed.

Thus, even before they had fully grasped what they had done, they had fallen prey to a mutual passion so profound that had *Madame* not arrived when she did they might have consummated it on the spot.

Did she wish to repudiate her agreement to marry him? No, she did not. Unwise it might be, but her own reactions to Ben's caresses had shown her two things. The first was that, however fierce he might be, however like his namesake the untamed wolf which roamed the forests, in appearance and manner, his lovemaking to her had been both considerate and kind to the untried woman that he knew she must be. And secondly, her own response to it had been breathtakingly spontaneous. She had proved herself not only willing to meet and match him in the lists of love, but that she was ready to dare all in marrying him.

Their fiery coming together had shown how tepid her relationship with Francis Sylvester had been: a mere extension of friendship with no passion in it.

She was prepared to be the wolf's mate—and would glory in being so.

Unknown to herself, her face told *Madame* everything. Later, alone for a few moments with Ben, she said to him with some severity in her manner, 'You must be kind to her, *mon cher*. Yes, I know she is a strong woman, but it is plain that she has not known what it is to be loved and cherished and you must supply that lack.'

'Oh, I will,' he told her, 'but, and I must tell you this, my own passion for her frightens me. She is so small and delicate, and I am so large. Wolfe my name is, bear I sometimes feel myself to be.'

Madame smiled a subtle smile. One thing Ben Wolfe did not know of himself was how much his face changed and softened when he looked at Susanna. She was prepared to bet that the desire to love and to protect his mate was strong

within him and would not be denied. She had long thought
that the woman whom he married would be lucky—but only
if she could meet his strength with her own quite different
brand.

In Susanna Ben had met his mate and his equal and it
would be her pleasure to see them flourish together, their
respective miseries long behind them. She could only pray
that the troubles which surrounded him would soon be over
and that their life together would be set fair.

Chapter Twelve

The buzz about Ben Wolfe's origins rose to a roar. Rumours flew about: that Lord Babbacombe wished to go to law, but pursuing a Writ of Ejectment through the courts would prove both long and costly and Babbacombe, unfortunately for him, was on his beam-ends. It was known that the moneylenders would no longer accommodate him and that no bank would advance him so much as a half-penny. He was in immediate danger of ending up in a debtor's prison since he had been living on tick and borrowed money for years.

Ben Wolfe, on the other hand, was rolling in it, as the saying went, and since possession was nine-tenths of the law, remained ensconced in The Den in the country and in his town house in London.

M'lord called in the Runners, but all their pushing and probing gave him no harder evidence than he already possessed—other than that there had been a country rumour about the time of Ben's birth that his supposed mother was not his real one—but no reliable witnesses could be found to testify that this was true. Another rumour was that a child had been born to Mrs Wolfe but that it had died immediately and an orphan brat had been substituted in its place to prevent Lord Babbacombe from being the then rich estate's heir. This, too, was supported by no witness whom a court of law might believe.

Lord Babbacombe, rolling his eyes and looking melancholy, said repeatedly to anyone who would listen to him that it was monstrous that a poor man like himself should be unable to do anything to right his wrongs, particularly when his enemy was so stinking rich.

'Ill-gotten gains,' he always ended mournfully.

He also stirred the pot vigorously by keeping the old gossip about Mrs Wolfe and Lady Exford alive.

Ben's defenders—who were not many, seeing that he was somewhat of an outsider owing to his strange career—were powerless to silence the uproar.

'You could bring an action for slander against him,' Lord Exford said, doubtfully, 'but once one goes to law the outcome is always uncertain.' He never ceased to believe in Ben, as did Jack Devereux who laughed scornfully at the very idea of going to law.

'Leave it,' he said. 'By next season there will be another *on dit* to engage the *ton* and by then Babbacombe should be safe in the Marshalsea—or worse.'

Ben, engaged in the preparations for his marriage to Susanna, was in agreement with Jack, although the whole rotten business distressed him, not for his own sake, but for that of his future wife's. He also thought that Babbacombe and his claque would not let the matter rest.

'It's *point non plus* for me, I'm afraid,' he told *Madame* and Susanna almost apologetically. 'There's nothing I can do to silence him, short of calling him out, and then he's likely to refuse to meet me on the grounds that I'm not really a gentleman, just some nameless bastard masquerading as one.'

'But Lord Exford says that you are the image of your father,' protested Susanna, Madame de Saulx nodding her agreement.

Ben grimaced. 'Oh, that proves nothing. Someone made

that point to Babbacombe and his answer was that I was
Charles Wolfe's bastard by a village girl who was conve-
niently handy for substitution. He has an answer for anything.'

'And many believe him,' said *Madame* sadly.

'Well, I don't.' Susanna was robust. 'You're not to let it
worry you, Ben.'

But he did worry, all the same. He did not mind people
giving him their shoulder, but it hurt him when they did it
to Susanna.

He knew that Susanna had met Amelia Western at Lady
Leominster's and that she had rudely accosted Susanna with,
'Can it possibly be true that you are about to marry that
impostor Ben Wolfe?'

She shuddered delicately while murmuring, 'You must
know that if you do I cannot possibly continue to receive
you when I am married. I am sure that you are aware that
I am promised to Sir Ponsonby Albright, who has the strict-
est notions of propriety—as I do, of course. I trust to your
good sense to cry off before you become a social pariah.'

'Having been a social pariah once, and survived it, I don't
regard that state with quite the same horror that you do,'
returned Susanna drily. 'And as I happen to be marrying
Ben because not only do I love him, but trust him, your
notion that I should cry off is repugnant to me.'

Amelia sniffed. 'You never showed much common sense
about these matters when you were my duenna,' she announced, 'so one can't expect you to display any when your
fortunes are so unaccountably changed. We part, I fear, not
to converse again.'

And what a relief that will be, thought Susanna, but did
not say so.

'I don't think that I ought to marry you until this is settled
one way or another,' Ben told her one afternoon in Hyde

Park when a peer who had been one of his friends, and had dined with him several times, cut him dead.

'Nonsense,' she said. 'I don't value any of these people. Think how they all behaved towards me when I was in trouble.'

'Nevertheless…' He sighed.

'No.' Susanna was definite. 'I will not have my life—and yours—at the mercy of a spiteful old man. I know that you need to live in London, but it is populous enough for us to choose for our friends those who do not believe these slanders.'

She reflected for a moment. 'In one way,' she said thoughtfully, 'it might be better if Lord Babbacombe were rich enough to bring a Writ of Ejectment against you. The whole thing would then be decided one way or another.'

'Except,' said *Madame*, her face troubled, 'that it still might drag on for months or years and if the Writ by some mischance resulted in the court finding for Lord Babbacombe, Ben might end up in prison for personation for fraudulent reasons by falsely assuming the Wolfe name in order to gain The Den and the remainder of the estate. Worse, he might also lose much of his hard-earned wealth by having to pay Lord Babbacombe heavy damages for depriving him of his property and forcing him to go to law to recover it.'

'*Point non plus* it is, then,' Susanna agreed ruefully.

It was not to remain so. The Duke of Clarence gave a great dinner for men only to which Ben, Lord Exford and Jack Devereux were invited. Lord Babbacombe was conspicuously not present. Before it, the Duke took Lord Exford on one side. 'What's this about my friend Ben Wolfe, what, what?' he demanded.

Lord Exford looked at him and wondered how to be tactful. Common sense took over. Nothing about His Royal Highness, William, Duke of Clarence, was remotely tactful.

So as precisely as possible he informed the Duke of the rumours and slanders which Babbacombe was promoting, the possibility of his taking out a Writ of Ejectment, and the difficulty of silencing both him and his son.

'Never liked the man,' bellowed Clarence. 'Played cards in an odd way—didn't do to say so, what! So my friend is in trouble and no way out.'

'He's at *point non plus*, in this matter,' agreed Lord Exford, echoing Ben.

'And raising the old scandal about your poor mama. Can't do anything about that, but the other, yes. Have Erskine to dinner, lean on him, eh? Don't want any more noble scandals, eh, what? Public getting restive.'

By Erskine he meant the law lord who had once been Lord Chancellor and was highly respected in consequence.

Lord Exford betrayed his puzzlement. Clarence said, his rosy face beaming goodwill, 'A private court of adjudication, what? If Erskine thinks that Babbacombe has right on his side—which I beg leave to doubt—then I shall help him with his Writ. If, on the other hand, he finds for Mr Wolfe, then Babbacombe must apologise and withdraw. Simple, ain't it?'

One thing was to be said for him, Lord Exford decided. Downright and slightly simple he might be, but he ordered himself and his life better than his much more clever elder brother, the Prince Regent, who lacked the unselfconscious and childlike honesty which was Clarence's hallmark.

'And will Lord Erskine agree to preside over such an unofficial court?' asked Lord Exford.

'He'd better,' retorted the Duke with a twinkle in his eye. 'Both parties would have to agree that his decision would be binding, of course. Otherwise, no point.'

What he did not say was that if either party refused to agree to such a request their social ruin would be inevitable.

'An impromptu court of law. Trust Clarence to think of anything so unlikely,' was Ben's first remark when Lord

Exford told him of the Duke's decision.

'Aye, but on the other hand it could bring the whole matter to a head. You would do well to prepare yourself for it.'

Susanna and *Madame* nodded their agreement. One way or another it would end what had become a constant irritant and would—if satisfactorily settled—mean that Susanna and Ben could be married without a shadow hanging over them.

'Suppose Lord Babbacombe does not agree?' Susanna asked Lord Exford. He shook his head before replying, 'He cannot gainsay a Royal Duke. The only way out for him would be to apply for a Writ of Ejectment immediately and he cannot afford to do that.'

'As for preparation,' Ben said, 'I have to tell you that I have had Jess Fitzroy and a couple of my most trusted men secretly investigating the servants and villagers who live around The Den to discover what they can about both the circumstances of my birth and the strange disappearance of my mother. I gather that Babbacombe has had a couple of Runners doing the same thing, but most of the local people are loyal to my family and have given nothing away. I ordered Jess to inform those whom he questioned that they must tell him the truth about these matters, however unpalatable it might be for me to learn it. I have no wish to be surprised by the revelation of events long gone either in a true court of law or an unconventional one such as the Duke proposes. I wish to know the worst, as well as the best, of my case.'

'Very wise,' agreed Lord Exford.

Susanna said to Ben when Lord Exford had gone, 'You are not happy about this, are you?'

'No,' he said, walking restlessly towards the window to look out of it at the busy street below. They were in a drawing room on the first floor of *Madame*'s house near Regent's Park. *Madame* was seated on the sofa before an empty hearth. She watched Susanna walk to where Ben was standing in order to take him by the hand.

'Lord Exford believes that the Duke is doing this to help you. He calls you his friend, Mr Wolfe.'

Ben gave a short laugh and turned to look down into her earnest, anxious eyes. 'I am not sure whether he will help me. I believe in letting sleeping dogs lie. I do not think that Lord Babbacombe will be able to find any evidence substantial enough to help his cause in a court of law—should he ever get there. Given time the whole business would, I believe, have blown over of its own accord. It is thirty-four years since my birth and twenty-five years since my mother disappeared. During that time people's memories have faded and become unreliable—my own included. In a sense the Duke, although he does not mean to, is indulging Lord Babbacombe and keeping the scandal alive.'

'I know,' she told him simply, 'and I agree with you. Nevertheless, the thing is done, and there is, as Lord Exford told me yesterday, no gainsaying a Royal Duke, and perhaps Lord Babbacombe may not agree to submit to such a tribunal.'

'Perhaps—but I think that he will. Looking on the bright side, our mutual friend, Lady Leominster, who was the direct cause of bringing us together, has invited us to dinner in order to demonstrate her faith in us. And the fact that *Madame*—' and he turned to bow to Madame de Saulx '—as well as Lord Exford, continue to be my friend is a plus on my side.'

'And your own character,' added *Madame* rising to join them at the window, 'which is that of an honest man. One thing is significant: there have been no more attacks on you since the failed one.'

Ben smiled wryly. 'Oh, there are two reasons for that. Babbacombe hopes to destroy me by spreading scandal, and the fact that I never move without a bodyguard has spiked his guns.'

'And the Rothschilds are still dealing with you,' said Susanna who was beginning to take an interest in Ben's business affairs, 'which must stand for something.'

'Only that a good business deal takes precedence with them over the whim-whams of the *ton*,' said Ben cynically. 'Nothing must interfere with the making of money.'

'Ah, that is truly a case of the pot calling the kettle black,' commented Susanna, her face full of mischief, 'since I believe that is your motto, too.'

'Minx,' exclaimed Ben, bending down to kiss her soft cheek, regardless of *Madame*'s presence—or rather because her presence meant that he could take his caresses no further. 'I see that I shall have a useful helpmate. If the future Mrs Wolfe is going to be as keen a businessman as her husband, I shall have to find her an office!'

'Which must wait until you are married.' *Madame* smiled.

'And that cannot be,' said Ben firmly, 'until this wretched business with Babbacombe is over. When I marry Susanna I want no cloud in my sky.'

'Which means,' said Susanna, 'that you anticipate giving Lord Babbacombe a legal black eye in this odd arrangement which the Duke has set up!'

'Exactly,' said Ben, kissing her again. 'And now I must leave you both. I have work to do before I call on you to take you to Lady Leominster's.'

'Oh, I do hope that he is right to be optimistic,' Susanna sighed to *Madame* when he had gone, 'but I cannot help but feel that the Duke has made him a hostage to fortune.'

'No need to repine,' returned *Madame*, putting an arm around her shoulders. 'My instincts tell me that Babbacombe must lose. You see, I don't believe that he ever intended to go to court—he simply hoped that he could drive Ben out of society by blackguarding him so much that he would turn the whole town against him. The Duke has forced his hand, and now he must prepare to back his slanders with evidence. That, I believe will be difficult—and almost certainly impossible.'

Nevertheless, Susanna went off to dress for the Leominsters' dinner with a heavy heart. It was for Ben that she feared, not herself. She had been through the fires of rejection and knew how much they hurt, and although she had come through strengthened, she knew that the fires had burned and changed her.

Her love had had a hard life and it was time that he found peace. It would be her duty, once they were married, to see that he achieved it. She was only sorry that he would not marry her until the enquiry was over, for she wished to demonstrate to the whole world how much she loved him, and that no stupid slanders could affect that love.

The Duke's court of enquiry moved at a greater speed than the courts in which a Writ of Ejectment would have been debated. Lord Babbacombe asked for more time to prepare his case: Ben, having heard from Jess, allowed that he was ready at any time that the Duke commanded.

The Duke, wishing to appear fair, gave Lord Babbacombe the extra time he asked for.

'But no more, mind,' he told m'lord sternly. 'I have set this court up to bring matters to a speedy conclusion, not allow it to drag on. It does society—and the country—harm to allow these matters to be aired so publicly and so lengthily.'

'Stretching it a bit, ain't he?' was one comment. 'What's Ben Wolfe's legitimacy got to do with the country's interests?'

'Only,' said Lord Exford severely, to whom the comment was made, 'that in these troubled times when the Radicals are gathering again, anything which shows the aristocracy and gentry in a bad light adds fuel to the would-be fires of revolution.'

Most of the cousinry—for the aristocracy and gentry were

heavily inter-related—agreed with Lord Exford. The only thing which they lamented was that the enquiry was to be held in private.

'Which means that we shall miss all the fun,' was the complaint of many.

Which was what the Duke intended. Later, when his brother's marriage to Princess Caroline was dragged through Parliament, the courts and the press, it was generally agreed that the Duke had shown wisdom in his arrangements.

Lord Erskine hummed and ha'd at this bypassing of the courts, but agreed with the Duke that since Babbacombe persisted in his slanders, and was not able to find the money to launch his Writ, this suggestion to end the matter was as good as any.

'Why does not Wolfe bring an action for slander against the feller?' he asked Clarence. 'That would settle things.'

'Pride,' said the Duke simply. 'I understand that he says that he will not waste his time bringing Babbacombe to book, for it would mean that he would be taking his accusations seriously. Since Babbacombe would certainly not agree to a duel with a man he claims to be a common impostor, then my friend Wolfe says, "To hell with him and his lies, I shall not demean myself by recognising him or them." This wretched business must not be allowed to drag on, so my solution is what lies before you in the document which my secretary has prepared. Both parties have agreed to accept your judgement, and after it, whichever way it goes, will let the matter die immediately.'

Lord Erskine was now an old man whose wits—honed by a lifetime in the law—were still undiminished by age. He fell in with the Duke's wishes after some mumbling and chuntering.

'Although I fear that you may find that the losing party will not keep to the agreement about letting the matter drop.'

'Oh, as to that,' said Clarence cheerfully, 'he will face social ruin if he goes back on his word. It would not be

well seen. You shall have a room at St James's Palace and
as many secretaries and aides as you please. You have only
to say the word.'

Lord Erskine said several words—as did the rest of society when the news of the enquiry became public—as it
inevitably did. Lord Babbacombe, when questioned, looked
noble, saying, his eyes rolling, 'I could not but agree to
anything which His Royal Highness might propose. We are
each allowed a counsel to represent us and may produce our
own witnesses. I could not ask for more.'

Ben said nothing. 'Better so,' he told *Madame* and Susanna. 'I shall save my remarks for the enquiry itself.'

Clarence decided that it was to be held at St James's
Palace and that ladies were not to be admitted, only a few
men who might be regarded as the cream of society and
who would be there to see fair play. Lady Leominster was
delighted that her Lord was to be among them, but annoyed
that she might not be there to enjoy the fun, although privately Lord Leominster had informed her that it would be
very dull. 'Lord Erskine will make sure of that,' he said.

'You may be sure,' she trilled at Ben, 'that Leominster
will see that you are not thrown to the wolves. And Lord
Granville will be there, which is very proper, for all the
world knows that he is not only shrewd but will, in his calm
way, see fair play for all parties. The spectators will not be
allowed to take part, of course, but their very presence will
act as a useful check on folly. Leominster says that witnesses will be called and that both parties have handed in a
list to Lord Erskine.'

Her Lord, standing by her, added his own gloss on the
matter. 'The Law Lords have been saying that it is all most
irregular but, seeing that Babbacombe cannot afford to go
to court and that Mr Wolfe will not, they agree that it is the
only way out of a dangerous impasse.'

Which seemed to be the general feeling. Society, sharply

divided as to who was right and who was wrong in the
matter, agreed only on that—and the fact that the Duke had
insisted that the matter be settled as soon as possible.

'Bad enough for the Princess of Wales to be a thorn in
everyone's flesh,' as Mr Canning said privately to Lord
Granville on hearing that he was to be present, 'without
having this scandal hanging over us for months. The radical
newspapers would fill their columns with screams about
"old corruption". That scoundrel, Leigh Hunt, has already
been gloating over it, reviving the old mystery about Lady
Exford and Mrs Wolfe.'

'So I understand.' Lord Granville was frosty. 'Fortunately, Exford is Mr Wolfe's friend, which ought to put a
damper on too much unpleasant speculation. Erskine has
told me that he has instructed both Babbacombe and Wolfe
not to discuss the matter with others either in public or in
private before the enquiry is held.'

'And a blessed relief that is,' said Mr Canning, agreeing
with *Madame* and Susanna, who were saying the same thing
to Ben when they were picnicking by the Thames at Richmond one sunny afternoon.

Susanna was charming in a simple white high-waisted
frock with a pale blue sash, and a small blue bow at her
neck. Ben was more formally dressed and had already com-
plained that 'the ladies are more able to endure the sun than
we are, seeing that they wear about half the quantity of
clothing with which we are encumbered.'

They had been speaking briefly of Lord Erskine's inter-
dict. 'Not that Ben has been giving anything away,' said
Susanna, laughing up at him. 'He's been keeping mum, but
I believe that he has been thinking quite a lot.'

She knew that he had been closeted with Jess Fitzroy that
morning, going over evidence which he had been collecting
in Buckinghamshire.

'None of it is substantive,' Ben said wryly. 'We shall be
trading in gossip and hearsay, and how the truth can be

arrived at in such a climate is beyond my comprehension. Jess has heard that Babbacombe has been secretly claiming that he has two witnesses who will win his case for him, but he cannot discover who they are. Neither can Jackson, the ex-Runner I have been using, so perhaps it's nothing more than Babbacombe's flimflam.' He added, still wry, 'At least, I hope so.'

'I wish that we could be there to support you,' said *Madame*. 'But I believe that the Duke is probably keeping the ladies away in order to ensure that the audience will be small and informal—which is probably wise.'

They had finished eating their cold collation and were reclining on the grass. Ben took Susanna's hand in his. She pressed it gently, both of them wishing that this wretched business had not arrived to delay their wedding. Each ached for the other. For the first time Susanna understood what the poets meant when they spoke of love as a flame. It was burning strongly inside her breast—and in Ben's.

Madame, watching them, suddenly declared that she was drowsy and would like to rest. 'But you, on the other hand, are both young and lively, so I suggest that you go for a stroll. There is a fine promenade by the Thames called Cholmondely Walk which will offer you some splendid views of Twickenham Bridge in one direction and Richmond Bridge in the other. Or you may meander into the pleasant grove which lies behind us. Arcadia is another name for the river at Richmond.'

And so it proved. First they wandered along the promenade, admiring the ducks and rails who were taking their ease on the river, before striking off into the trees where they found themselves alone.

'At last,' murmured Ben, taking her into his arms. 'I think that *Madame* knew what a temptation you presented to me in your pretty summer frock and provided us with an opportunity to indulge ourselves.'

He ran his right hand through her hair before gently kissing her as passionlessly as he could.

'I must restrain myself,' he muttered into her ear, 'for I am in danger of celebrating our wedding night, here on the grass, before the parson has made all legal and proper.'

Susanna knew how he felt for she was experiencing the same wild desire as Ben was. She had not truly known herself, she decided ruefully, for always in the past she had thought of herself as cool and contained and now her whole body was throbbing, demanding a fulfilment which it had never known before.

'Alas, this is not the time or the place,' she said sadly, breaking away from him. 'If we were simply a shepherd and his love in the Arcadia of which *Madame* spoke, then we might have met and loved in innocence—with no consequences. But we are not—and must wait. Fortunately, we may not have to wait long.'

'Yes,' he said, standing back. But he could not prevent himself from putting out a tender finger and running it along her upper lip. Susanna turned her head to kiss the caressing hand.

Ben stood spellbound. For one brief mad moment he thought that both *Madame* and propriety must wait. And then sanity returned. He dropped his hand to take hers again, to swing her towards the path back to the world where duty waited for them.

'Not long,' he agreed with her. 'Next Monday we meet at St James and, please God, matters will be settled once and for all.'

The sun made shifting patterns of light on the river and threw a golden glow over everything. Men and women in their summer finery passed them chatting happily. A dog ran towards them and barked defiantly at Ben, who bent to stroke it behind the ears. It stood passive, allowing him to caress it, and when he stopped nuzzled at his boots asking for more.

An elderly lady walked up to claim him, smiling at the handsome pair Ben and Susanna made in the peace and quiet of the early afternoon. When they reached her, *Madame* was resting on the grass, half-asleep. One of the footmen was standing guard.

She opened her eyes as they walked up. 'Back so soon,' she murmured drowsily, 'I would have thought that you'd have been away longer.'

'Another time,' said Ben gently, 'another time. We shall soon return, I trust, to pay the river homage. Now, I fear, we must leave for Jess told me that Jackson would be back later this afternoon, and I must not keep him waiting. Duty calls.'

It would always call Ben, and he would always answer it, thought Susanna as they were driven home. Which is one of the reasons why I love him.

Chapter Thirteen

'Nothing so far,' said one disgusted gossip to another of what was now known as Lord Erskine's enquiry. 'My information is that so far it has been all guesswork, rumours and hearsay. First Lord Erskine addressed them all on the rules of the court and then the attorneys spoke at length—and so two days were taken up. Then some affidavits were read when Lord Babbacombe's action began, mostly from those too old and stupid to appear in court. Lord Erskine ruled that their evidence should be struck out as it consisted merely of country gossip. Lord Babbacombe made no objection as he said that there was better evidence to come.'

'And that was that?'

'So I understand.'

'Much ado about nothing, then?'

'So far,' agreed the first speaker, 'but we are only at the beginning. My informant said that Ben Wolfe looked ready to sleep by the end of the day.'

'He's confident, then?'

'Appears to be—which is not the same thing.'

Ben, whom *Madame* had invited to stay with her for the duration of the enquiry, but who had refused on the grounds that he wished to give his enemies no ammunition with

which to accuse him of impropriety, chose instead to call at
the end of each day with the latest news.

'So far,' he told them at the end of the third day, 'you
have missed nothing. We are proceeding as in a normal trial.
First Lord Babbacombe will state his case, and then I shall
state mine. At the end, after due consideration, Lord Erskine
will give his judgement. So far it seems likely that we shall
remain at *point non plus* for Erskine has so far heard nothing
to enable him to come to a conclusion. On the other hand...'
He paused and frowned.

'What is it, Ben?' Susanna said as calmly as she could.
She thought he looked ill, and wondered how well he was
sleeping.

'Nothing? No, that is a lie,' he said energetically. 'The
evidence today from some old woman who used to work in
the kitchens at The Den had a strange effect on me. Of
course, I can have no knowledge of what my father may or
may not have done at the time of my birth, since I was then
a newborn babe. But...'

He paused again. 'The oddest thing is happening. I have
never been able to remember much of my childhood and
virtually nothing of what happened when my mother disappeared, but suddenly memories of that time are flooding
back. I remember playing battledore and shuttlecock with
her on the terrace at The Den, that she watched me when I
was taught to ride. I remember my father praising me because I learned so quickly... All that had gone, apparently
beyond recall.'

Again, he fell silent. Neither Susanna nor *Madame* said
anything. He turned away from them for a moment before
turning back to continue. 'I could not even remember her
face, or whether I grieved at her disappearance, but now I
know that I did, and that from his behaviour my father became a broken man. It is as though what happened was too
terrible for me to hold on to. Now, even as I speak, more
and more of the past comes to life again. Yesterday I could

not have told you what my mother looked like—my father destroyed all her portraits, he could not bear to look at them—but today I could see her in my mind's eye, a woman younger than I am now, who would be in her fifties if she had lived... I am convinced that she died either on that day, or soon after.'

There was such a look of anguish on his face that Susanna rose and went to him, to put her arms around him, regardless of *Madame*. She felt him shudder at her touch and, when he bent his head, his hot tears fell on the hand which she put up to comfort him.

'I never cried then,' he said, 'and I suppose that I forgot because it was too painful to remember. Besides, my life was hard once my father died and it took me all my time to endure and survive in the present without grieving for the lost past.'

He took the tiny handkerchief which Susanna offered him, and dried his eyes with it.

'You will think me maudlin and unmanly,' he said ruefully, 'but I cannot ever remember crying or grieving before—it is a new sensation for me. Perhaps I should try to forget the past again.'

'No!' exclaimed Susanna and *Madame* together.

Susanna, indeed, added her gloss. 'You surely do not wish to lose your mother for the second time. It cannot be hurtful to remember past happiness with her and your father—and if the enquiry has restored them to you, it cannot be a bad thing.'

'Wise girl,' he said, his eyes dry again, and he bent his head to kiss her tenderly on the cheek. 'You have a touch of my mother about you and I never knew that until today. You are not at all like her in looks but in your brisk, but loving-kind, manner.'

He guided her to the sofa where they sat decorously side by side. 'Jess tells me,' he said at last, 'that one of Lord Babbacombe's two key witnesses will be on show tomorrow. She worked in the nursery when I was born, and later married one of the workers on his estate. She refused to talk to Jess and told him that what she had to say was for m'lord Erskine and no one else. He thought that she was extremely hostile when speaking briefly of my father. Jess joked that his own famous charm made no dent on her patent dislike of him. Jackson had a go at her and fared no better.'

'If Jess cannot charm her, then no one could,' Susanna declared. She could see what attracted other women to Jess even if he did not in any way affect her as Ben did. She had long ago decided that she liked large, dark and fierce men more than smooth, fair and mild ones.

'So tomorrow may be a crucial day,' commented *Madame*.

'Very much so. It will be the first hard evidence offered. On the other hand—' he paused again '—on the other hand, what has passed so far is difficult to refute—or prove— simply being rumours which left Babbacombe with little hard ammunition to shoot at me. Still, we shall see.'

'And you will stay for supper?'

'If I may?' His eyes were on Susanna as he spoke. 'I must tell you that I never valued the company of women until I enjoyed that of yours and Susanna's. You may both take the credit for civilising me.'

It was plain that he meant what he said. Susanna, remembering what he had hinted earlier about his hard life, understood that the softer side of human intercourse had been missing from it. The women whom he had met as a common soldier and then, later, as a hard-working merchant were unlikely to have had the same interests—and advantages— that she and *Madame* had been blessed with.

Hard though her life had been after Francis had jilted her, she had always remained in polite society, even if only at the edge of it—Ben, on the other hand, had been banished to the outer depths.

Supper over, *Madame* offered him a bed for the night

because she thought that there was a desolation about him. He shook his head at her. 'No ammunition for Babbacombe,' he announced, more cheerful than he had been all evening. 'I shall call on you tomorrow—and with good news, I hope.'

Ben had no real hope of any such thing. Both Jess and Jackson had prepared him for the worst well before the enquiry.

'The woman was undoubtedly present at your birth. She is the only reliable witness that they were able to find. Your father's steward agreed that Mrs Harte was indeed the Joan Shanks who assisted at your mother's accouchement. We can't attack her as an impostor coached by Babbacombe and his men—only as a possible liar.'

Ben's attorney had agreed with them. 'We have to break her,' he advised. 'Try to catch her out, suggest that Babbacombe has bribed her. She is their strongest card.'

She was to be the first—and possibly the only—witness of the day. It was cold and grey for summer: rain was sliding down the panes of the long windows. Inside, the candles in the chandeliers had been lit and a fire was blazing in the large hearth. Lord Erskine was seated at a long table covered with law books, his clerk by his side busily taking down every word.

A large armchair placed at an angle to the table accommodated the witnesses. The major participants in the action were seated on each side of a gangway which ran the length of the hall. Behind them was the small audience of gentlemen and noblemen, all of them grave and reverend signiors, who behaved themselves impeccably throughout the hearing as befitted their station and their years. Lord Granville was on the front row. When he cared to attend, the Duke of Clarence and his suite were seated in a gallery at the back of the room from where they could look down and see all that passed.

An usher called out in a loud and important voice, 'Mrs Thomas Harte', and a stout woman of middling years was escorted to the witness stand by a footman. She was dressed in a decent black gown with a white linen fichu, edged with lace and fastened by a small brooch, her only piece of jewellery. Her answers were given in a clear, composed voice touched with a rural accent. Any hope that she might be awed into making mistakes by her grandiose surroundings and the presence of the great men who were listening to her soon disappeared.

Lord Babbacombe's attorney, a Mr Gascoyne, took her gently through her story.

'You are Mrs Joan Harte, are you not, formerly Miss Joan Shanks?'

'Yes, sir.'

Mr Herriott, Ben's attorney, leapt to his feet. 'M'lud, may we have evidence before us that this woman is who she claims to be?'

Lord Erskine looked towards Mr Gascoyne. 'You have this evidence, I assume, Mr Gascoyne.'

'Indeed, m'lud.'

'And it has been shown to Mr Wolfe and his attorney?'

'Indeed, and I believe that Mr Wolfe remembers this woman as being part of the household when he was a boy.'

Lord Erskine addressed Ben. 'Do you confirm that, Mr Wolfe?'

Ben remained silent for a moment. He was staring at Mrs Harte. Something about her troubled him, but he could not say what. He was silent for so long that Lord Erskine said testily, 'Did you hear me, Mr Wolfe? Do you remember this woman? Can you confirm that she was Miss Joan Shanks, who is now Mrs Thomas Harte?'

Ben jumped. More than one of those present thought that it was unlike him to be so *distrait*.

'Forgive me, m'lud. Yes, I believe her to be who she says she is.'

If his answer was a trifle equivocal it was deliberately so. He could not say what it was about her which troubled him, but something did. An elusive memory rode at the borders of his mind and refused to be identified.

'You may continue questioning the witness, Mr Gascoyne,' snapped Lord Erskine, not best pleased by Mr Ben Wolfe's absent-mindedness which he considered derogated from his court's dignity.

Mr Gascoyne smiled reassuringly at Mrs Harte and began his examination.

'You were employed as an assistant nursemaid to Mrs Wolfe before her accouchement?'

'Yes, sir.'

'And you were present throughout the delivery of her baby boy?'

'Yes, sir.'

She had been well coached. Her answers to Gascoyne's questions were all brief and to the point, without embroidery.

'What happened after the baby was delivered?'

'The doctor and the midwife were alarmed because it was not breathing properly. It was the wrong colour they said. Blue, not pink.'

Listening to her, Ben found that it was difficult to believe that they were talking about him in the long ago, before he had either memory or real consciousness.

'And did this condition continue?'

'It did.' Again the brief, stark answer giving nothing away.

'Were the doctor and the midwife alarmed?'

'Yes.'

'How long did this go on?'

'For two days. The little boy, Ben, they called him, could scarce suck his mother's milk because of his difficulty in breathing.'

'And what happened at the end of two days?'

'The child began to fail. The doctor said that he was not long for this world.'

'But the child did not fail—or so the gentleman calling himself Mr Ben Wolfe claims.'

Mr Herriott jumped to his feet and protested at this. 'That is a most improper statement. I must remind you, m'lud, and Mr Gascoyne, that nothing has yet been proved affecting Mr Wolfe's legitimacy.'

'Very true,' said Lord Erskine. 'Please refrain from making such statements, Mr Gascoyne, and address yourself solely to your witness's evidence.'

'I obey you, m'lud. And did the boy die, as the doctor prophesied?'

'He did, sir. On the third day.'

For the first time there was noise in the court as this stark answer sank in.

'You were present?'

'Yes.'

'What happened then?'

'Mrs Wolfe screamed that Ben had stopped breathing. The midwife ran over to the bed and took the child from her. Mr Wolfe was sent for.'

She stopped. Again she had been so simple and straightforward when she answered that everything she said seemed to bear the ring of truth.

'And what happened when Mr Wolfe arrived?'

'He took the child from her and left the room.'

'Did he return?'

'Yes, but not before Mrs Wolfe had a screaming fit.'

'What happened when he returned?'

'He brought in a baby wearing Ben's clothes and laid it in Mrs Wolfe's arms.'

Again there was a murmur. Ben leaned forward. What was it about the woman? Dame Memory flashed her skirts at him again, but would not show her face. His puzzlement over this prevented him from being shocked at her evidence which proclaimed him to be an illegitimate impostor—albeit unknowingly.

'You say a baby wearing Ben's clothing. Was it not Ben?'

'No, sir. This baby was like him, but he was bigger and he was the wrong colour.'

'The wrong colour? How so?'

'He was pink. The true Ben had always been blue. At the end he was purple.'

'Did no one question this apparent exchange?'

'No, sir.'

'Why not?'

'Mrs Wolfe was too far gone to understand and the midwife was tiddly.'

'Tiddly?' queried Lord Erskine, his voice austere.

'I believe she means drunk,' explained Mr Gascoyne, while Mrs Harte nodded agreement.

'Very well. Continue.'

'Where did the new baby come from?'

Mr Herriott leapt to his feet. 'I protest at a question which asks the witness to assume something. If she has no direct evidence of an exchange, she cannot answer the question.'

Before Lord Erskine or Mr Gascoyne could say anything, Mrs Harte explained mildly, 'Mr Wolfe's by-blow by Lucy Withers, one of the parlour maids, was born on the same day as Ben Wolfe. Her baby was so big and strong it killed her. It was very like the true Ben Wolfe. Mr Wolfe exchanged the two babies and gave it out that Lucy Withers' baby had been the one that died.'

She came out with this although the two attorneys and Lord Erskine were all trying to silence her. Ben doubted whether Mr Gascoyne was trying very hard and believed that it was more than likely that he had instructed her to continue with her account if ever he was challenged.

If true, Mrs Harte's story was a hammer-blow for Ben. Lord Babbacombe was grinning, George, seated by him, was clapping him on the back. Here was no village rumour, no hearsay, but a decent, quiet woman who had been present at the birth, the death and the substitution. Lord Babbacombe's witness was like to win the case for him.

The woman herself sat there quite still, in no way discomfited by having every eye upon her. She apologised to Lord Erskine for having continued to speak after Mr Herriott's protest. He accepted her apology, saying sharply to Mr Gascoyne, 'Pray instruct your witness not to volunteer information unless she is first asked to offer it by you.'

Mr Gascoyne also apologised to m'lud, his head suitably bent, adding afterwards, 'I have no further questions for Mrs Harte, m'lud, her evidence now speaks for itself'—earning himself yet another rebuke from Lord Erskine, but gaining the advantage that the woman's last words would be remembered as destroying Ben's case.

Mr Herriott, invited by Lord Erskine to cross-question the witness, murmured something to Ben, to which Ben nodded agreement, before he rose to say, 'In view of the grave nature of Mrs Harte's evidence and the fact that neither my client nor I were aware of its nature until she gave it, I would ask m'lud to adjourn the court so that we may determine what course of action we need to follow to counter it.'

Lord Erskine stared at the ceiling as though asking God to advise him, before looking up at the gallery at God's nearest representative on earth, the Duke of Clarence, for guidance. He took the Duke's imperceptible nod to mean that an adjournment should be granted and so ruled.

'You may have until tomorrow morning, Mr Herriott. In view of the gravity of the evidence of which you have spoken, I must ask all present not to discuss what has passed today with anyone outside of this court. That is all.'

He rose, and swept out of the chamber.

'You knew nothing of this?' demanded Mr Herriott of Ben that evening after they had dined in Ben's London home. 'If you did, you should have informed me at once.'

'Two of my people questioned her,' Ben said. 'Both of them are skilled in such matters, one of them being an ex-Bow Street Runner, Jackson by name. Neither of them got any change from her.'

'Jackson, hmm, a good man,' murmured Mr Herriott. 'That woman's a cool piece. You're sure she was employed at your home when she said she was—and in the capacity which she claimed?'

'Both of my men were sure that she was. They went to a great deal of trouble to check that. The devil of it is that most of the servants at the time are either dead or gone elsewhere and cannot be traced. It is on her evidence—and her husband's—that Babbacombe's case relies. We have no one to counter them with.'

Mr Herriott sniffed. 'Whether she's telling the truth is quite another matter, of course. Now, let us sit down and take her evidence to pieces. If either of your men is here, send for them at once.'

Ben nodded. He had had to forgo his nightly rendezvous with Susanna, sending her and *Madame* a brief letter informing them that something quite unexpected had occurred during the day's hearing, and that he needed to spend the evening with his lawyers planning their next moves.

Jess was sent for and was questioned ruthlessly by Mr Herriott, but the lawyer could not fault him in any way.

'So, what do we do next?' he asked. 'For once, Mr Wolfe, your guess is as good as mine, perhaps better.'

'I don't know,' said Ben slowly. 'If I did, I would tell you. The thing is, there is something *wrong* about that woman, something I can't put my finger on.' He did not tell Mr Herriott what he had once told Susanna—that he could smell wrongness and evil. With Mrs Harte it was the former—but what about her gave him that impression he could not think.

Mr Herriott stared at his puzzled face before saying, 'If anything occurs to you, you will, of course, inform me. We really need some hook, some device or ploy, to break that woman's confounded certainty. She's the best kind of witness. Doesn't say too much, keeps her head. One thing, Fitzroy said that she married one of Babbacombe's people. Could Babbacombe have bribed her through him? Who exactly was Tom Harte?'

Jess said, 'He succeeded the agent who disappeared after the disappearance of Lady Exford and the murder of Mr Wolfe's mother.'

'Did he, now? That might bear investigating. Had this Harte a good reputation?'

'The best,' said Jess reluctantly. 'That's the devil of it. He and his wife are both highly regarded, being good churchgoers with well brought up, well-behaved children. They can't be faulted. I suspect that he's Babbacombe's next key witness'

'So—' Mr Herriott swung on Ben '—it's up to you now—try to think what's wrong with her—it might help us, or it might not. God knows we need help. Or the sort of miracle that doesn't happen nowadays. Tomorrow I'll try to break her, but as it is, it's bricks without straw.'

But next morning, sitting there, demure, in the big chair, Mrs Harte looked more unshakeable than ever when Mr Herriott took her once again through her evidence. Questioning everything she said, he was quite unable to disturb her.

The devil of it was that she never repeated anything—exactly—something which might have hinted that she had been coached. Ben, watching her, was more baffled than ever as she ran rings around all Mr Herriott's clever tricks by being apparently transparent and truthful in all her answers.

Only once was she a little shaken. He had asked her how

she could be certain that the baby Mr Wolfe had brought back was not the one he had taken away. 'You said that it was because the new baby was pink, whereas the old baby had always been blue—'

He paused.

'Purple,' she offered helpfully. 'I said that he was purple at the end.'

'So you did. You appear to have an excellent memory for what happened over thirty years ago...' He paused again. 'What puzzles me is this: if you knew that Mr Wolfe had switched the children, why did you never tell anyone? Lord Babbacombe, for instance. He was the heir and his man, Harte, was courting you at the time. You must have known that Mr Wolfe had committed a crime—and against your future husband's employer.'

It was the first time that she seemed to be a little wrong-footed. She did something that Ben had seen her do before when a question momentarily took her by surprise. She put up a hand to fiddle with the brooch which fastened her fichu—and as she did so, Ben's memory took on a life of its own, and he knew, at last, what it was about her that was wrong.

'I was afraid of what might happen to me if I told the truth,' she said at last.

While she spoke Ben was thinking furiously, testing his newly won memory until he was certain that it had not deceived him. Mr Herriott, pausing temporarily in his cross-examination of Mrs Harte, bent down to pick up a piece of paper on which Jess had prepared some questions for him. As he did so, Ben caught him by the sleeve.

'A moment,' he said urgently.

'What is it?' Mr Herriott was irritable. 'M'lud will not like it if we hold matters up.'

'This. Will you allow me to question her? I have just realised what is wrong with her, but it would be lengthy and difficult for me to instruct you at this late date. If I begin to make a fool of myself, I promise to sit down immediately.'

'Very well. Desperate situations demand desperate measures and, God knows, ours is desperate enough.'

'M'lud,' he said, appealing to Lord Erskine, who was about to protest their whispered conversation, 'my client begs leave to question Mrs Harte himself. He has new and vital information relating to—' He turned to Ben and hissed, 'Relating to what, for God's sake?'

'Her truthfulness,' Ben whispered back.

'Her veracity, m'lud,' translated Mr Herriott into legalese for m'lud.

'Very well, Mr Herriott.' Lord Erskine was reluctant, but was wishful to appear fair. He knew, like everyone in the room, that Mr Ben Wolfe was nearly dished.

Indeed, when both participants to the enquiry, and their lawyers, had entered, shortly before Lord Erskine came in, Lord Babbacombe had smirked at Ben, exclaiming loudly and exultantly, 'I wonder at you, Wolfe—or whatever your true name is—still having the gall to continue with this matter. Better to cut line and cut losses. The longer this case goes on, the bigger the damages I shall claim when I go to the law courts to win it.'

Ben had said nothing; had simply given him his shoulder. Now he rose to his feet to walk slowly towards Mrs Harte. She showed no emotion when he smiled at her and said, 'I have not seen you since I was a little boy and you were Joan Shanks, but I should have known you anywhere.'

Her only response was to stare stonily at him.

Ben made nothing of that but simply continued to speak, in the same even tones which the lawyers had used. 'I believe that you were somewhat of a favourite with my late mother, were you not?'

Her right hand rose to finger her brooch nervously before she replied, somewhat reluctantly, 'Yes, I suppose I was.'

'I knew my memory could not be at fault,' he told her gravely. 'I think, however, that yours might be.'

Mr Gascoyne leapt to his feet. 'I protest, m'lud. Mr Wolfe is going nowhere. He is simply making speeches, not asking questions.'

Ben bowed first at him and then at Lord Erskine who said sharply, 'Do not make speeches, Mr Wolfe. Confine yourself to asking the witness questions.'

'I do beg your pardon, m'lud. I am not versed in the law, but now that you have so kindly instructed me, questions it shall be.'

He turned again towards the witness. 'That is a very pretty brooch you are wearing, Mrs Harte.'

Her hand dropped from it as though it had been scalded. Mr Gascoyne leapt to his feet, howling, 'I protest, m'lud, he is making speeches again.'

Before Lord Erskine could reply, Ben forestalled him by saying, 'Grant me a little patience, m'lud. I shall now ask Mrs Harte a question.'

It was her turn to be bowed to before he threw a gentle question her way, his voice honeyed. 'Pray tell me, Mrs Harte, who gave you that trinket? I believe that I have seen it before. It is an inexpensive fairing, is it not?'

This time the jack-in-a-box which Mr Gascoyne had become was almost gibbering. He shouted in m'lud's direction, 'What the deuce have these questions got to do with anything in the case?'

'Something which I am asking myself,' said m'lud, gazing severely at Ben. 'Is there any point to all this, Mr Wolfe? Because if there is not, I must ask you to cease this line of questioning.'

Beside Ben, Mr Herriott was moaning gently to himself. He saw his case—and his reputation—declining into ruin.

'It is very much to the point, m'lud, and if you will instruct the witness to answer it, you would earn my undying gratitude.'

Mr Herriott's moans grew louder. He rested his head in his hands, declining to look at his principal, or the court.

Lord Erskine said frostily, 'I don't want your gratitude, Mr Wolfe, undying or otherwise, but to please you and in the hope of bringing this matter to a speedy end I shall instruct Mrs Harte to humour you. Were we in a real court of law I should not do so.'

He leaned forward to say gently and kindly to the witness, 'Pray answer Mr Wolfe's questions, madam.'

She stared at Ben before saying, defiance in her voice for the first time, 'Why, your mother gave it to me. It *is* inexpensive, tin and glass, but I treasure it in her memory.'

'Do you, indeed? That is most gracious of you. Tell me, when did she give it to you?'

She smiled at him for the first time. 'That is easily answered, sir. The day I was promised to Tom Harte.'

'Which was?'

'A fortnight before she disappeared.'

'A fortnight before she disappeared. You are quite sure of that?'

'Quite sure, sir.'

Mr Herriott, agonised by this series of *non sequiturs*, pulled at Ben's coattails to urge him to sit down. Ben ignored him and tried not to catch the eye of Lord Erskine or the by now baleful glare of Mr Gascoyne.

Instead he said to her, his voice still honeyed, 'Do you know, Mrs Harte, I do believe that you are not telling me the truth, the whole truth and nothing but the truth.'

Her hand flew to the brooch again. 'Oh, but I am.'

'No, and I can prove you to be a liar. If I am not mistaken, that brooch was bought at Lavendon Fair and given to my mother on her birthday, the very day she disappeared, and I was the one who paid for it, and gave it to her. I bought it out of my pocket money.'

She was now as agitated as she had been calm. 'No, it is you who are lying. You have been living a lie all your life.

It was as I said, she gave it to me on the day I was betrothed to Tom.'

Pray God, thought Ben, that time has not betrayed *me*, nor erased my handiwork of over twenty-five years ago.

'You see,' he said, and his kind smile never wavered, 'I was only a little boy of nine then, and I was so proud of my gift that I scratched my name and the date on the back. I don't suppose that you ever saw it, or, if you did, thought that the marks were other than random. Pray give m'lud the brooch that he may inspect the back of it.'

He knew that he was taking an enormous risk, but as Herriott had said the night before, they needed a miracle and perhaps here was one for the asking—if the marks were still there.

'You see,' he said, more into the silent room than to the now-unhappy witness, 'I gave my mother that brooch a fortnight *after* the day on which Mrs Harte claimed that my mother gave it to her. Two points must follow from that false statement. One, that if she has lied about that, then she can lie about anything, including my birth, and two, when I kissed my mother goodbye on that last terrible afternoon she was wearing my brooch to please me—so how did Mrs Harte come by it?'

Everyone was staring at the pair of them. Ben was still smiling his now terrible smile at the white-faced woman who was shrinking away from him in her chair.

Lord Erskine said at last, 'Pray hand me the brooch, Mrs Harte, so that I may inspect it.'

'No,' she wailed. 'It's my brooch. I made a mistake...my husband gave it to me...'

She got no further. Lord Erskine had motioned to one of the ushers who came forward, his hand outstretched, ready to take it from her. Her face a rictus of shame, she unfastened it and handed it to him.

Regardless of whether or not Ben's childish marks were

on the back of it, she had given herself away by trying to change her story.

Lord Erskine took the brooch, turned it over, picked up a quizzing glass and inspected the back.

'What do you claim to have scratched there, Mr Wolfe?'

'My name, Ben, and the date, 12.6.94.'

M'lud bent his head, raised it and said, 'The marks are just visible, Mr Wolfe, and confirm that what you have said is true. Bearing in mind your second point, I shall ask the court's tipstaff to detain Mrs Harte for questioning in connection with your mother's death, which, I understand, has been a mystery ever since the day you gave her your present. I am afraid that the court must retain it for the time being.'

Mr Herriott's face was one smile. Mr Gascoyne was shaking his head ruefully, and Lord Babbacombe looked ghastly as his strong case against Mr Wolfe dissolved before his very eyes.

Chapter Fourteen

'That was deliberate, was it not?'

Ben smiled, a lethal smile. 'What was deliberate, Mr Herriott?'

'All that clowning which you did. Pretending not to know the rules of evidence, bringing Lord Erskine into the case, making the witness think first that you were harmless, and then that you were not.'

'If you say so, Mr Herriott.'

'Oh, I do say so. You did not make a great fortune out of mere guesswork, I am sure.'

'No, indeed. But I also took risks. The brooch was made of tin. Mrs Harte has been wearing it for over twenty-five years. I took an enormous risk in assuming that the marks were still legible enough for m'lud to read them.'

Mr Herriott shook his head admiringly. 'By God, that *was* a risk.'

'But one worth taking, you will agree. You will be admired as the man who had the sense to allow his principal to take over, and the case to be won thereby, will you not?'

For, after hearing Mr Harte's halting evidence, and warning him not to incriminate himself in matters not relevant to the court of enquiry, Lord Erskine had given judgement.

'Unless Lord Babbacombe has further direct evidence to

present, which I understand is not the case, his action against Mr Benjamin Wolfe must fail. Without independent evidence to support that of Mrs Harte and her husband, it would be dangerous to find for him, given her proven lack of veracity in relation to an even more important matter.

'I now declare this court of enquiry closed and urge both parties to keep to their agreement that, whatever the result, they will not take any further action regarding the question of Mr Ben Wolfe's legitimacy and will refrain from comment on it. The matter of Mrs Wolfe's reappearing brooch will be passed on to the proper authorities for investigation.'

The usher shouted 'All rise,' and Lord Erskine left the room. Lord Babbacombe swung round to address his attorney. 'And that's it? Have you nothing more to say?'

Mr Gascoyne shook his head gravely. 'No, m'lord. Mr Wolfe sank your witness. Or, rather, she sank herself by lying about the brooch. Whatever can have possessed her?' and he fixed Lord Babbacombe with a glittering eye.

'But that,' persisted Lord Babbacombe, 'did not necessarily mean that she was lying about Wolfe's birth.'

'No, indeed, but you heard what his Lordship said—that it meant that her evidence could not stand on its own. Since we could produce no other witness to the birth, he was compelled to disallow what she had said—and so your case could not be sustained.'

'But she told her husband—'

'What she said to her husband was hearsay and, as such, could not be admitted into an English court of law.'

Lord Babbacombe, in an agony of frustrated rage, would not be silenced. 'A more nonsensical rule I have never heard—and besides, this was not a true court of law.'

Mr Gascoyne began to gather up his documents, 'Unfortunately you, and Mr Wolfe, both agreed that the rules of an English court of law should obtain at this enquiry. No, I am afraid that you must grin and bear it—'

'Pray cease patronising me, you damned pen pusher,

snarled Lord Babbacombe, 'and do not trouble to send me a bill for your inefficient conduct of my action for, thanks to you, I have nothing left to pay you with.'

He stalked off, his head in the air, his unhappy son George trailing after him.

'Could have told you he would turn nasty if you lost,' remarked Mr Herriott cheerfully, 'which you were bound to.'

'No such thing,' returned Mr Gascoyne, snarling nearly as fiercely as his late patron. 'Nearly dished you, didn't we? And would have done so if that silly bitch had held her tongue.'

'Ah, but you hadn't coached her on the questions Ben Wolfe asked her, had you? How much did Babbacombe pay her to lie for him, do you think? Or was it only a promise of money in the future? For sure, she will get none now—and, by the by—how did she come by the brooch?'

Which sally he repeated gleefully to Ben when talking to him in the anteroom outside the court. He was still laughing when the Duke of Clarence walked in, his royal hand out-stretched towards Ben.

'Never enjoyed m'self in a courtroom so much before, Wolfe. Wouldn't have missed it for the world. A pleasure to watch you demolish that lying old besom. My congratulations, didn't believe a word of what she said, although she said it well. Too well for my money, but you pinned her down royally.'

He laughed heartily at his own pun. 'Royally, since I was there—and at last you may find out what happened to your poor mother. Erskine said we weren't to gossip about to-day's excitements, but I'm willing to bet they will be the talk of the town tomorrow.

'And now you can marry your pretty girl with a light heart, what, what! I'll send you a fine piece of silver for a wedding present. No tin and glass this time, eh, what!'

* * *

'Did he really say that?' asked Susanna when Ben visited Stanhope Street that night to tell them that he was still legitimate Ben Wolfe, and the melancholy news that his mother's death was to be investigated again.

'Indeed, he did.'

'And this woman, Mrs Harte, I suppose that the fairy stories about your birth which she told yesterday were the reason why you did not visit us last night. How could she lie so convincingly that you nearly lost your case?'

Ben shrugged. 'I suspect, and Herriott thinks so too, that she was well paid to do so by Lord Babbacombe.'

'You're not happy about your mother's death becoming a topic for rumour again, are you?' asked Susanna shrewdly.

Ben, who looked better than he had done for weeks, said slowly, 'Not really, but you must understand that the discovery of the brooch changes things completely. For where did it come from? Mr Herriott swears that Lord Babbacombe must be involved—although I understand that there was no question of that at the time. Mrs Harte began to say that her husband had given it to her. Was that the truth—or another lie? She's lodged in Newgate tonight and tomorrow the law will harry her until she does tell the truth—if she knows what truth is.

'What is strange is that the strains of this enquiry, as I told you a few days ago, caused me to remember a great deal about my life both before and during the day on which my mother died, things which I had completely forgotten. A week ago I could not have identified Joan Shanks as she then was, and I had no memory of my birthday gift to my mother. That I fortunately recovered in court whilst she was testifying.'

Madame, who had so far said nothing, now rose and walked to the fireplace to look down into the empty hearth, her back to Ben and Susanna, who stared at her breach of manners in some astonishment—she was usually so circumspect.

'There is something of which I should have told you before, Ben,' she said in a low voice before turning to face them both. 'It was wrong of me to keep quiet. I did not think that anything I knew was important and, like you, Ben, I had forgotten, almost deliberately, much of what happened on the day that your mother disappeared.

'You see, at the time I was staying at Lord Exford's, the daughter of his cousin who had married a Frenchman who became an *émigré* during the revolution of '89. I was then twenty years old. I am sure that you have no memory of me, for what little boy of nine would know much of one young woman among many, and one who took little interest in him.

'Later I married another *émigré* who had become an India merchant and there, in India, I met you again, much changed from what you had been when I last saw you. I saw no reason to remind you of the unhappy past, the less so when you helped me when my husband died suddenly. Like you, I wished to forget that unhappy day.

'But now, I too, must try to remember it, for as your memory saved you in court today, mine might contain something which did not seem important to me at the time, but which might help to solve the mystery surrounding my two lost friends. When I asked Susanna to recover La Rochefoucauld's *Maximes* for me I was, for the first time, revisiting the country of my youth.'

'But why should you feel regret,' Ben said, 'at saying nothing to me of this? It does explain, perhaps, the affinity which I felt for you when we met in India—and the many kindnesses which you have done for me since—including helping me when I found myself in difficulties after kidnapping Susanna.'

'You must understand,' said *Madame*, 'that in some way I felt that I owed you something, having known you as a happy child before your life fell apart—and you ended up, penniless, in India. I could not but admire your courage and resolution in making yourself such a successful life after such an unpromising start.

'And, more to the present point, although Lord Erskine would undoubtedly not accept it as evidence, I never heard anything to suggest that you were other than Charles Wolfe's legitimate son. You are most remarkably like him.'

She resumed her chair before going on, 'As to your mother's disappearance…since you told us of the mysterious reappearance of her brooch I have been trying to recall something of that day. I do remember that I had a slight summer cold; consequently, when your mother asked me to accompany her and Lady Exford on their walk, I refused her kind invitation. Would that I had not—perhaps my making it a party of three might have averted a tragedy. But how can I logically assert that? As it was I watched them walk down the terrace steps and into the Park, not knowing that I was never going to see them again.

'I also remember your father leaving us to visit Lord Beauval. He usually accompanied your mother on her painting and sketching expeditions and reproached himself bitterly afterwards for having not been with her that day.'

She stopped, to put her head in her hands for a moment. Neither Ben nor Susanna said anything, except that Susanna went over to her to take her in her arms. *Madame* lay there for a moment before continuing.

'I have been trying to remember whether or not I saw Lord Babbacombe that day. I don't think that I did. You must understand that he was then a handsome young man and I was very taken with him until, one day, his dog snarled at him and he beat it cruelly with his crop—he thought that he was alone. He did not know that I had seen him coming up the drive and was on my way to meet him. I turned back and went into the house. I never felt the same about him again.

'There was one thing, though. You remember that I told you that Lord Babbacombe testified that Lord Exford and

Mr Wolfe had had a fierce argument at a dinner he gave the night before, which Lord Exford always denied—well, I was at that dinner and I can remember no such argument. What I do now remember is that later, after dinner, Mrs Wolfe went upstairs to the room which had been set aside for the ladies' coats, jackets and shawls, saying that she was feeling the cold. I was careless of servants those days and would have sent a maid to collect it—and so I told her.

'She laughed and said that Jane, her lady's maid, deserved to enjoy her evening in the Babbacombe kitchens and that she was strong enough to climb the stairs and collect her own shawl. When she came downstairs again she seemed very agitated. So much so that I remember asking if anything was amiss. She said ''no'', but when Lord Babbacombe returned from some errand she asked him if he would allow her and Charles to leave early—she had begun to suffer from a slight megrim, she said. I thought nothing of it at the time, and it was only this wretched business of a court of enquiry which set me trying to recall the past again.

'What if the fierce argument was not between Lord Exford and Mr Wolfe, but between Lord Babbacombe and Mrs Wolfe? Did he try to accost her when he found her alone? Both of them were certainly absent at the same time. Lord Babbacombe had taken it very ill that your mother had refused him, Ben, but later he appeared to forget his anger and he became friendly again with both your father and your mother. He said that he would never marry, having lost the woman he loved, and indeed, he did not, until after your mother's death.

'None of this may mean very much, I know. Lord Babbacombe was never suspected of being involved in your mother's disappearance and was only lightly questioned by the authorities. His agent testified that they had spent the afternoon together at Babbacombe House and that it was on his way home shortly after that he saw Charles Wolfe when he was supposed to be some miles away.'

Ben, who had been listening eagerly to her, his face fierce, said, 'Suppose that the agent was lying? At Lord Babbacombe's orders. Is it preposterous to suppose that Lord Babbacombe was behind the disappearance of my mother and the attack on Lady Exford?'

He struck his hands together. 'So far we have no evidence of any such thing—other than the ferocity with which he has pursued me—and the fact that my mother's brooch has reappeared on the breast of the wife of one of his servants. Until Mrs Harte and her husband have been questioned, we are making bricks without straw. We must contain ourselves and wait for the tidings which tomorrow will surely bring us. I have never felt so helpless before.'

He was thinking that always before in his life, once he had reached manhood, he had been in control of events. Even in the enquiry it had been he, who in the end, had dictated matters, he who had blown down Lord Babbacombe's house of cards. He wanted to do—what?

There was such a look of anguish and frustration on his face that Susanna was now compelled to leave *Madame* and comfort him.

'Come,' she said, putting her arms around him and stroking his warm cheek gently, before releasing him in order to sit by his side again. 'You have been patient all your life. You can be patient a little while longer, I am sure. Neither you nor *Madame* have anything to reproach yourself with.'

'I have,' *Madame* said sadly. 'I should have told Ben the truth about myself long ago, but I said nothing in order to spare him. We both thought that the past was over and done with and that we could forget it.'

'We were both wrong,' Ben said. 'Once I returned to England it lay in wait for me. Whilst I was a nobody in India it hibernated, but when I arrived here, rich and relatively powerful, it revived again. While I was on the other side of the world Lord Babbacombe must have felt safe— indeed, he *was* safe. But when I returned one of my first tasks was to try to account for my father's sudden ruin, and after much investigation I found, to my surprise, that Lord Babbacombe had engineered it.

'That was when I tried to revenge myself on him by kidnapping his son's rich bride and marrying her—but I ended up by kidnapping Susanna by mistake! After that I decided that revenge, too, was a mistake and decided to let the past stay dead. But Lord Babbacombe was a fool, for he allowed his hatred of me and mine to remind the world of it by constantly attacking me so that the old ghosts began to walk again, clamouring for justice. The only thing which surprises me is that I never thought to connect him with my mother's disappearance before.'

'Ah, but he thought that he could destroy you, didn't he,' said Susanna sensibly, 'by proving you to be both illegitimate and dishonest? Let us pray that by making that mistake he may have destroyed himself.'

'The Duke of Clarence said that you were my pretty girl: he did not know that you were my wise girl, too. He also told me to marry you straight away,' said Ben. 'Will you? I think that I was wrong not to marry you before. I must not let my past destroy my present, and with you by my side I think that I could face anything.'

'Tomorrow, if you wish,' exclaimed Susanna joyfully. 'Yesterday would have been better!'

Ben's face cleared as she uttered this naughty joke. The misery he had worn on it since he had destroyed Mrs Harte's credibility, at the cost of reviving his anguish over his lost mother, disappeared.

'You are right. Life must go on. All I would ask is that we should wait until the Hartes have been questioned. I should not like the prospect of their revelations hanging over our wedding day.'

'I'm willing to agree to that,' Susanna told him. 'Only if, whatever happens, you marry me as soon as possible afterwards. No further delays, if you please. At least Francis

Sylvester managed to get me to the church—we have not been in sight of it yet!'

'Oh, but even if we marry in church, I want the ceremony to be as private as possible since church has unpleasant associations for you. I certainly don't want many curious spectators who have only turned up because we have both been objects of scandal. If *Madame* agrees that we can be married from here, I propose that we invite only our most immediate friends—like the Dicksons and Lord and Lady Devereux. The only thing is, I can't offer you a honeymoon at present, I've too many deals tied up—but once they have been concluded then you may choose to go where you please: France, Italy or the moon!'

'Wherever you are, is where I please to be,' Susanna told him, her face rosy with suppressed joy. 'I think that the moon might be taking things too far. Later on we can arrange together where we might like to take our ease.'

They had forgotten *Madame*. She watched them, a wistful expression on her face while she remembered her own happy hours with her dead husband.

'Of course, you may be married from here,' she told them when they at last came down to earth again. 'And I approve of the wedding being as soon as possible. You have both already waited far too long to be happy.'

Tom Harte was in a small dark room in Newgate Prison, facing two Bow Street Runners. He had been arrested shortly after his wife and taken for questioning. He was a big, burly man, usually rosy faced and jovial, but on the morning after the collapse of the enquiry he was neither of these things.

Immediately afterwards he had tried to approach Lord Babbacombe to ask him for help and advice, but m'lord's lawyers would not allow him within yards of their client, having him escorted as quickly as possible out of St James's Palace. After that rebuff he had considered fleeing London, but had rapidly decided that he had no stomach for living as an outlaw.

Now, facing his interrogators, he had no notion of what his wife might have told them on the previous day. His face grey, his manner hangdog, he at first tried to deny that he had given her the brooch.

The larger of the two men laughed. 'That is not what she says. She asserts that you gave it to her not long after Mrs Wolfe's disappearance, saying that you had found it.'

'So I did,' he said eagerly, 'Now I remember. That was it.'

'She also said that you told her to tell anyone who was curious about it that Mrs Wolfe had given it to her a fortnight before her death—although why you should have thought anyone would be curious about such a trumpery thing…' He paused before saying with a nasty grin, 'Unless, of course, it was because you knew that it had been in the possession of a woman whose disappearance was a mystery.'

Tom Harte closed his eyes in agony. To tell the truth would free his wife—but would destroy him. Who would have thought that a worthless trinket, carelessly given to his wife, would have the power to bring him into the shadow of the gallows.

The second Runner saw his face change, and his head begin to hang.

'Of course,' he said slyly, 'if you were not a principal in the matter of Mrs Wolfe's disappearance, but merely an unconsidered servant who felt compelled to defend and obey his master, then to confess all might be to earn something of a remission from the utmost penalty of the law. To that end I will inform you that there is a warrant out for the arrest of Lord Babbacombe on a charge of murder and kidnapping.'

He leaned forward to tweak Tom Harte's slovenly cravat to pull him forward a little in order to thrust his face into his victim's, growling, 'Have a little common sense, cully, and save yourself. You cannot save him!'

Tom Harte was not to know that unless he confessed the notion that Lord Babbacombe was involved had no hard evidence to back it—only Mrs Harte's tearful cries and recriminations and that the warrant had been sworn simply to compel m'lord to answer questions relating to Mrs Wolfe's disappearance.

His face turned from dirty yellow to dirty white.

'I wasn't there,' he stammered, 'not I. Vincent was, I know. M'lord's agent, he was. Him as lied about seeing Charles Wolfe where he wasn't. He and m'lord were as thick as thieves. Used to go hunting the common molls together—both in the town and the country. Vincent was m'lord's poor relation who been at Oxford with him.'

This information came out in a frantic rush. The Runner said, 'Whoa, lad, steady on. A little more slowly. My fellow cannot hear you properly. What happened—"there", I believe you said?'

'Seems that they'd been drinking all morning and went for a walk—to clear their heads, Vincent said. Very merry they were, laughing and singing. They found Mrs Wolfe painting on her own, by the river, t'other lady had gone for a walk.'

He put his face in his hands. 'I don't know exactly what happened. Seems that m'lord said something wrong to Mrs Wolfe and she answered him sharply. M'lord was tipsy and took it amiss. He struck her in the face and she was knocked to the ground, half-stunned. He laughed and fell on her—and then someone screamed, Vincent said. It was Lady Exford who had come to rejoin Mrs Wolfe.

'M'lord shouted, "Silence her, damn you"—or something like that—so Vincent did. And since m'lord was having his fun with Mrs Wolfe, he had his with Lady Exford. Only when it was over they found that Mrs Wolfe was dying—she'd struck her head on a stone when she fell—and that Lady Exford was unconscious, and likely dying, too. That's when Mr Vincent fetched me. They dragged Lady Exford into the undergrowth to hide her, and m'lord ordered me to carry Mrs Wolfe to the mausoleum in the grounds of Babbacombe House where we opened one of the old stone coffins and put her in. She was dead by then.'

'And before that,' said the Runner savagely, throwing him violently to the ground, 'you took the brooch from Mrs Wolfe's dress and later gave it to your wife—adding grave-robbery to your crimes.'

'It weren't valuable,' howled Tom.

The second Runner, who hadn't yet spoken, said coldly to him, stirring him with his foot, 'You disgust me. Tell me, was it you who did for Vincent—or m'lord?'

'It weren't me. I swear God it weren't. We thought we were home dry when Lady Exford was found and couldn't remember anything, but then Vincent got the shakes. He couldn't sleep, he said, the women were haunting him and he was all for giving himself up. I know he told m'lord so—and then he disappeared. M'lord told me him and Vincent was drunk and so were not responsible for what they had done. "T'were an accident," he said. And then m'lord said that Vincent had shot himself in the mausoleum and that was the end of that. "We are safe," he said, "now that there are only the two of us." And then he made me agent.'

Runner number one said, 'Take him away. Be a pleasure to see him swing.'

Tom's howls increased. 'You promised...if I talked...if I told, you said...you know you did...'

'More fool you. And your biggest folly was to steal a tuppenny fairing and give the law the chance to do you. Stand up, man.'

'No,' he wailed, 'no.'

So they dragged him from the room.

* * *

All this Mr Herriott told Ben Wolfe when Ben visited him in his chambers the next afternoon.

Ben listened in silence as the dreadful events of that long-ago afternoon were slowly unfolded.

Mr Herriott nodded. 'I am grieved to have to tell you this sad news, but better I than another. The officers of the law were sent to Lord Babbacombe's home with a warrant for his arrest even before Tom Harte had confessed, but he had fled it the night before. Another set of officers have gone to Babbacombe House with a warrant to search it and the mausoleum. Babbacombe's flight, however, would appear to prove his own guilt and the truth of Tom Harte's story.

'And had you not recognised your mother's brooch, the mystery would still remain a mystery. Both Babbacombe and Harte must have felt safe after all these years.'

'Until I returned to England and began to unravel the true cause of my father's ruin. No wonder I was pursued so relentlessly. M'lord was undoubtedly the man behind the attack on me.'

'It would seem so. It is, alas, yet another scandal in high life. Babbacombe will have to be tried by his peers in the House of Lords—the last time that happened the wretch, one Lord Ferrers, was found guilty and hanged with a silken rope.'

Ben said grimly, 'Which would hardly lessen the magnitude of the sentence.'

'Indeed. I am sure that you will be glad when this sad business is over.'

Ben said, 'I hope that you will not think me heartless, but I intend to marry as soon as possible. I am in process of arranging for a special licence. My future wife is a sensible young woman who will be a great comfort to me—as she has been already.'

'Then you are a lucky man, sir. And I wish you well.'

'In return for which, Mr Herriott, I will send you an invitation to the ceremony which will be held as privately as possible. You deserve that for having to suffer my amateur attempts at usurping your role in the enquiry.'

'Best not let the Duke of Clarence know,' remarked Mr Herriott with a grin, 'else he will demand to be present, and, if I know him, that will certainly put paid to any attempt of yours to keep it private!'

He and Ben enjoyed the joke together, before Ben left to call at Stanhope Street and take Susanna for an airing in Hyde Park. The strange thing was that, now he knew the truth, terrible though it was, a huge burden which he had not known he was carrying had been lifted from his back.

Chapter Fifteen

Any hope that Lord Babbacombe would be swiftly caught and brought to justice soon faded. He had disappeared completely. The Runners sent to track him down reported that the rumour was that he had left England immediately and disappeared on to the continent.

Their investigations at the Wychwood mausoleum on Lord Babbacombe's estate proved that Tom Harte's story was true, and Ben and Susanna's wedding was delayed yet again when they went north to Buckinghamshire to give his mother's remains a Christian burial. Vincent was given a suicide's one, at a crossroads, even though Lord Babbacombe might possibly have killed him.

Custom and etiquette should have made them delay the wedding even further, but Ben would have none of it. 'I have grieved for my mother for twenty-five years,' he said, 'and for me she died on the day on which she disappeared. I shall love her and grieve for her no less if I love and marry Susanna. Remembering her, it is what she would have wished.'

Since he had unlocked his memory, recollections of his lost past had come flooding in. In them he was playing cricket with his mother and father on the lawn before The Den, holding her hand at the Fair where he had bought her the brooch, and watching her enjoy herself at the coconut shy stall. He remembered, too, that she had lifted him up on to her shoulder the better to see Mr Punch perform.

She had been jolly and kind, and he was sure that she would have approved of Susanna if only because Susanna greatly resembled her in her liveliness—as Madame de Saulx confirmed.

More than one person—for many came to congratulate him on his victory in the enquiry and to commiserate with him over the news of Lord Babbacombe's destruction of his family—remarked that he must be greatly wishful to see his accuser brought to book before the House of Lords.

'Yes and no,' he replied. 'I would like to see him punished, but on the other hand I hate the notion that the whole dreadful business will be rehashed again—and in public, too. If it could be done in private and without fuss—that would be different. No mummery of a trial and of silken ropes for execution can bring my mother back.'

Many could not understand him, but Susanna did. 'You are really a very private person, Ben,' she told him when they were, at last, preparing for the wedding, 'but because you are big and strong and powerful in every way most people think that you have no tender feelings at all. *Madame* and I both know better than that.'

'You always think the best of me,' he said gravely. 'You forget that I am a hard businessman.'

'Most sensible of you,' returned Susanna, 'for if you were not you would not be so successful and I should not be marrying you—or you might be marrying me for my money, which you only retrieved for me because you *were* a hard businessman—with tender feelings.'

'Oh, I do like the idea that I am marrying such a hard-headed wife,' he returned, kissing her and beginning to make gentle love to her, for *Madame* had left them alone for a little and as a couple about to be married they might be allowed to enjoy themselves without prying eyes following them about.

Five minutes later Susanna sat up and began to rearrange herself. They were both finding it harder and harder to prevent themselves from anticipating their wedding day.

'Which we mustn't,' she told him severely, 'because think of the *on dits* which would run round if we had to put the wedding off yet again and our indiscretion meant that we had an early baby. I don't worry for my sake, but for yours. We must have no scandal of any kind attaching itself to us which might give the gossips another field day at our expense.'

'Goose,' he said, kissing her affectionately before retying his cravat which she had pulled undone. 'We need fear no further delays, I am sure. Jackson told Jess and myself yesterday that they had quite certain information that Babbacombe boarded a packet for Calais on the morning after he fled. Harte and his wife are in Newgate, awaiting trial and George Darlington, like his father, has also disappeared. There was talk that he might buy a commission in the Army, seeing that his father has been declared bankrupt. Once the news of Babbacombe's infamy became known, the banks and the moneylenders foreclosed on him at once.'

'Nevertheless,' persisted Susanna, 'I have the oddest feeling that all is not yet quite over. I suppose that it comes from living with uncertainty these last few months—and years, for that matter. I woke up with gooseflesh this morning after a bad dream. I can't remember what it was, just that it was bad. No, you are not to look at me and tell me that I am suffering from female whim-whams!'

'I wouldn't dream of daring to do any such thing. What I do think is that the sooner we are hitched, the better.'

'And so do I.' Susanna was fervent. 'Jess talked about you being turned off—which I thought was slang for being hanged, but he said no, that it was also used to describe a man when he was about to be married, for being married was, for many men, equivalent to a hanging! I asked him what the equivalent slang was for a woman, but he didn't know.'

'Oh, Jess,' said Ben dismissively. 'He had a bad experience with a woman in India and tends to see them and marriage through jaundiced yellow spectacles. I did worry once that he might be after you.'

'Well, worry no longer. I like Jess—but not to marry. He must find his own young woman.'

They were still engaged in happy badinage when *Madame* came in and reproached them both for not spending the day having the final fittings for their bridal wear.

'After all,' she told them severely, 'you have the whole of the rest of your lives in which to gossip together. At this rate you will both be wearing what you stand up in—and that would never do.'

Despite all Madame's predictions their wedding day found them both in splendid fig. Susanna's dress was made of a delicate cream silk. It was high-waisted, in the latest fashion, and boasted a boat-shaped neckline. Her only jewellery was a small necklace of pearls. Her little kid slippers were cream with silver rosettes. She carried a bouquet of cream and pale pink carnations and a tiny wreath of them circled her head.

Ben, who never normally cared to rival any of the dandy set, had surpassed himself. His cream breeches, his black coat, his cravat were all so splendid that Jess told him that he was barely recognisable. As for his hair, his barber had excelled himself.

'You look a proper gentleman at last,' Jess said approvingly. He, of course, was as well turned out as ever.

'I look a proper noddy,' grumbled Ben. 'I thank heaven that I don't have to deck myself out like this every day. Everything's so tight I should never get any work done and we should all starve and be turned out into the street—you included.'

'Not me,' said Jess sweetly. 'Thanks to you I've a little something of my own for the first time in my life. Now, one more twist to your cravat and you'll be fit to be presented at court. Oh, by the by, did I tell you that the Duke of Clarence has invited himself to the ceremony? He will respect your wish that you have a private party at The Lair after it, but he does insist that he has a right to see you turned off, seeing that it was his court of enquiry which saved your bacon. His words, not mine.'

Ben closed his eyes. His wishes for a quiet informal ceremony were, it seems, not to be heeded by anyone. He would have preferred to be married in his working clothes with Susanna in the pretty cotton dress which she had worn at Richmond. Well, it was not to be, but no matter, by evening they would be safely hitched, and he and Susanna could get down to the real business of marriage.

Even thinking about it ruined the tight and perfect fit of his breeches. He could only hope that Jess was so busy chattering that he didn't notice, or, if he did, that he would have the common sense not to say anything.

The church they were being married at was not too far from Croft House, Ben's home in Piccadilly, now always jokingly referred to as The Lair since Susanna had christened it that on her first visit. It was a medium-sized mansion, a little set back from the road, with a small drive, bordered with shrubs and trees, which led up to an imposing front door. He could hardly wait to walk up to it with Susanna on his arm, his wife at last.

And who would have thought, on the day which had seen Susanna kidnapped by mistake, that he would ever be doing such an unlikely thing—he who had vowed that he would never marry!

He was still wondering about the mysterious workings of Fate when he was at last in church waiting for Susanna to arrive. His Royal Highness, the Duke of Clarence, and his suite were already seated in the front rows. Behind them were Susanna's mother, her stepfather and their two pretty blonde girls. The groom had no relatives other than Madame de Saulx so his part of the church was given over to Jess, Tozzy and numerous others of his staff. Ben's wish for a private marriage was being only partly met.

Mrs Mitchell, delighted that Susanna was marrying wealth and birth, as well as a man whom a Royal Duke called friend, had graciously forgiven Ben for restoring her fortune to Susanna. She, the girls and Mr Mitchell had spent the previous day at *Madame*'s and it had been agreed that the past should be forgotten. Ben refrained from saying that great wealth and consequence gilded everything—if one's daughter was marrying it, that was.

Afterwards, Susanna remembered little of the ceremony. She only knew that Ben was with her and that she was with Ben. The contrast with her previous failed wedding day could not have been greater. The Duke came up to them after they had been pronounced man and wife and the parson had given them his blessing, in order to add his congratulations.

'I would have entertained you all at St James's Palace, Mrs Wolfe,' he roared, 'except that your husband does not wish to share you with anyone and insists on taking you home with as little ceremony as possible.'

'He is a very private man, Your Royal Highness,' replied Susanna demurely, as she had earlier said to Ben, 'and ceremony does not sort well with him.'

'Oh, he's a true old soldier, one sees well, blunt and down to earth. Well, well, let me wish you both happy, eh, what? And if your husband should ever wish a favour he knows where to find a friend in need. You hear me, Wolfe. I always mean what I say.'

'You know...' said Susanna when they were finally

seated in Ben's splendid new curricle, decorated with white ribbons to celebrate his wedding, in which he was to drive her to The Lair. The rest of the party and the carriage in which she had been escorted to the church, were to follow behind. 'You should not mind that the Duke invited himself. The moment I informed my mother that he was going to be present and that he counted himself your friend, all was forgiven. The man who was the friend of a royal prince was not to be sneered at and must be recognised. Even Mr Mitchell was won over. My mother said that he had acquired a new post, down at the docks, which was enabling them to live in a little comfort.'

She looked sideways at her husband. 'I wonder who found that for him.'

'No, you don't,' he told her, skilfully negotiating a herd of cattle being driven by a sullen boy, 'you know—or, rather, you guessed—that it was I who arranged it. He does not know that, and you must not tell him—or your mother.'

'No, they would not like it. My mother even hinted that you might not be best pleased that he had found employment. Why did you do it?'

'She is your mother, and the girls are your half-sisters. I did not do it for them. I did it for you.'

That did not need saying, Susanna thought, and said aloud, 'It was a kind action, all the same.'

Ben said simply, 'I did not wish to see you unhappy at the thought of their poverty and squandering your money on them. This way we are all happy.'

'Indeed we are, particularly me.'

'I refuse to allow you the particularly. It is I who am particularly happy,' he teased her.

'Both particularly happy, perhaps?' she teased back.

'Agreed. Both of us. So noted, as I say to my clerks.'

They had reached The Lair and outpaced their followers. Their grooms who were wearing white wedding cockades on their jockey caps, jumped down to hold the horses for them.

Ben leapt out to hand down his bride. She was still clutching her bouquet of pink and white carnations. In the excitement of the Duke's intervention at the end of the wedding, she had forgotten to throw it to her sisters.

'You may do so later at the wedding breakfast,' Ben had told her.

Now she took his arm and they began to walk towards the door.

Afterwards, Susanna was to ask herself why the premonitions of disaster with which she had been plagued had disappeared completely on her wedding day. Excitement no doubt, she later concluded.

So it was that, when they were halfway to the front door, which was being held open by two footmen, she was almost as surprised as Ben when a man jumped out from the trees and bushes in which he had been hiding to wave a pair of pistols wildly at them.

It was Lord Babbacombe. His clothing and appearance were as wild as his behaviour. Ben held Susanna's arm firmly, wondering what action he could take. He could only be grateful that Babbacombe had not shot them down on the spot, for his intention was plainly evil.

His first words revealed his fell intent—and the reason for his delay. 'Well met,' he cried. 'I would not have had you, Ben Wolfe, go straight to your maker without knowing that I had repaid you for ruining me and making me gallows meat.

'Stand aside, Mrs Wolfe. I should not like to shoot you by accident.'

'No—' began Susanna defiantly.

She was silenced by Ben, who said gently, without taking his eyes from Lord Babbacombe, 'Do as he says, Susanna. Madmen should always be humoured.'

'And who made me a madman,' roared Babbacombe, 'but

you and your mother! She should have married me—and then none of this would have happened. Well, at least if I hang, it shall be for killing you—and you shall not see me swing. Why did you not stay in India, why?'

He raised one of his pistols.

Susanna, who had obeyed Ben and moved a little away, knew that she was about to lose him.

'No,' she shrieked, 'you shall not kill him,' and she flung the bouquet which she was carrying straight into Babbacombe's face as, startled by her cry, he turned his head in her direction.

It was enough for him to be so disorientated that he involuntarily fired the pistol he had raised, and for Ben—the shot going high and missing him—to leap upon him and to try to wrest the second pistol from his grasp.

They both fell to the ground, struggling. Susanna, delighted that her intervention had saved Ben from certain death, now had to watch him trying to overcome Babbacombe. As they writhed on the ground there was a second shot.

For a moment the world reeled about her at the thought that Ben might have been killed, until he stood up, unharmed, his bridal clothes torn and awry while Babbacombe lay supine on the ground. Susanna hurled herself on Ben, exclaiming, 'Oh, Ben, I thought I had lost you!'

And then, 'Is he dead?'

Ben held her for a moment, their two hearts beating as one, sharing the joy of danger passed.

'You saved me,' he said at last, kissing her. 'You, the Wolfe's mate, saved me. And no, I don't think he's dead, just sorely wounded.'

The footmen, paralysed by the sight of their master and mistress in danger, were now running towards them. The outriders of the wedding party, who had arrived in time to see the end, also ran up.

'What is it? What is it?' they cried, at the sight of Lord

Babbacombe lying on the ground, semi-conscious, blood running from a wound in the chest.

Jess, who together with Jack Devereux had reached them first, said shortly. 'Stand back, everyone. It's Lord Babbacombe. He tried to kill Mr Wolfe—and failed. I'll send for the Runners. Leave me to deal with matters, sir, while you and Mrs Wolfe go into the house.'

Ben, used to being the one in charge, was ready to argue until Susanna said, her voice shaking, 'Yes, indeed, very sensible of you, Mr Fitzroy. We owe a duty to our guests. Come, Ben, you know that Jess is quite capable of looking after matters properly for you.'

Ben, oblivious to those about them, put an arm around her and kissed her, saying, 'Since you saved me, my love, you shall have your way.'

'Saved you?' exclaimed Mrs Mitchell shrilly—she had arrived well after the whole matter was over. 'Whatever can you mean?'

'We shall explain to you once we are indoors. Do not let this wretched business mar our happy day,' said Ben urging them all in, except the footmen who were placing Lord Babbacombe on a makeshift stretcher.

'Carry him into the summer house and you, Tozzy, find the nearest doctor and bring him here,' were the last words Susanna heard as Ben ushered her through the front door of her new home.

Madame de Saulx was on her left, not clucking and exclaiming like her mother, but saying gently, 'What a brave and resourceful creature you are my dear, I arrived in time to see you throw your bouquet at that murdering wretch. I picked it up for you since it deserved not to be trampled on but to be preserved as an emblem of your courage.'

'I wasn't brave,' responded Susanna numbly. 'I did what I did without thinking.'

'The truest bravery of all,' said Ben kissing her again. 'Take that from an old soldier. And now if the company

will excuse us for a moment, let us retire upstairs in order
to repair the damage which recent events have done to our
bridal wear.'

Jess and Jack Devereux watched them walk away. 'I tell
you, Fitzroy,' Jack said, 'that young woman is a fit wife for
Ben Wolfe. I would never have thought that he would find
anyone who could match him for sheer courage and initia-
tive, but he's certainly married a nonpareil.'

Jess nodded and said briefly, 'I know—and once she
looked at him any hopes I had of winning her dropped dead.
I wish that I could say the same of Babbacombe. He's still
living—just. For Ben Wolfe's sake, I hope that he doesn't
survive to go to trial. Ben doesn't deserve to have the whole
wretched business rehearsed again.'

'Agreed,' said Jack, taking his wife by the arm, 'but now
that he has a helpmate worthy of him, she can share his
burdens.'

It was a good epitaph for his own lost hopes regarding
Susanna, Jess thought, and then set about organising matters
indoors until Ben and Susanna came down, looking re-
freshed, and ready to face the congratulations of their guests,
not just on their marriage, but on their very survival.

Later, much later, the house to themselves, Ben and Susanna were at last alone in their bedroom.

Susanna had exchanged her cream silk wedding dress for
a cream cotton nightgown. Ben was wearing a linen one,
open at the throat. Trying to overcome her natural shyness,
she said, laughing, 'We are nearly as muffled up in our
nightwear as we were in our wedding clothes.'

'True,' said Ben slyly, 'but not for long, I hope. No, do
not blush, my darling. No woman who has just saved her
newly married husband's life should blush.'

'Oh,' she said, turning her face into his chest as he put
his arms around her, 'you are over-praising what I did. I'm

sure that you would have found some way of overpowering him if I had remained a mere spectator.'

'No,' replied Ben, his voice sober. 'For he was about to shoot me—and would have done so had you not thrown your bouquet into his face. I know the look in an enemy's eye when he feels ready to attack. Who would have thought that he would have deceived everyone by hiding himself away in England, and waiting for an opportunity to murder me?'

'Yes,' said Susanna, shuddering. 'It is wrong and un-Christian of me but, like you and Jess, I hope that he does not live to be tried. And now, may we forget him, for he failed and what started nearly thirty years ago is over, and we may make our own lives with that shadow removed from it. You can remember your mother as young and lovely, and I can forget Francis Sylvester and the pain he caused me.'

'You are right, my love—which is a distressing, but useful, habit of yours. Yes, tonight is ours and the future. Come to bed, Mrs Wolfe, and begin to celebrate it.'

Celebrate it they did, and the last memory of the unhappy past disappeared when Lord Babbacombe died of his wound in prison. The Den and The Lair became happy homes again, full of joy and laughter when Susanna and Ben raised what Ben called their wolf pack.

'The wolf and the wolf's mate must have cubs to carry on the line,' he said to Susanna one fine afternoon at The Den some years later, watching their children playing on the lawn, 'and make the future secure for all the Wolfes to come.'

'None of whom,' riposted Susanna naughtily, for she loved to tease him, 'would have existed if, on a long-ago day, you had not kidnapped the wrong woman.'

'The wrong woman then, but the right woman now—and forever,' was his loving reply.

'I have no answer to that,' she said—and kissed him.

* * * * *

Silhouette
bestselling authors

KASEY MICHAELS

RUTH LANGAN

CAROLYN ZANE

*welcome you to a world
of family, privilege and power
with three brand-new love
stories about America's
most beloved dynasty,
the Coltons*

Available May 2001

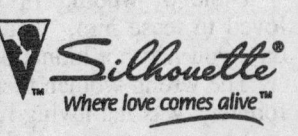
Where love comes alive™

Every mother wants to see her children marry
and have little ones of their own.

One mother decided to take matters into
her own hands....

Now three Texas-born brothers are about to discover
that mother knows best: A strong man *does* need a
good woman. And babies make a forever family!

Matters of the Heart

A Mother's Day collection of
three **brand-new** stories by

Pamela Morsi
Ann Major
Annette Broadrick

Available in April at your favorite retail outlets,
only from Silhouette Books!

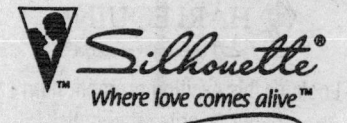

Where love comes alive™

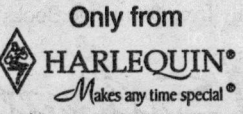

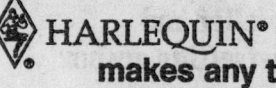